THE ISLAND OF LOST WORLDS
Mike Chinn

Damian Paladin hauled himself through the tear in the fuselage. He flopped into warm surf, salt water stinging a variety of cuts and bruises. Staring at the ditched Lockheed 10 Electra he whistled in disbelief. Apart from the hole in the fuselage and both engines looking pretty done in, the airplane was surprisingly intact.

"Any one you can walk away from," he muttered, getting to his feet.

Leigh Oswin appeared, framed by torn metal. She looked like Paladin felt: pale, bruised, her blonde curls a fright. Her fancy duds—all ready for Cuba's nightlife—were a mess. But at least she'd made it; more than could be said for the two pilots and other passengers.

Her eyes flickered up the beach the Electra had smashed into, towards a line of exotic trees under a pale blue sky. "Havana's not what I expected."

"I figure we're a little way off course, princess."

Leigh dug a pack of cigarettes from her purse. "Gee, you think?" She stared hard at the calm sky. "And what happened to the storm?"

He'd been wondering much the same. Less than a half hour from Havana their flight had been hit by a sudden tropical squall, tossing the small passenger plane like a kid's toy. Somehow the Electra had set down more or less intact, but it wouldn't be getting back up again.

"Guess we'd better see if we're alone in this lost paradise." Paladin stepped towards the line of trees, wishing he'd brought his Browning and Mauser 9mm automatics. "Let's ankle."

Passing into the trees' shadow brought a cool silence. The sounds of the waves receded to a gentle murmur. There was no perceptible breeze, and the underbrush hung still and heavy. If there were bugs around, they were keeping out of it. Hints of a strange perfume teased Paladin's senses.

"We should have brought machetes!" muttered Leigh as she stumbled over a concealed root.

Paladin helped her up, at the same time gesturing for quiet. He'd spotted something just to their left: an area around the size of a doorway which appeared to shimmer and glow with a pearly opalescence. It gave him a bad feeling.

A picture of nonchalance, he strolled up to the shimmering patch, grabbing up a fallen branch. At arm's length, he poked at the area with the branch: it passed through, not appearing on the other side.

"Say!" Leigh spotted what Paladin was doing, and its peculiar effect. "What is that?"

Paladin glanced her way. "I'm hoping it's—"

The branch was snatched from his hand, vanishing into the opalescence. Paladin jumped back. He waited; nothing more happened. The branch didn't reappear; nothing popped through to take its place.

Leigh stepped closer and stared over his shoulder. "Some kind of gateway?" she whispered, coming to the same conclusion he had.

He looked at his scratched palms. "And one way." Which made him feel kind of relieved. "Storms that come out of nowhere and go straight back; an island with a portal to … somewhere…"

"No coincidence, huh?"

He shook his head. A moment later he spotted something which immediately drove away his sense of relief: a castle. Halfway up a rise and surrounded by a landscape that was just missing a giant ape and a couple of dinosaurs, the place was a designer's bad dream. Half-assed Gothic and medieval rubbed alongside Modernist white-painted concrete and high, curved windows. Then there were the crazy towers and castellated walls that didn't belong to any school of architecture Paladin recognised, looking more like they'd been grown than built. Finding a castle in the middle of a jungle-covered, tropical island was crazy enough; this place was on a whole new level. It made Paladin's teeth ache.

"Another coincidence," he muttered.

They headed towards the strange building. Paladin kept his eyes open for any more of those one-way portals. They may have been a way off the island, but it was far too risky.

There was a short bridge leading up to a towering arched entrance. It looked like fossilised tree fronds, the entrance far too much like a screaming mouth. There was a suitably huge wooden double door with a heavy iron knocker. Paladin banged it. The sound echoed for a moment before falling abruptly silent. He glanced at Leigh; she stared back.

"I think I saw this movie," she muttered.

Paladin was about to knock again when one of the doors swung inward. Its hinges should have creaked.

Standing just inside the open door was a tall, skeletal figure draped in dull clothing that barely fitted him. His dark, hooded eyes seemed lifeless—though Paladin thought he detected a flicker when they swung his way.

"Sorry to bother you." Paladin was sorry: every cell in his body was

Weirdbook

VOL. 2, NO. 19   ISSUE 49

Features

Short Stories

Poetry

Artwork

FROM THE EDITOR'S TOWER

It's 2025, and I'm having trouble wrapping my head around the idea of living during all these "science fiction" years. Think about it. 1984? That's history. 2001? Ditto. *Blade Runner*, *Soylent Green*, and even *Rollerball* take place in a past that never came to be. I feel somewhat displaced. I mean, a quarter of the 21st Century is almost in the past now.

And (as of 2017), 42% of the world's population was under 25 years old. In other words, almost half of the people on this planet were not alive during the 20th century.

So, what am I getting at?

Well, when I wore a younger man's clothes, I couldn't imagine fantasy and horror literature continuing to exist in a future world of spaceships, robots, and flying cars. But here we are. Fantasy and horror are still going strong. No matter how much the world changes, some things remain the same. We need scares and thrills to distract us from the *real* horrors the future has delivered.

Are these two genres thriving despite or because of the forestalled expectations of what the future would bring? I wish I knew.

Ray Bradbury showed us in stories such as "Usher II" and "Pillar of fire" that horror and the fantastic will do just fine even in a bright and shiny future. I'm guessing our tired and dirty future is no threat. But that might just be because we still don't have our robot servants (which might be for the best), flying cars, or Werner von Braun space wheels to vacation on.

Look on the bright side. At least things aren't quite as awful as we were told they would be.

May our prophets, at least in this case, be wrong.

—Doug Draa, Editor

Staff

PUBLISHER & EXECUTIVE EDITOR

John Gregory Betancourt

EDITOR

Doug Draa

CONSULTING EDITOR

W. Paul Ganley

WILDSIDE PRESS SUBSCRIPTION SERVICES

Sam Hogan

PRODUCTION TEAM

*Sam Hogan
Enid North
Karl Würf*

telling him this was a bad idea. "Our plane crashed on the beach. We—"

"Please. Come in." The figure's voice was thin as he was: reedy, with an odd background buzz, reminding Paladin of fingernails down a chalkboard. Stepping aside the gaunt figure gestured at a hallway which was as mixed-up and sprawling as the place's exterior.

"You have a phone?" asked Leigh.

"This way." The skeletal figure loped towards a door to their right. He pushed it open. In the room beyond were couches in a variety of styles and fabrics, dark bookshelves lined the walls, and lacquered screens stood in corners or next to a wide, empty fireplace. Low tables dotted the polished wooden floors, alternating with throw rugs that were decorated in some South American, Pre-Columbian pattern. Green, jungle-tinted light filtered through a tall, narrow window. It was like the library in some exclusive country club.

Standing by the bookshelves was a man whose impossibly handsome face was in stark contrast to his stunted, badly proportioned body. He wore a simple dark suit with an immaculate cut that did its best to hide its wearer's defects. For a moment the guy looked perturbed. Pale green, almost yellow eyes stared up at Paladin, fixing for the longest time on Leigh. Then he smiled: the kind Hollywood producers had been looking for since motion pictures began. Paladin knew Leigh had instantly fallen for him—just a little.

"Thank you, Sylax." His voice matched his matinee looks. He had an accent, but Paladin couldn't place it. "Food and drink for our guests. And dry clothes, I imagine."

The cadaverous figure bowed and left.

"Very good of you," said Paladin.

The small guy shrugged. "You are not the first to have been wrecked on this island. The weather is very unpredictable. Dangerous. Many is the time ships have been wrecked by squalls."

"We were in an airplane." Leigh settled herself on a black leather couch. She drew out a pack of cigarettes.

"Indeed? I think this the first time an aeroplane has crashed, Yes, I am sure of it. Oh—forgive me—!" He limped towards Leigh, removing a lighter from his coat pocket. He lit her cigarette. "Let me introduce myself: Yuziel Cabal. I am from the Argentine. And you...?"

She replied before Paladin could stop her. "Leigh Oswin. And he's Damian Paladin."

Cabal's strange eyes fixed on Paladin. "The renowned occultist and monster hunter? I have heard of you, of course. I am honoured, sir." He bobbed his head.

"Been a while since anyone called me an occultist." Paladin returned

Cabal's smile, though his unease was growing by the heartbeat.

"Indeed. Many years, I imagine." Cabal stared at him just a moment too long before consulting a huge pocket watch. "Where is Sylax with your refreshments and clothing?" He turned and left the room, closing the door gently behind him.

"Odd little stiff." Leigh grinned up at Paladin. "Though his face is quite dreamy."

"Uh-huh. Pretty sure Cabal—if that's his real name—can't be trusted."

Leigh stubbed out her cigarette. "Jealous?"

"I know Cabal's type. What he is and where he comes from—"

"Argentina."

"Yeah—he made a big point of mentioning that, didn't he? He may have been there recently, though I think he goes way back."

"You don't think he's human?" She'd caught up and was racing ahead. "And what kind of screwy name is Sylax?"

"Cabal's as human as I am." Which didn't mean much.

The door opened again and Sylax entered. He dumped a pile of clothes on an empty couch. "There is a variety here; some should fit you." Straightening, he left the room.

Leigh stood and checked the pile over. "Men's and women's: all sizes." She held up a faded blue cloche hat. "Maybe no longer all that fashionable." She sorted out a deep red Cossack style shirt and black pants and retreated behind a tall chinoiserie screen to change.

After a moment's thought, Paladin decided to stick with his own clothing. He'd live with the damp.

"Wonder where Cabal got the clothes?" Leigh commented as she re-emerged from behind the screen. The Cossack look suited her.

"He did say there had been shipwrecks," Paladin murmured as he walked towards a bookshelf. "Maybe you're wearing drowned sailor duds,"

Leigh ran her fingers down her silky black pants. "I doubt any sailor would wear something like this."

Paladin slid a heavy tome off a shelf. The black leather binding was scuffed, gold letters peeling. He made out enough—filling in the rest from memory. Haverford's *Mundorum Transgredi*. Not a rare book, even outside arcane circles, but normally not found beyond dusty university library shelves. Same with Felinus Tullius's *Veritas Ædis Partem Ambiebat*. But the anonymous *Lagen van de Internering: Hun Vele Paden en Vallen* was a new one on him.

The door opened again and he slid the books back in place. It was Sylax again: this time laden with a tray that looked far too heavy for his gaunt frame. He placed it on one of the tables, leaving them silently. There was fruit and cold meat, and a crystal decanter of pale red wine. Leigh glanced in Paladin's direction. He gave her the smallest shake of the head.

"Mickeyed?"

"Maybe."

"You have a suspicious mind." She lit another cigarette. "So who is this Cabal? Or what?"

"Just a gut feeling. His appearance, his books."

"What about them?"

"He's very curious about the Tiers of the Internection. The realities beyond this one, the infinite layers—and the gateways into them."

"Ah-hah! Like that doodad outside?"

"I'm guessing it's not alone."

Leigh took a drag on her smoke, looking thoughtful. "So what about his appearance?"

"The warped body along with a—shall we say—inhumanly beautiful face. That's sometimes the sign of—" He considered his words. "—mixed birth."

"As in—?"

"The union of a human mother with an Eternal. The mother can't always process the essence of the Boundless: the baby's features may be divine, but the body becomes damaged, warped. All too often, it dies."

She gave him a hard look. "*Your* father was—"

"An Eternal, yes—"

"Worked out okay in your case. Except for the divine features."

"Thanks. Guess I was one of the lucky ones. But then my family does have a history. Remind me to tell you about my grandfather some time."

"Sounded like he recognised you."

"The name, anyhow. Whether he'll put it all together..."

Leigh stubbed out her smoke. "Maybe he'll welcome you as a long-lost cousin."

Or maybe the stuff on that tray's loaded with something kind of permanent, he thought. And because we aren't playing ball, Cabal might go ahead and get creative.

* * * *

Cabal limped into the room, followed by Sylax. Paladin watched through slitted eyes. Cabal faced the couch where Paladin and Leigh were playing possum.

"Please cease the pretence, Mr Paladin. Of course neither of you is unconscious."

Leigh and Paladin dropped their act. Paladin stretched.

"So what's the story, Cabal? You collect wreck survivors and feed them to whatever's on the other side of your portals?"

Cabal smiled. Paladin felt himself wanting to surrender to that smile. He searched for a hidden vein of anger and mined it.

"Nothing so crude. I am alone here on this island—aside from Sylax. I require diversion."

"By which I guess you mean wrecking ships, or planes and—" Paladin stared hard at Cabal "—well, doing exactly *what* with the survivors?"

The stunted figure flopped onto a couch. His left leg jutted, clearly unable to bend. "There is a steam yacht moored in a small bay to the north. It is spacious and well-provisioned. All my guests need to do is reach it, and they may sail to any port in the Caribbean."

Leigh snorted. "That easy, huh?"

"There are, of course, what Mr Paladin refers to as portals."

"We spotted one," she pointed out. "Don't look so hard to dodge."

Paladin shook his head. "I'm guessing they're not fixed, princess. They open up in random spots, without warning."

She tutted. "I'm beginning to think you're not a nice guy, *Señor* Cabal."

Cabal shone his smile on her. She stared back like the novelty was starting to wear off.

"What's on the other side?" asked Paladin.

Cabal shrugged. "I have no idea. The destination is also random. Any one may be a gateway to a heaven—or a hell."

Paladin sat upright. "That's still not the full story though, is it? This island is on no map I've ever seen, which means you're keeping it hidden, and have been for some time. You just conjure up a storm every now and then, when you want to play hide and go seek with peoples' lives."

Cabal just smiled his dazzling smile.

"So you're hiding." Paladin gave back his own smile: predatory, all teeth. "And not from anything on this world."

Cabal didn't flinch.

"Yet transitioning the Veils isn't just like stepping through a door—there's a response; an acknowledgement. Every time some poor soul is ambushed by one of your roving portals, it sends a message across the Internection. A message that can be received only in the most rarefied Tiers."

This time Cabal's grin twitched with an atom of uncertainty.

"Nobody who's in hiding goes around shouting *I'm here!*—which is what each transition amounts to. That adds up to just one thing: smoke and mirrors."

The dazzling smile faltered. Cabal's yellow eyes flickered.

"Whatever's after you keeps getting close—and you need to distract them. You know damn well where the Veils open: the most remote corners of the Boundless. Every soul sacrificed sets off an alarm: always somewhere different, and always as far across the realities as possible."

Cabal's handsome face twisted with anger. He slipped off the couch and to his feet. "I should have realised!" he spat. "I thought there was something of the Boundless about you! You're one of them! How did you slip past my wards?" He raised mismatched hands and made a complex gesture. For an instant the room was bathed in a purple light.

Paladin smelled ozone, and he couldn't move.

Cabal gestured towards Leigh; Paladin could have sworn he saw sparks dance on his fingertips. Leigh froze.

"Never mind," muttered Cabal, breathing hard. "Surprise is still the best weapon. So—" he hobbled to where Paladin sat, their faces level. "—who are you? This creature—" he indicated Leigh "—called you Paladin, so that will not be your true name. What is it? You may speak!"

Paladin felt his mouth relax. "You got it all wrong. I've lived many lives, had many names—just like you, I guess. But I'm the same as you: half human, half Endless."

Cabal looked Paladin up and down, clearly not believing him. "Oh yes—we are so much alike!"

"You want a name? Okay. One I got stuck with the day I was born: Raven's Son. Maybe you've heard it?"

Cabal took an uneven step back. "*You* are the Raven's Son?" He limped to the couch and leaned against its padded arm. "From my understanding of your sire, he is an inveterate meddler in the affairs of the Boundless—"

"You got that right."

"—And from what I have heard of Damian Paladin, he is little better."

"Now you're being nasty."

Cabal was thoughtful. His smile returned, this time tinged with malice. "I have a proposal, Raven's Son. Your powers against mine—for the sake of Miss Oswin here."

A sick feeling began gnawing at Paladin's gut. "You mean magic? I don't do magic."

"If you and I are bastard cousins of the Boundless then we must both share some of its puissance. You have sampled my talents—are yours so much less?"

"I told you: I don't do magic...!"

"Indeed?" Cabal left the couch and crossed to Leigh. He stroked her immobile cheek with one deformed hand. "Then this lovely creature will, I am sure, be shortly experiencing the worst agonies the Internection can provide."

"I said I don't do magic," Paladin murmured, "not that I can't. Simple spells, sure: charms, divination—kid's stuff I've done countless times. But the true magic—that which comes from the essence, the soul... I've seen what it does to the practitioner."

"Like your father?" Cabal's eyes were alight.

He knew Cabal was goading him. "On some Tiers the dumb inhabitants worship him as a god, if that answers your question."

"Then it is a simple dilemma. I will set Miss Oswin free to reach my yacht. If she can. You will do your best to help her; by all the means at your disposal. I will try to stop you."

Paladin wished he could get up and punch that handsome face raw. But Cabal was powerful, clearly able and willing to expend his innate magic like a true Eternal. Almost. Paladin's few tricks would be nothing against him.

Against his better judgement he said "Deal."

* * * *

Leigh was feeling pretty evil. It had been bad enough when that good looking runt had put some kind of whammy on her, leaving her frozen while he and Damy argued. Then the walking skeleton had slung her over his shoulder like she was weightless, and dumped her like so much garbage in a dingy room not much bigger than a closet.

Worse, she was stuck in the same position she'd been on the couch: sitting back, one arm raised. She felt like a forgotten storefront dummy.

She tried to lower her arm, to stretch her legs and lay flat. It was no use. Her body was unresponsive as a bar of steel.

She let anger envelope her: there wasn't much else she could do. Somebody, she decided, was going to pay. Once she got movement back, that Cabal bird was going to suffer. Hell yes!

A light came on in the closet: dazzling bright. She looked for a lightbulb, but there wasn't one. It took a moment for her to realise *she* was the source. Her whole body was glowing with a cold, white light.

"Now what'd the little creep do?" she muttered, the words out before she appreciated she was talking. Her hand touched her jaw. Dammit! She could move, too!

She got to her feet, expecting her legs to knot into a charley horse. Nothing. In fact, she felt better than she had all day.

The light dimmed, and with it some of the high. She still felt pretty good, though. Had Damy pulled some kind of stunt? In all the time she'd known him, he'd never used any kind of hocus-pocus. Magic rings, sure. Fancy powders, crystals, amulets—even the odd spirit summoning. Never any of that Chandu the Magician wavy arms, beams from the eyes spell casting. He always preferred his twin heaters. After meeting Andy Raven—Damy's charming, slightly scary dad, and seeing what he could do without thought or consequence—Leigh was pretty much on Damy's side. Just because you could incinerate someone with a thought didn't mean you had to.

She pushed at the closet door. It opened with a soft click.

Leigh stepped into a panelled hallway that was cluttered with figurines, paintings and oddly-shaped chunks of sharp metal that had to be weapons of some kind. Everything gave her the creeps. It was all just so *wrong*.

She slipped a hand into a pocket in her black pants, taking comfort in the weight of the small .38 automatic she'd stowed there when she'd changed. Like Damy, she put her faith in packed heat.

Now for Cabal.

* * * *

They were standing on a kind of parapet. It looked as if it had been built from cotton candy which was starting to melt in the sun, and grow things. Paladin kept his hands tucked in his pants' pockets so he couldn't touch anything. Cabal had given him back his mobility, though a simple gesture could likely take it all away again.

Cabal was pointing across the jungle spread out below them. Every now and then pearly lights would flicker through the canopy, dancing on and off like lightning bugs.

"The bay lies due north of here. My yacht is moored to a short jetty. The boiler is fired, a good head of steam already building."

"And I just take your word."

"I do not see that you have a choice."

He was right, of course. "When do we start?"

"Shortly. Sylax will be reviving Miss Oswin about now. We will join her at the entrance hall. Then the games will begin."

"I won't need innate magic to get her safe—or to beat you."

Cabal's smile was huge. "If that is what you believe, you are a fool, Raven's Son. And something of a hypocrite. You have senses far and above those of other humans. True?"

Reluctantly Paladin agreed.

"And an affinity with all magical paraphernalia? You are able to use them with almost reckless ease?"

Paladin nodded.

"And how is that different from the natural, sorcerous talents of any member of the Boundless?"

Paladin stared at the green horizon and the harbour somewhere out there. "What's the difference between a slingshot and a Tommy Gun?"

"Death, I imagine." Cabal turned. Sylax was stepping out from a high, twisted cylinder that was probably meant to be a turret. "Is she ready?"

"She has escaped." Sylax's reedy voice was petulant.

Cabal's smile faltered. "Then find her and bring her to the main hall!"

Sylax folded his gaunt frame in an awkward bow and left.

Paladin found himself grinning. "That's my girl." He didn't wonder how Leigh had shaken off her paralysis. Maybe Cabal had been careless.

"She cannot get far. My home is not so large—and Sylax is a stubborn bloodhound."

"Leigh's just stubborn."

Cabal muttered something Paladin didn't catch. He started to limp along the parapet, away from the warped turret, and down an uneven staircase. "This way!" he barked.

Paladin fell in behind, before Cabal decided to force him, taking the dangerous steps easily. He whistled softly to himself.

* * * *

Leigh could hear voices ahead. Or she thought they were ahead. Sound didn't travel along the odd hallways like it should. She wouldn't put it past Cabal to have put some kind of whammy on the place to ball up her senses.

Now the voices were coming from behind. Rats! She retraced her steps; this time the voices died altogether. Swell. She was just going to have to press on and hope she fell over a way out. She couldn't trust her ears; maybe not even her eyes.

She reached a four-way junction. Two routes led off into shadowed hallways that glistened in an unpleasant way. The third could have been a twin of the one she'd just come along. Likely, it was. Even though the odds were she was being railroaded, she took the third hallway.

A couple of yards from the junction, the hallway suddenly grew dark. Cussing up a storm, Leigh lit a match. The panelled walls looked soft and bulging, the angles where walls meet floor and ceiling disappearing. It looked more like a tunnel.

But at least there was none of that slimy, glistening look.

She turned around. The hallway behind was gone: replaced by impenetrable blackness. Her world had contracted to a sphere of pale light cast by the match. It burned her fingers.

Swearing, she dropped the match. The dark closed in. To her left she heard an odd, wet rubbing sound. Or was it to her right? Or behind her?

She lit another match. In the flare nothing showed. Not even the floor she was standing on. She could have been floating in space.

The flame seared her fingers. The match fell, its light engulfed by the dark.

That rubbing sound came again. It may have been nearer.

Leigh's hand grew tight around her .38's grip. On a good day she could shoot the eyelashes off a June bug. But she needed to see it.

There was a faint glow. The darkness fell back a little. Like before, the light was coming from Leigh herself. The moment she realised that, it flared: searchlight bright. The hallway was picked out in sharp relief, stark black shadows against a white light.

Leigh wanted to laugh. The whole thing was so dumb, yet so exhilarating.

A shadow moved, sliding down the soft, bloated walls. It rose up, apparently boneless, towering over Leigh. It was Sylax, his gaunt features more skeletal in the white light. His black eyes were slitted.

"You will come with me," he hissed.

"I don't think so, bub." Leigh raised her automatic. Sylax snatched out a bony arm and she fired.

Somehow, he twitched aside. Even in the overwhelming light it was hard to see his movements. Like a lanky cobra: fast, unpredictable. Leigh loosed a clipful of shells, missing every time. Despite his outward human appearance, Sylax was clearly anything but. His body was as fast and invisible as a cracking whip.

He swatted the empty pistol aside, free hand twining around Leigh's throat. He hauled her up, leaving her feet dangling. It felt like she was being strangled by a mass of wiry vines.

"You will come with me!"

Leigh tried to make a smart-aleck reply, but the words couldn't squeeze out her throat. Even so someone was talking: a strong voice which rang with authority.

"You should not be here. The Sylax are forbidden from ever leaving the Cinrollyc Permanence!"

The grip on Leigh's throat slackened a little. Deep inside Sylax's black sockets there was a flicker of doubt. "What do you know?"

"I am she who cannot be escaped. The sublime balance. On his plane I am known as Adrestia."

Sylax allowed Leigh to drop to her feet. "You have come for him!" There was no doubting the fear etched across his thin face.

"I come for everyone eventually. Be gone Sylax."

The thin creature stepped back, his gaunt body wriggling. He leapt for the wall, starting to climb like a huge, four-legged spider.

"You know there can be no escape."

Leigh watched, fascinated, as a hole opened in the bright-lit wall: a silvery glowing pin-prink which rapidly grew to the size of a cellar door. Within the pale, metallic sheen she could make out vague, wriggling shapes.

"Return, Sylax. Redress the balance."

"No!" He tried to squirm away, scuttle for the few shadows the harsh light allowed. The silvery portal followed him, growing ever bigger.

"Return. Never come back."

Sylax leapt for the arched ceiling. The expanding portal flared wider, its brilliance matching the magnesium flare burning from Leigh. Sylax was consumed: a bug gulped down whole. A moment later, the portal vanished.

The light blazing from Leigh dampened, dying by degrees. Her insane elation faded with it. She propped herself again the wall, the hallway once again free of both darkness and blinding light. She'd never wanted a cigarette more.

What had just happened? Who or what in hell was Adrestia? That light, that voice—she knew it had come out of her, somehow—scared her. Hell, it terrified her. But the feeling of power, the high it gave her—that terrified her more.

Damy had a lot of explaining to do when she caught up to him.

* * * *

Paladin followed Cabal into the entrance hall. The deformed creature looked around. He wasn't happy.

"Sylax should be here by now!"

He raised his right and made a florid gesture. It looked to Paladin like he was sketching a question mark in the air. Showboating.

"Problem?"

Cabal shot him an angry, confused glance. "I cannot locate Sylax. Or Miss Oswin."

"Losing your grip already?" Paladin didn't like the sound of Leigh going missing. Not in this place.

"Not your concern."

"I beg to differ."

Cabal pointed at the huge doors. "I will locate Miss Oswin and bring her to you myself. No more time wasting."

The double doors swung open. The smell of the jungle flowed into the entrance hall.

"I will give you thirty minutes, then the hunt begins." Cabal smiled a dentist's dream. "Did I neglect to mention that the Veils are sentient, and they have a basic predatory instinct? Their behaviour appears random and unpredictable—yet I have reason to believe there is also cunning at work."

"I thought you wanted to go face to face."

Cabal raised a hand. Paladin felt his body gripped by something unseen. Like a clockwork toy he was turned and marched towards the open door.

"In the fullness of time," sighed Cabal.

Leigh had to admit she was lost. From the outside, Cabal's joint was big and rambling; inside it felt twice the size and harder to get through than a maze. All the hallways looked the same—although they were no longer draped in shadow. Lined by dark wooden panels which seemed to be warped and bloated by rot and fungus, they rose, fell and twisted for no reason. Sagging bookcases, fly-spotted cabinets, statues and stuffed animals like nothing Leigh had ever seen masked the walls. It was worse than that book about Alice she'd looked at as a kid. She was getting frustrated and angry.

"Adrestia? That your name?" she whispered, wondering why she was keeping her voice low. "I could do with some help right about now. A signpost would be real neat."

There was nothing. No bright light, no voice. She'd expected nothing less.

Leigh stumbled over something: a bust in black stone. Roman or Greek. It had two faces, staring blindly in opposite directions. She banged it down on a shelf alongside two dark brown statues of young boys, one with a lion's head. Almost stubbing her toe hadn't improved her mood any.

A flicker of movement caught her eye. On the opposite wall was a kind of mirror. The back was peeling, the glass dirty and chipped. As Leigh stepped closer, the pale blur of her reflection twitched and rippled, like in a fairground mirror.

"Jeez," she muttered. "I could sell the entire contents of this dump and still not have enough for bus fare."

The reflection stabilised, staring back at her. It took Leigh a moment to realise the face wasn't her own.

She swore, flinching. The not-reflection frowned, watching as Leigh levelled her reloaded .38. The face was delicate-featured, so fine-boned Leigh thought it could have been spun from white glass. Cold, pale blue eyes were angled above cheekbones Leigh might have killed for. The hair was long, and appeared to be the same pale blue as the eyes.

It had to be some kind of gimmick: a fake mirror, mounted in a framed alcove behind cheap, distorting glass.

Leigh pocketed her automatic, turning her back on the icy face. Those cold eyes didn't track her movements—it was an effect of the distorting glass; the head didn't give a birdlike tilt to keep her in sight.

It was just Cabal's place giving her the heebie-jeebies.

* * * *

Paladin felt Cabal's control slip away. He was deep in the jungle, surrounded by towering fronds. Thick-boled trees hung overhead, their trunks and branches twisted into agonised shapes. Even though Paladin had been counting from the moment he'd been marched from Cabal's mansion—just over two minutes ago—it was nowhere in sight.

He slipped off his belt, running a finger down a seam in the back. It peeled open and he felt around for the tiny compass stashed away. He may not be ritzed up in his work clothes, with its modified cartridge belt containing a treasury of gadgets, but that didn't mean he couldn't sport a few hidden gizmos. He quickly found north.

There was a high-pitched whine. Paladin winced. A patch of jungle turned opaque: a crude oval of opalescence, expanding rapidly.

Paladin dropped to the ground. The glowing portal drifted no more than a yard above him. There was something predatory about its movements. After a moment it turned—almost like it was looking back—seemed to twist in on itself, and vanished.

Paladin got to his feet, checking all around and above. There was nothing.

He took another step. There was a high whine that made his eyes water. A moment of nausea. The ground below him dissolved, and he plunged through.

* * * *

Leigh couldn't help looking back over her shoulder: certain there was someone behind her; more than one someone. It felt like half the hallways were suddenly full of rubberneckers, watching her go by. But there was no one. Just the usual clutter. Although it did seem all of the blackened statues and faded paintings were of women. Pallid, blue haired women with eyes that followed. Maybe they always had been; she just hadn't noticed.

She couldn't help thinking she was heading in a circle. Or a spiral, anyhow. All the hallways had started bending to her left, and the floor was definitely rising. Was Cabal behind it? Was he bringing her straight to him?

Leigh shrugged; she didn't seem to have much choice. She pressed on, the invisible crowd close behind.

* * * *

Paladin went face first into dust. He smelled something like sulphur and spat sour grit from his mouth. Rolling over he sat up.

A desert stretched away in every direction: flat, featureless. Bright ochre in colour, strewn with thumbnail sized purple rocks. Wind blew constantly, whipping up dervishes of grit. Overhead the sky was a bloody red, fading to orange at the circling horizon. Despite the heat and overall brightness, there was no sun. No stars at all.

He was on some other plane of existence. A particularly hellish Tier of the Internection. Next time, he'd watch where he put his feet.

He stood; it didn't change the perspective much. If there was any other life around, it was way out of sight. No portal, either. Likely snapped shut the moment he dropped through.

He was going to have to get back, though. Somehow. There was nothing stowed in his belt to help him. He was going to have to do it the old fashioned way. And passing through the Tiers was no more natural to him than using innate magic.

He'd tried only once before—and then he'd had help. Even with two of them, neither an expert in transcending the Veils, Paladin had struggled. Alone…?

If he could remember how it had felt. How he'd visualised it.

The ground shook. There was a deep rumble he could feel, up through his feet. Something huge and black was rising above the horizon. It grew ponderously, from a wide dome to a broad pillar. Even though it was shadowed by the invisible light source, Paladin could just make out colossal features as they appeared. Eyes, a spreading nose, lips, a gaping maw.

The ground shuddered again. Paladin half fell. The planet sized face looked bigger—or was it closer—?

It took him a moment to realise the massive face wasn't approaching him: he was being drawn towards it. The rough, dusty ground was a tongue, and he was being hauled straight into that yawning mouth.

On one knee in case he fell, Paladin closed his eyes, trying to ignore the vast presence dominating half the sky. He allowed his senses to reach out, to feel for the geometry of the portal, lying at strange, mathematically absurd angles to the world he was in. For the folds and inclines of a multi-dimensional shape that had no name.

And found it.

He opened one eye: the vast face was above him, so huge he could no longer discern its features. Only the mouth was clear: a cavern higher than the tallest mountain, growing ever closer.

Paladin shut his eye. He wrapped his mind around the bizarre angles, seeking the gap: the sphincter sealing one reality from another. He probed. Something gave.

He risked another glance. The mouth blotted out most of the sky, leaving just an orange semicircle against the shrinking horizon.

Paladin pushed. The world pushed back. Mentally, he wrenched, tearing at the sphincter—

He opened his eyes. Fronds hung over him. A faint breeze, spiced with that strange perfume, wafted past his face. He closed his eyes again.

"So much for the easy part."

* * * *

The hallways' arc was growing tighter. It was like rounding an endless corner: impossible to see what was coming. As Leigh stepped around the latest in an infinity of Greek goddess statues, she met Cabal, limping from the opposite direction. They both froze: Leigh raising her .38, Cabal his mismatched hands.

"Hold it, short round," she muttered. "We got unfinished business."

Cabal smiled. "Indeed we have, Miss Oswin. Now, lower that gun, if you would."

She found herself doing just that, despite her best efforts. Perversely, the rest of her body wouldn't move. Here we go again, she thought.

"I could have understood the Raven's Son breaking my hold, despite his protestations. But you…" Cabal stepped closer, his handsome face peering up at her. "How did you…?"

His eyes glowed yellow. Leigh felt spidery legs brushing through her head. She wished she could shudder. Memories blurred past, too quick to focus on. One image stabilised: her walking through a simple Bowery church gate—which at the same time was something much worse. A second was shuffled out: pierced through the body by a vast aerial hook, almost dragged from her cockpit seat. She felt the pain all over again; saw the final darkness close in. A third memory: waking up amid a dazzling rainbow, carried by Damy. Reborn—

The memories shut off abruptly. Cabal stepped back.

"You transcended the Tangential Gate!" Some of his cockiness had evaporated. "Both ways. You died, and came back—but not alone…!"

He was making as much sense as Damy when he got excited. And his concentration must have been shot, because Leigh could feel her paralysis melting away.

"Adrestia," she mumbled, for no reason she could figure.

Cabal retreated another couple of steps. "So the Greeks named it. Daughter of war, sister of fear and dread. The balance between good and evil; just retribution and revolt. The handmaiden of Nemesis. But it is so much older than that. So much more."

Leigh found she could raise her .38 again. "You think *I'm* this Adrestia dame?"

"Part of you. Yet—" He was staring at her again, his composure returning. "—so far it is new to you. You have little control … no understanding." His grin spread. "Sylax. Yes—he was no match for your nascent powers, but I—"

His arms whirled in a dazzling pattern. Leigh fired her automatic. Cabal winced, clutched at his left arm. The circular hallway spun tighter, eating itself.

The world went away.

* * * *

Paladin checked his compass for north. He pressed on, being extra cautious now he knew the portals might come from any direction. He hadn't gone a hundred yards when he felt it. Last time there'd been no warning, so what the hell was this?

His ears popped in the violently displaced air. Right in front stood Cabal and Leigh; both looking like they were fraying round the edges. Cabal was pale, and he clutched at an arm. Pale, watery blood oozed around his fingers. Paladin didn't need a wild guess to figure how that had happened.

"You changing the rules again?" He braced himself for another immobility spell.

"It has come to my attention that Miss Oswin is possessed of certain … talents." Cabal grinned like he'd just cracked the world's greatest gag. "Also, that these talents may well be amplified by my island's unique topography."

Paladin was baffled. What talents? He shared a look with Leigh; she shrugged, looking confused as he felt. Swell. Maybe someone would fill him in before life got any more complicated.

Cabal was still talking, half to himself, almost feverish. "She has no control over Adrestia: the avatar manifests almost on a whim. She is a wild card—one I may not allow to remain any longer. Hence, this game is brought to a premature end. You understand."

Bright purple light built up around his hands. The air screamed. Paladin was forced to his knees, hands rammed against his ears. Somehow Leigh remained upright.

The screaming stopped. Purple light enveloped the jungle. Paladin felt like it was crushing him. He flopped onto his back, gasping. Above them the sky was tearing open: a jagged black rent in the blue sky. It gaped wider. Paladin was unpleasantly reminded of a huge mouth. It yawned, black and impenetrable, covering the heavens.

Another flash half-blinded Paladin: a pale, lustrous blue which engulfed the blackness. He thought he heard Cabal yelling something—then the blue void tore through the heavy purple light—

Paladin blinked back tears. He felt weightless. He came to his feet, squinting at his new surroundings.

The jungle was gone—replaced by vegetation unlike anything he'd seen before. It looked more crystalline than plant, there was no green anywhere. Reds and oranges predominated. In the distance, sharp-edged, slatey mountains menaced a violet sky. The smell of cinnamon was carried on a warm breeze.

Leigh was standing next to Paladin. She looked around at the bizarre landscape, half-smiling, eyes wide with delight. "There's something familiar about this place. I think Cabal messed up—or his little spell was intercepted."

Paladin shook his head. "Now I know how I sound. Level with me, princess."

Her smile widened. "Apparently, ever since you and Saint-Germain brought me back, I've just not been myself. How come you didn't notice, Damy? And from the moment we crashed on this island I've felt like someone's watching me—"

"That would be Cabal."

"Nuh-huh." She tapped her forehead. "Much closer than that little creep. Stuff's happened to me—been done by me—like you wouldn't believe. Apparently, I'm half a goddess."

"That is a very parochial term—but true, in as far as it goes."

Paladin whirled. The speaker was several feet above him, standing on air. Pale, delicate features, sharp-pointed ears, pale blue hair and eyes; dressed in dark clothing that glowed with a black light. Something like a twin-bladed skeletal axe hung from their waist.

Paladin was suddenly very uneasy. He knew what the being before him was, what it represented. An Inquisitor. Born of the Internection to redress equilibrium and right wrongs—both real and perceived. Both masculine and feminine, whilst being neither. Implacable.

He dropped to one knee and lowered his head. "Whom do I have the honour of addressing?"

"I am Arqyell." The voice was oddly pitched.

Paladin cleared his throat. "I am—"

"I know who you are, half-breed. I know your father, and I know of his father. It is by these graces alone that you are presently allowed you to live. Rise!"

Shaking, Paladin got to his feet. Arqyell was stepping down: descending an invisible staircase. The Inquisitor passed Paladin with scarcely a glance. Only Leigh held any interest for the pale creature. They stood face to face. Even though their features were nothing alike, Paladin had the craziest notion he was looking at twins.

"You know me." Arqyell's words were a statement.

"Adrestia?"

"The handmaiden of Nemesis?" Thin fingers caressed Leigh's cheek. A brief smile twitched across Arqyell's pale face. "Perhaps. Once. But I am also you, sister. The Endless was invoked when you transcended the Gate: its essence invigorates you—as it does all who walk the Tiers of the

Internection. Even that mongrel to which you have allied yourself." The Inquisitor's features hardened. "But the Raven's Son is not my concern. That resides wholly with the creature calling itself Yuziel Cabal. In this you may be of help."

"Forgive me." Paladin knew he was pushing his luck, but he asked anyhow. "There is no part of the Internection that an Inquisitor can't reach. Or so I was told. Why do you need help? Why not just walk right into his crazy mansion?"

"Cabal's manipulation of the Boundless is equal to that of the one who sired him." Arqyell never took their pale eyes off Leigh's face. "He has surrounded himself with an interwoven network of one way portals. All lead away from him—none back."

"I managed it."

Arqyell half turned and fixed Paladin with a stare that froze his guts. "Naturally. You are your father's son, after all." The Inquisitor turned away.

Paladin wondered if Arqyell had just handed him a half-hearted compliment. Then the importance of the Inquisitor's words struck him.

"Cabal's father was an Inquisitor." It would explain why his life was considered forfeit. Potentially too powerful, too unstable. "His mother must have been something special."

"His mother was a Russian peasant who died giving him life." There was no doubting the contempt in Arqyell's voice.

"And he's been on the run ever since—however long that is." Paladin had to hand it to Cabal: dodging this cold-hearted son of a bitch for centuries was no mean feat.

"A flight which is shortly to be ended." Arqyell removed the axe-like thing from their belt, offering one of the blades to Leigh. "Sister."

Leigh put a hand to it. "Now what?"

"Now you take us to Cabal."

"Just like that, huh?" Leigh looked doubtful.

"As you say."

Leigh glanced Paladin's way. He could guess what she was thinking: that Arqyell didn't sound like someone you argued with. "Sure. It'll be a breeze," she murmured.

Soft blue light sprang from the thin axe, enfolding both Leigh and Arqyell. The axe itself grew brighter, becoming a blinding pinpoint.

"All aboard." Leigh's voice trembled just a little. "Guess this train's about to leave."

The soft light spread, wrapping itself around Paladin. He heard a distant chanting or singing; hard to tell which. It sounded like a melding of Leigh's soft tones with the Inquisitor's harsher voice, creating a third.

The crystalline landscape melted away like a photograph in a flame. Beyond was a more familiar jungle.

Cabal stood exactly as he had when they'd been engulfed by the portal. His pale blood dripped onto a frond by his feet. It took a moment for his expression to catch up with events. The moment his yellow-green eyes locked on Arqyell the heart-throb features dissolved into blind terror.

He tried to run. Paladin caught him easily, swinging him around to face Leigh and Arqyell. Energy rippled out of Cabal, tossing Paladin aside.

The deformed figure drew himself upright, grasping for a shred of dignity. "Then it is not to be a fair fight? Two against one."

"This is not a fight." Both Leigh and Arqyell spoke together, voices as one. "It is the erasure of a mistake, long overdue."

"I will not die easily!"

"I would expect nothing less from a spawn of the Boundless—even one so corrupt." Leigh/Arqyell raised the strange axe. It was more dazzling than the sun.

Cabal struck a defensive pose. Wounded, he was even more ungainly.

Light blazed. Magical power surged around all three figures, probing, intertwining, pushing; soft blue against deep violet. They soon became nothing more than silhouettes, lost in the inferno. The ground shook.

Paladin dragged himself out of range. He'd heard of this kind of duel: sometimes the participants got so caught up in the fight, bystanders were forgotten. Fatally.

It looked evenly matched. Cabal, despite being wounded, seemed able to ward off Leigh and Arqyell's combined assault. Maybe he'd had plenty of time to prepare himself; maybe Leigh's inexperience was holding the Inquisitor back.

Magical bolts seared the air and smashed against each other. Thunder hammered.

Arqyell stepped on a leafy frond and slipped, falling to one knee. Cabal stepped forward, his confidence boosted. The blinding axe ripped up, shearing through Cabal's guts. He staggered, belatedly recognising the feint. His dark violet aura faded. Like a pricked balloon, Cabal sagged to the ground, the yellow light fading from his eyes.

Leigh snatched her hand off Arqyell's axe. She looked sick, kind of scared. Paladin got to his feet and hugged her, offering what comfort he could. He knew it would never be enough.

Arqyell nudged Cabal with a black foot. The small guy groaned and rolled onto his back.

"He's not dead?" murmured Leigh.

The Inquisitor stared at her, cold blue eyes surprised. "Should he be?"

"We just— That axe thing—"

Arqyell hefted the skeletal weapon. "His non-human essence is destroyed, if that is your meaning. Cabal is now merely human, no longer a hybrid with command of the Veils. He will live out a brief mortal existence."

Paladin watched the deformed creature struggle to his feet. His haggard features were no longer handsome, his eyes a muddy brown. He looked tiny and frail.

"You might just as well have killed him."

Arqyell stared back. Paladin didn't fool himself the Inquisitor wasn't considering a similar fate for him.

"Why? It was not his human soul which had transgressed."

The Inquisitor slashed down with the axe. A jagged tear appeared where one of the blades sliced between the worlds. "Farewell, Leigh-Adrestia. Raven's Son. I trust there will be no need for us to meet again." Arqyell stepped through the tear; a moment later it faded.

Paladin sighed in relief. He raised Cabal's arm: the blood was now a deep, normal red. It was bad, but if the bleeding was gotten under control he'd most likely be fine. The small guy was still too deep in shock to even whimper.

"Give me a hand, princess. There's a yacht waiting for us, and somewhere out there a hospital."

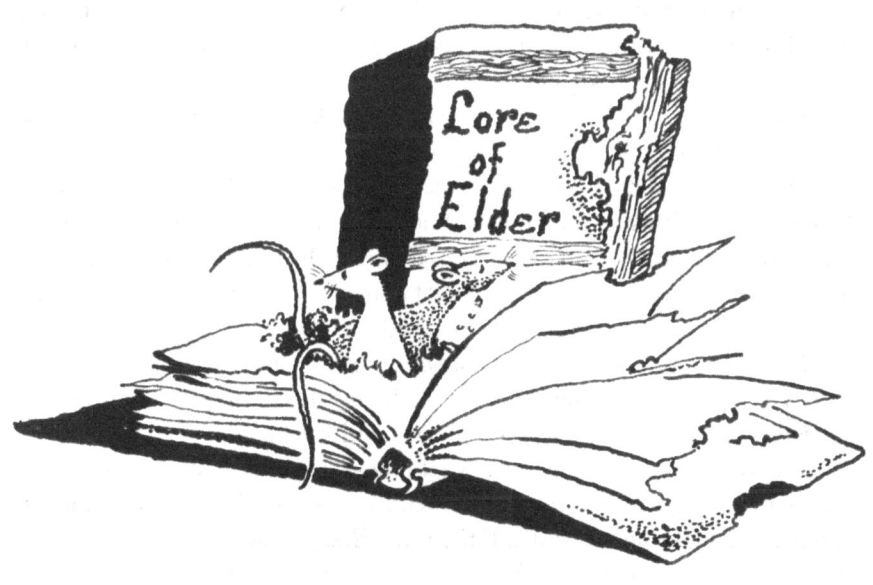

EVENTS AT A STRANGE HOTEL

Adrian Cole

I'm a man who is not easily shocked. I've experienced things in life that would turn some people's hair grey, and that's not an idle boast. My own hair is grey—I'm fifty now—so maybe that's not all down to things I've seen and heard—and felt. I would say I've grown fairly thick-skinned, but I'm not complacent enough to imagine for a moment that I've seen it all. Now and then something bumps into my life to remind me that the darkness has still got plenty of surprises, some of them far more chilling than we could imagine.

I've won a small reputation in certain circles, although I prefer to play it down. I'm not a crank and I don't want to attract the kind of misguided attention that invariably associates itself with the things I deal with.

I'm known as the Ghost Whisperer.

Yes, I talk to ghosts. I'm not a priest. In fact, I'm not inclined to religion, at least, not the organised kind. My own beliefs are complicated, even to me. I prefer to stick with what I know, based on experience. That way I'm better prepared for the curved ball. I talk to ghosts—sometimes they come to me because of what I can do. Those are the cases I am obliged to deal with. I can always refuse a human request for help, although if it's genuine—and I know when it is—I rarely pass.

Which brings me to Starkwalls Hotel. A place that redefined evil for me in a way that I never thought possible.

I had a phone call from one of the proprietors, a Miss Emily Milton-Belgrave. Something in the timbre of her voice suggested that she wasn't a young woman, although even down the phone she exuded a kind of vivaciousness. Very well spoken, somewhat conspiratorial, as if I'd known her all my life, certainly a potentially intriguing person.

"I understand, Mr Mars that you specialise in spiritual matters."

It's not quite how I'd have sold myself, but she told me I'd been recommended to her by one of my saner clients, so I let it pass.

"We seem to be experiencing what one might term disturbances," she said, managing to imbue her words with just about the right amount of drama. "I suppose one would call them psychic phenomena."

"Have you spoken to the local priest, ma'am? I rarely intrude on someone else's patch without their knowing about it."

"With the greatest of respect, Mr Mars, I don't think the local Reverend takes my sister and me seriously. He thinks we're a couple of daft old crones who're frightened of their own shadows. I assure you, there's more to us than that. And there is definitely something not quite right about Starkwalls."

It was September, and one of those warm ones that more than ever these days have replaced August as the last month of summer. August had been a washout and my so-called holiday, away from the city, hadn't been much of a success. I'd spent more time indoors than out and never seemed to be dry. So the call from Starkwalls from the elderly damsels in distress—in a remote part of the South West—was more than tempting. I told my secretary, Myra, I was going to check things out. She grinned her encouragement.

"I've got more than enough catching up to do." She tapped an enormous heap of papers. "Go and enjoy yourself. Make up for that crappy break you had." She was more like a mother than a secretary, despite being a lot younger than me. She knew what made me laugh, what made me growl with anger, how I should dress for whatever occasions—all that and more. She'd have made a good wife, except that she already had Stan, and he was twice my size and all muscle to boot, a builder with a heart of gold. Dependable, which probably isn't me.

So I set off into the sun, driving slowly and chewing over the information Miss Emily Milton-Belgrave had given me. Starkwalls was a home of sorts, or as she put it, a sanatorium, a very special place with its own unique way of looking after its clients. I made the mistake of referring to them as patients and she was quick to put me right about that.

"Guests, Mr Mars. An important distinction."

I wasn't about to argue. She'd booked me in for a week, all expenses paid, so I was cool with that. Starkwalls was in the small town of Westeringham, on the north coast of Devon, nestled at the end of a wide bay, under the rim of a wooded escarpment and sitting in lavish gardens, walled off from the rest of the town—it had once been a teeming centre for tourists, before its slow decline as cheap European holidays became the norm. Now that the summer had officially ended, there wasn't much life here. The main source of energy seemed to be with the surfers, who spent more time in the heaving seas than on land.

The hotel had once been a splendid affair, rising several stories, huge bay windows, wide oak doors beyond the portico, an orangery running off to one side of the gardens. All that kind of Victorian splendour. I parked the car in a surprisingly crowded car park and studied the building. I always get certain vibes from a place, but this pile gave me absolutely nothing, and that wasn't right. My skills, such as they are, often stir up buried emotions in a locale, but Starkwalls was as much a psychic void as deep space. Which meant it was hiding something. Probably something unsavoury.

In the lavish interior I met up with the Milton-Belgrave sisters, and I could have been forgiven for thinking I'd stepped back a century. They were in their late seventies, dressed dramatically, sparkling with jewels, faces made up—very successfully—to play down their age.

"It's such a pleasure to have you with us, Mr Mars," said Emily, offering me her hand. Naturally I took it and pressed my lips gently to the bony fingers. The gallant gesture would not be lost. It wasn't. Emily introduced her sister, Amelia, and I repeated the process. Her hand was far colder than her sister's, and there was something in her eyes that brought the faintest of shivers to my spine. Not a pleasant experience.

"We'll get you settled in your room," Emily said, beaming. "We've given you one of our loveliest views of the bay. When you're ready, do come down and have dinner, Mr Mars. Shall we say in an hour?"

I had the feeling that everything here would be done by the clock, following a long tradition. I decided to play ball—I'd been offered a ridiculous fee for my services, and a good advance, so I had no intention of killing the goose that was laying that particular egg.

From the wide window of my room I could look out at the spectacular sweep of the bay. The tide was out, exposing a wide expanse of sand that disappeared into misty distance. A grey pebble ridge rose up beyond what would be the tidal limit, curving slightly away. I could see a few individuals walking along its top, enjoying an afternoon stroll. The sea sparkled with foam. Surfers, crouched on their boards, rode those waves expertly, zigzagging shoreward. They made me feel cold. Even so, I felt drawn to the beach, as though it, too, held secrets.

I was about to quit the room, when I noticed the tall standing mirror beside the door. It was on its own stand, fitted so it could swivel from its middle, its frame a somewhat gaudy example of curlicue, rather vulgar. As I approached it, straightening my tie, my reflection imitated me. However, there was something very odd about it. I stared at myself and saw immediately what it was. In the mirror image I'd lost a score of years. I patted my stomach—a not too obvious pot—and nothing had changed. On the one hand it was flattering to see myself in the mirror as I had been, but on the other hand, it was disturbing. The eyes, in particular, were almost alien to me and seemed to stare back at me coldly, with a glint of hostility.

I left, assuring myself that the image of the younger me had been wishful thinking, triggered by a memory of happier days when holidays had been more fun. It didn't explain those eyes, though.

In the splendid dining hall I was surprised at the number of people—residents as it turned out—present at dinner. And even more so by the fact that almost all of them were women, well advanced in years. Not that I commented on the fact. It was also noticeable they all seemed in very good shape. Maybe it was the sea air, the exceptional food, and the unmistakable atmosphere of well-being that permeated everything. It was quite heady—indeed, infectious. My earlier unease was calmed as I settled down to enjoy the wonderful food and very fine wine.

As one of the few male diners, I attracted several admiring glances. I wondered if the sisters had revealed to their guests the nature of my business. It usually fascinates people, though not always for the right reasons. When Emily and Amelia Milton-Belgrave joined me, some of the ladies actually scowled, as though they were piqued at their arrival and monopolising of my attention.

Emily poured wine and spoke softly so our conversation wasn't shared. "What do you think of our little establishment, Mr Mars?"

"Call me Gideon, please. It's a beautiful building. I'm surprised how marvellously you've maintained it. There can't be many places like this."

"That's very kind of you—Gideon," she said, smiling. Her lips were very red, her facial skin rouged, though she'd taken a lot of care to show herself off to her best advantage. I wondered what she'd been in her younger days. An actress, perhaps. A model—it wouldn't have surprised me. Her hair was extraordinary, probably dyed to some extent, but still silky and I was sure it was no wig. She was conscious of my appraisal and seemed to approve of it.

"So—you have a few problems with Starkwalls," I said.

She nodded. "In simple terms, Gideon, we have ghosts. I think there have always been ghosts here. I did find some old records that referred to exorcisms—minor affairs—many years ago. Apparently whatever happened then was dealt with. These manifestations are more recent. I think it has something to do with what my sister and I are trying to achieve here."

"A health spa?"

"In a way, yes. You'll have noticed that most of our residents are ladies. Mature ladies," she added, diplomatically. "While we don't claim to have found the fountain of youth, we do pride ourselves on our ability to help our ladies make the best of themselves. Health, fitness, youthful vigour. You'd be surprised at the ages of some of our ladies. Of course, none of them looks young, but you won't find a soul among them under eighty."

"That's remarkable," I told her, genuinely. Whatever my hosts' methods, they were effective.

"And the ghosts?"

"Recently there have been quite a few sightings. Mainly on the upper floors, down the main staircase at night and in the main reception area. Sometimes a single phantom, at others a group of them."

"Are they recognisable?"

She frowned at her sister and it struck me that they were both hiding something. It wasn't unusual in such cases. People rarely like to admit they're aware of ghosts. They often expect me to dismiss the concept, relieved when I accept such things as I would any normal intruder.

"No," said Amelia. "We don't know who they are." There was a cold finality about the statement. Her taciturnity was, I supposed, part of her nature, but there was something else in her attitude—that coolness—that seemed to me to be almost hostile. She didn't like me.

"They're looking for something," said Emily. "We have no idea what."

"Any hint of hostility?"

Again they shared that covert look. "Not obviously," said Emily. "But their mere presence is unpalatable. We'd like to be rid of them."

* * * *

It was still light after I'd eaten, so I decided to go for a walk on the nearby beach. The sun had dropped deep down in the west over the sea and already an evening mist, a feature of this time of year, had diluted the light's glare, banks of yellow curling and uncurling across the waves of a gentle tide. The air was still, the temperature just beginning to drop after what had been another very warm day. I seemed to be the only person availing themselves of the beach: no doubt the locals knew it well enough. The tide was incoming, its little waves rushing quietly up the sand, leaving small deposits of weed and other minor debris as they retreated.

The line of the pebble ridge ran ahead of me for two miles or more, a gentle curve into a haze where the river estuary spilled out into the bay. Occasionally a gull passed overhead, or crows organizing a last bit of scavenging before winging it back to the woods high over the cliffs behind the town. It was a unique stillness, set apart from the world in its own little bubble of time. I looked across the sea for surfers, but of course, with hardly a wave to ruffle the water, there were none. I was alone. It was extraordinarily relaxing.

I walked a long way over the sand, conscious of the sea's slow approach. Soon it would cover the sand and I'd have to pick my way back to the hotel over the lower pebbles of the ridge. The sea mist was weaving patterns, swirling and twisting in tidal motions of its own. As I turned to retrace my steps, I realised that it was closing in along the tide line, several wispy arms unfurling over the grey pebbles. These clattered underfoot as I hopped on to them to avoid a sudden rush of foam.

Looking back down the beach, the small town now appeared to be half hidden behind a veil of mist. What had been an indefinite haze had now become something very different. The sea mist had sculpted itself into a row of shapes that bobbed and pulsed along the water's edge, spectres drawn from mist and foam alike. The falling sun through their transparent forms imbued them with an eerie life.

They were not here by chance. It was my presence that had summoned them. My strange affinity with such things—my so-called gift—had evoked them from their marine inundation. I couldn't see the eyes of these shapes, but I knew instinctively their attention was focused on me. I walked on slowly, hampered by the pebbles, which shifted underfoot and threatened to trip me. I reached a point where I couldn't avoid the progeny of the mist.

Each individual shape gradually became more tangible, recognisable as a human form, and I realised with a start they were all young people, in their teens, mostly girls. They were cautiously surrounding me. I waited, transfixed. They had faces and I picked out certain features, all cast in despondency, a grim hopelessness that chilled the air.

They didn't speak, or send telepathic messages—that's not how it works. It's more a case of emotional transmission, a surge of pulses that relay energy in the form of feelings. Often it's sadness, despair at some personal dilemma surrounding their passing from our world to whatever grey limbo has trapped them. Sometimes it's anger.

This group was suffused with both sadness and anger. It fuelled their purpose in gathering about me. There was no menace in them, not towards me. I was to be the conduit for their suffering. My unique psychic affinity for these spirits gave a form to their circumstances. They thought of themselves as lost, rejected or ignored. Something in their collective lives had set them apart, sparking this confused afterlife, this way station. There were perhaps a dozen of them, and I sensed they had all died in my world in the last few years. I probed those deaths cautiously, and knew at once I'd found a deeply disturbing area.

All of them had been murdered.

The details were too sensitive to probe—I had no mental anaesthetic to ease that pain. It was what they wanted, though. Recompense, a reckoning, something to assuage the terrible thirst for justice, which might release them. They understood my position, that I was a potential ally. For now, it was enough for them. We would help each other—it was understood.

As the mist and its occupants pulled back, I walked towards the town, the sky darker, the sun very low. Time had moved more quickly—the tide was already receding, exposing the sand again as the waters ebbed. Near the end of the beach I saw one last spectral figure, hovering above a disturbed area, where kids may have been churning up the sand to make a miniature castle, except that there had been no kids here today.

I studied the sand. Something had been scrawled there, as if by someone who could barely write. Two words. The first was 'BEYOND'. I struggled with the second, but then it came to me, probably prompted by the shape that lingered close by, the last of the mist. It was 'MIRROR'. I stood back, assessing the weird message. I'd no doubt it was for me.

I used my foot to rub out the message, as if someone might find it and start asking unwanted questions. This had become my private affair, between me and the ghosts. Ironically I had been brought here to Westeringham to seek out ghosts only for the ghosts of the sea to find me. I stood at the top of the ramp back to the empty amusement arcade and appropriately the penny dropped. Were these the ghosts I'd been summoned to find and dispel? These things are never certainties, but it was a reasonable conclusion.

* * * *

I had an early night—the sea air acted on me like a sedative. I must have dropped into a deep sleep. I woke the next morning fresh and eager to be on with the business. I'd brought a laptop with me so I could plunge into the Web and do as much research as I wanted. However, I preferred to get away from Starkwalls for at least the morning. After a full English breakfast and a brief, cheerful exchange with Emily Milton-Belgrave, I set out for a nearby town that had a library and a section on local history.

I was looking for missing persons. I had little to go on—just the impression of faces I'd seen the previous evening in the mist—and trawling national sources, mainly through newspapers, didn't have any success. So who were the ghosts I'd seen? Homeless souls, kids estranged from a normal life, sleeping rough, not on anyone's records? There must be something. And if they'd disappeared, someone must have missed them. I thought about checking with the police, but that could be a treacherous business without positive facts to give them—a photo, a name, anything concrete. I had nothing. I'd be considered a crank, or worse, some kind of pervert.

I'd almost given up when I found something, in a local paper, dated a couple of years back. The face drew me, a blurred black and white photo on an inside page. A girl called Lucy Wells. Fifteen. She may have been one of the similarly opaque faces I'd seen in the mist. Missing. She'd been part of a group of foster kids re-housed from the Midlands, staying in a large house converted into flats in Westeringham. There'd been a police search for her but she'd never been found. The conclusion, no doubt the most convenient one for the authorities, was that she'd gone back to the Midlands, or maybe tried her luck in London. Whatever, she'd been swallowed up. Lost to the world she'd known here.

I checked out the place where she'd been housed, but it had closed down months ago, a victim of local government cuts. The trail was dead before it began. I had almost nothing to go on. Almost.

I dug out one last, small, article about her disappearance. It mentioned that Lucy Wells had a brief job, working in the kitchens at a local hotel, as they put it. Starkwalls. She'd worked there for a few months, prior to her disappearance.

* * * *

At Starkwalls, Emily Milton-Belgrave almost pounced on me, flanked by the pale shadow, her sister. "Gideon! I hope you've had a useful morning. I'm sure you'll want a tour around, now you've settled."

I was ready to take a look at the building and had made a note to look out for mirrors. I'd studied the one in my room that morning, turning it around and trying to find anything attached to its back, or caught in its frame. My mind still itched with the odd message I'd read in the sand, BEYOND MIRROR. Nothing on the mirror's reverse or wall beyond it had shed light on the mystery. I'd left the mirror—a garish thing—turned to the wall.

I then spent the best part of two hours visiting the various rooms and corridors of Starkwalls. My hostess was a bundle of energy, chirpily describing every feature and tossing in as many historical anecdotes about the place as she could call to mind, as though she'd lived here since the place was built. Her sister remained largely silent, occasionally called upon to verify something the more garrulous Emily had said. It was obvious if Amelia'd had her way, I wouldn't be here.

We didn't go into any of the bedrooms, but the visitations, as Emily called them, had been restricted to the hallways, corridors and stairwells, mainly on the lower floors—in the large dining room, reception area and several stores off the kitchen. The kitchen itself was surprisingly large, presided over by a colourful woman, Mrs Bowering, who hardly stood still for a moment. She drove her staff on with an unflagging enthusiasm that I'm not sure they shared. The team were used to preparing food for significant gatherings.

"Do you have a big turnover of staff?" I asked Emily.

I felt Amelia's eyes boring into my back, but she said nothing.

"Well, they come and go," said Emily dismissively. "Why do you ask?"

"Would they have been disturbed by the ghosts? Is that why any of them left?"

"Oh no, dear. Not here in the kitchen. Only a few of us have seen them. And we've kept it very quiet. You can imagine the effect it would have."

"And no one recognises any of the ghosts? Or knows who they were?

I'm just trying to establish a reason for their being here. Why Starkwalls should attract them. If I knew that, it would make it easier for me to—deal with them."

"Yes, I see. I'm afraid we can't help."

I managed to persuade Emily I needed to spend more time wandering around on my own, getting a feel for the place. Although she seemed hesitant to agree, she and the surly Amelia left me to it. When I was sure they really had gone, I slipped back into the kitchen and diplomatically cornered Mrs Bowering.

"Did you have a Lucy Wells working here?"

She disguised her surprise at my question. I sensed, rather than saw her inner discomfort. "Don't think so. Oh, she might have been one of our summer temps. Some of them only last a week or two. They realise quick it's not for them. Too much like hard work."

I passed it off with a smile. "I can see that."

One or two of the staff, young waitresses helping with the food preparation and a kitchen porter—a boy barely into his teens—were watching me, uneasily I thought.

I left. I'd had my answer. Lucy Wells had been here.

Shortly before dinner, I met up again with the two sisters. Something was on their minds—I could feel apprehension seeping out of them like perspiration, or a slightly over-applied perfume.

"Do you think you'll be able to perform the exorcism soon, Mr M— Gideon?"

I veiled my own unease with a practised smile. I hadn't actually mentioned exorcism. "I need a little more information. Possibly tomorrow evening."

"Ah," said Emily, her voice rich with disappointment. "That could be awkward. We're having a rather special dinner. A local society. Very formal. It's all arranged —"

"I quite understand. I'll keep well away. The soul of discretion."

Amelia gave me one of her acerbic expressions.

* * * *

Dinner was served—excellent traditional fare—and as a persistent drizzle had settled over the bay and town I thought better of taking another stroll along the beach. Instead I retired early to my room and combined further research with watching TV. There was a knock on my door and I was surprised when one of the waitresses entered with a tray and a particularly fine bottle of wine, a corkscrew and a glass. It was the same wine I'd shared with the sisters when I'd first eaten with them—I'd expressed my pleasure at its quality.

"Compliments of Miss Emily, sir," she said, setting the tray down on a small table.

"Thanks. Oh—I wonder if you could help me with something?"

The girl—a pale creature, little more than sixteen—looked around the room uncomfortably as though she had no business being here. She obviously wanted to get away.

"There was a girl working here. Lucy Wells. Did you know her?"

Her eyes betrayed her. The truth was there, but she lied. "No, sir." She shook her head, her body stiffening slightly. I let her go. I uncorked the wine, which had been suitably chilled. It was very good.

Little of note happened the following day. Starkwalls was utterly devoid of spiritual visitors in the day time at least. There were no traces of them, but it didn't surprise me—they had achieved their initial purpose in confronting me on the beach. I'd found a number of mirrors, some like the one in my room, and they all had an oddness to them, an atmosphere, something a little unsavoury, but I couldn't fathom it. I wondered if they were part of an elaborate watch.

The elderly sisters were noticeably on edge when I bumped into them during the morning. My presence had suddenly become something of an embarrassment, even to the gushing Emily, and I happily took the hint and went back into the town and beyond it in search of more information. The ghosts—spirits of the murdered—were all connected to Starkwalls. Had they died within it? Because of it? Why?

The only way I was going to find out, was by calling the ghosts, and I would have to do it in Starkwalls. If their human fate was inextricably tied to the place, they would only give up their secrets within it. It wouldn't be an exorcism as the sisters understood it, more likely expiation. But who would be settling debts?

I ate out in a local restaurant that would have been stuffed with tourists a few weeks previously. The manager was glad of my custom, but no more forthcoming about Lucy Wells and other youngsters who might have worked at Starkwalls. "Summer trade," he said. "The population of Westeringham doubles during the season. God knows where some of them come from—or go. I remember there was a bit of a fuss about some girl gone missing, but the police don't have the resources to follow these things up unless they have something to go on. Your girl—Lucy was it?—probably went back to the city. More likely to find winter work there."

It was a reasonable enough explanation and everyone around here, including the police, seemed satisfied with it. They wouldn't have known the truth.

Back at Starkwalls I had a job parking—the car park was full. Some of the cars were very expensive models. Clearly a lot of the local money had arrived for this 'society' dinner. I guessed it was something to do with the work of the sisters and their successful invigoration of the elderly. Maybe there'd be a few sponsors along from the vitamin industry.

Unnoticed, I went up to my room. I sat at the bedside table and took out my notebook. I'm still old fashioned enough to use pen and paper when I'm out and about, scribbling notes which I can later convert on my laptop. I plugged the machine in and set to work. I'd not been at it long, when there was a familiar knock. It was another waitress—not the young girl of the previous night—but an older woman. Her set expression, warned me not to ask her anything. I wondered if the girl of last night had told anyone I'd asked about Lucy Wells.

"Compliments of Miss Emily, sir," she said, putting down a tray with yet another bottle of wine on it before leaving.

Eventually I reached for the corkscrew. As I was about to pierce the cork, I felt an odd breeze ripple the air around me. As I paused, the wine bottle in one hand, something touched the back of my hand. Cold, almost solid. It was a warning. I realised with a start that one of the ghosts had materialised. Faceless, incorporeal as smoke, it hovered at my side. I felt emotions radiating from it. Anxiety—fear. Fear for my safety.

I put down the bottle and corkscrew. The phantom shape hung back. I reached for the bottle again and again that cold touch on my hand warned me off.

The wine! Last night's bottle had been fine. Not tampered with. But tonight's bottle—what? Drugged? They wanted me out cold, was that it? While they held their grand meeting.

I heard something behind me. Scraping the floor. Metal being dragged. I swung round. That mirror—I'd turned it to the wall on my first night—was partly turned back. The spectral presence had pulled away into the shadows in the corner of the room, afraid of something. The mirror?

I gently pulled it round, facing the glass. My reflection was shadowed, my image and the room's blurred as though the actual light couldn't properly penetrate the surface. I stood back. The reflected figure was as distorted as the one I'd first seen, aged and diminished, slightly repellent. Something about that struck me—repellent. As though the mirror itself didn't want me peering into it and its secrets. Secrets that, perhaps, the ghosts *did* want me to understand.

I pushed the mirror round again, so its back was to me, and waited. The spectre that had warned me reacted. Beside the mirror frame, it exerted its limited power, gradually turning the mirror to face me again. I pressed my fingers to the glass and the thing beyond drew back, independent of me. Not a reflection at all, but something far more sinister. It had unquestionably been trying to deter me from looking into the mirror. And more than that.

My fingers slipped beyond the glass, into it, as if into a cold pool, not water but thick, coagulating air. Fascinated beyond being afraid, I pushed forward. I could sense the apparition beside me, close to my shoulder, encouraging me to go on. *Beyond Mirror.* Of course. This was what the ghosts wanted. I let myself be absorbed into the room of this other dimension. There was a brief moment of transition, a vague buzzing suggestive of electricity, and I stepped out of a wall mirror into the corridor beyond my hotel room. I knew, however, it wasn't part of my world.

The negative thing that had tried to deter me, had gone, but my attendant ghost had not. It had taken on a fuller shape now, its face that of a young, teenage girl, very pale, hollow-cheeked, the eyes alive, the whole being alert, nervous as a gazelle about to take flight.

I recognised Lucy Wells.

She put a finger to her lips, warning me against making a sound and slipped down the corridor. I followed into a well of silence. As we descended the first flight of stairs, I sensed rather than saw other shapes at the edge of things, more ghosts, former tenants of this strange hotel. They had come here from the sea that had swallowed their murdered bodies, as though I was the beacon they'd been waiting for, rallying to me, stirred by my vitality.

There were no signs of human activity. I'd no idea what to expect in this mirror dimension, if it were that. In my world, there was a society dinner in progress. We were near the huge dining hall, but the place was also silent. I stood in its entrance. There were no lights on, but moonlight washed in from the tall window overlooking the bay. The chairs and tables, neatly arranged and set with fresh tablecloths, were unattended. They were picked out by the soft light like so many rows of tombs.

Across the hall, a huge mirror dominated the wall, its wide frame carved with voluptuous shapes. A trick of the light made them writhe, golden and garish. In the mirror, there was no reflection, just opaqueness, as though I were looking at a flat, watery surface, a grey sea.

The ghost of Lucy Wells drifted to it and turned to me, waiting expectantly. Again I heard the faintest whisper of gathering shapes, as the ghosts in this place pressed behind me. They had brought me here for this. It was this mirror they wanted me to inspect, to see behind.

I approached it and pressed both my hands up against its clammy surface: it felt like flesh. As with the mirror in my room, it yielded to me and I knew I could step through it, back into my own world. I could feel a mounting excitement in the spirits clustered behind me. If they'd been corporeal they would have shoved me forward, only now able to follow, whereas previously something had barred them, something set around the mirror in the way garlic is supposed to deter a vampire.

Gently I moved through the mirror gate and emerged into a deeper darkness. I knew I was in my own world again. Abruptly I heard sounds from far away, as if I'd entered a cavern, hewn out of the rock behind the hotel. As my eyes adjusted, I could see flagstones on the floor and walls reinforced with stone blocks. The ceiling was vaulted, not unlike a church, and there were modern strip lights in the walls.

Lucy and the other ghosts remained behind me, a soft tide of mist, following apprehensively as I went down the nave-like path towards the sounds. It was not the chaotic noise of people enjoying a revel or meal, more a synchronised singing, the voices in harmony. All female. It was an incongruously cheerful sound, as if I'd stumbled across a gathering of the Salvation Army.

I moved along the edge of the passage, cloaked in shadows. A wide set of steps led down into another chamber, a high place, vividly lit by more strip lights. Bodies were clustered here like worshippers in a church, heads raised, mouths open. Somehow the gathered elderly women, with their enthusiastic singing and glowing, joyous faces, seemed wrong, even dangerous. My instincts warned me to remain out of sight.

The rock wall forming the far end of the chamber had a tall statue carved from it, dark as obsidian. I guessed it must be a representation of a goddess, though of what age I couldn't say. I concentrated on the singing, and it was only now I realised the words were in some ancient tongue, not one I was familiar with. A Celtic variant, Gaelic? I didn't think so.

Below the statue was an area that could have represented an altar, a cleared space, around which some of the crowd had gathered. I recognised the two Milton-Belgrave sisters, both dressed in robes that put me in mind of Druidic uniform. They would have looked slightly ridiculous, but for the nature of the occasion. As I looked at the cleared space, my suspicions were validated.

Stretched out in that open area, apparently tied in place, was the young kitchen porter I'd seen. He'd been stripped naked, his pale body pathetically vulnerable. Amelia stood behind his head, raising her face, for once a smile—grim and terrible—twisting it. Her hands were like claws, distorted in the glare: she was more feral than human, gloating over the youth's naked body. The company pressed forward like the tide, blotting out my view. The singing was no longer harmonious, but had a ragged, snarling tone.

I could feel the pulsing breath of the ghosts behind me, radiating like heat from a fire, fuelled by years of frustration and fury.

The youth let out a high pitched scream which was quickly smothered by those gathered about him as they fell on him like rats on a carcass. I was transfixed long enough for the crowd to accomplish its work.

I saw—to my horror—what that was. A score of bare arms were raised up from the melee, glistening. It was clear enough in that light—they were slick with blood. There was a unified shout of rapture, a frightful, spine-numbing sound, all the more horrible because of the age of the women. A dozen faces gazed upwards and I saw a transformation in those ecstatic features—an injection of youth, vigour, the revelation of their secret. I caught one last glimpse of the kitchen porter, my stomach lurching.

He had become a shrivelled mummy, desiccated and dry, like something unearthed from an ancient Egyptian tomb.

They closed over the corpse a last time and I knew where they'd be taking him. To the sea, for an ignominious, anonymous burial. As with Lucy Wells and all the others.

Before I could react, the ghostly shapes behind me surged forward, released here by my opening of the mirror-door. They boiled down the steps, a churning cloud of raw anger that swept past me in a devastating blast of energy. The gathered women below turned as one to face the spectral wave, every one of them singled out by a spirit.

Again I was transfixed. Each of the women was assaulted by a spirit-shape. The ghosts *poured* into the bodies, like molten lead into moulds. It was possession of the most horrifying, destructive kind. Every single one of the gathered host was infused by the vengeful spectres and I watched as the bodies were shaken so violently I thought they would break apart, fragile as dolls in a high gale.

The women had become wild—creatures of darkness—their eyes blazing hatefully, screaming that hate, witches burned by the fires of hell. They were tossed this way and that, unable to fend off the monstrous revenge of the ghosts. All around the chamber the women were collapsing, smashing into the stone pillars, heaped up like so much rubble after a demolition. Overhead the strip lights started popping, gradually reducing the light, bringing a dark veil over the murderous carnage.

The ghosts had used me and my peculiar gifts, making me the sluice through which they flooded. I had no control and I felt battered, almost to my knees, caught in a merciless storm, or an irresistible rip tide. I crawled back from the chamber, every movement an agony.

Slowly I got away, going back to the entrance doorway. It was open and I could see beyond it the large dining hall—my own world—silvered by moonlight. I was quick to return to it and glad of the silence abruptly wrapping me. I paused for a few moments, gathering my wits. I was soaked in sweat. When I was able to turn around, I was facing the original mirror, its surface opaque. All I could see in it now was a vague reflection of the hall where I stood.

I had to get the hell out of that place. In my room I quickly gathered my stuff together. There was nothing more for me to do here: the spirits of the victims of the Milton-Belgraves had no further use for me in their ghoulish retribution. God knew what the police would find. I'd worry about that in the morning.

As I went hurriedly back down to the reception area, I heard a commotion beyond. A weird murmuring, low and confused, the sound of a crowd, though muted, compressed. I waited as the first shapes emerged—agonisingly slowly—from the main door into the hotel. In the poor lighting I made out a number of shapes, writhing on the floor. Like oversize, maimed spiders, they clawed their tortured way toward me. Among the first were the Milton-Belgrave sisters, but no longer as they had been. Now they were hideously ancient, small sacks of bones with their skin stretched across them, wrinkled and cracked. The years had been drained out of them in an accelerated reversal of the frightful process they'd set in motion.

One of them slowly raised a withered arm, like the rotting branch of a small tree. Its fingers clasped at air, its face a shrunken mask. Whatever it said was lost in a rattle deep in its chest. Behind it came a carpet of similarly stricken guests, their last vestiges of energy seeping away into the night.

I turned and left. As I got into my car I was aware of shapes across the car park, a thin line of watchers. It was a silent adieu from the ghosts of Starkwalls. They, at least, bore me no malice. The last sound I heard as I pulled away into the night was the sound of waves breaking on the shore, calling the dead back to its misty embrace.

✗

OFF TO SEE THE WORLD
Franklyn Searight

Angela woke up screaming as though her guts had been yanked and twisted by nighttime thugs invading her dreams. She sat up and looked around, her bedroom faintly lit by the clock radio on her nightstand.

She had been racing through the corridors and chambers of her mind, pursued by the awfulness within, until breaking through to a conscious level. Her forehead was wet and sticky and her heart pounded like a hydraulic hammer. Tentatively, she swung her feet over the side of the bed, resting them on the floor until they stopped twitching.

My God, she thought, this nightly torment must end. There seemed to be no surcease to the anguish she was forced to endure, tormenting her enough to drive her into a madness from which she might never escape.

"Keep it up and you'll be in a sorry state like your cousin," her mother had cautioned her only three days earlier when Angela had told of another awful dream.

Lester was an unwilling resident in the state institution for the criminally demented. The papers had been recently signed declaring him legally insane, committing him to their questionable methods of thereapy Would whatever tortured him never leave until the moment of his demise…and even then? But death was improbable for the man, still in the prime of his life, his physical health not an issue unless something unforeseen occurred. Almost certainly, he had many years of intolerable life remaining in which to suffer.

The very notion she might end up with the same malady reduced her to a sullen sulk lasting for the rest of the day.

"Arachnophobia," said Angela's mother, repeating her pronouncement as they sat across from each other in the breakfast nook. "Say it often enough and it'll become a part of your everyday vocabulary."

"And why would I want to say it every day?" was Angela's response. "Wouldn't once be enough?"

Joyce Daniels chuckled pleasantly, happy to enjoy time with her daughter. As a successful journalist and a part time bibliophile, often up early and usually on her way before Angela had even awakened, she seldom had the opportunity.

"You never know when someone will bring it up in conversation. Suppose Professor Millard were to tell you he stepped on one yesterday?"

"I'd ask him if it were Fruity or Spearmint, or some other kind of gum."

Joyce chuckled even heartier. "Silly! You know, as well as I do, it refers to a fear of spiders."

"Well, maybe I do—so what?"

"So maybe that's your problem, dearie, and why you turn and gyrate on your bed half the night…and cry out in anguish."

"I doubt it, Mom. But what if it is? Just because I'm able to define a word doesn't mean it has any connection with my dreams at night, does it?"

"Doesn't it? It might. Why don't you talk with Millard about it?"

"Why don't you go to work before all the news has been reported?" she returned testily, "or through the first edition of Christie you bought yesterday?"

"Hmmm. Perhaps I will. This being my day off, I'm my own person and can do whatever I choose. I just might decide to go back to bed and enjoy a few more hours of slumber."

"Maybe I will, too. I can't remember being this tired after a full night's sleep."

"But it wasn't a *good* sleep, dear. I could hear you leaping and spinning in your bed every time I woke up for a moment last night. You really didn't have a satisfying snooze, did you?"

"No, but if I went back to bed now, or took a nap in front of the TV set, I probably wouldn't sleep any better."

"Maybe not.

"Isn't it time you were going? Those animals you look after won't be happy until you're there to feed them. If they snap at Dr. Millard out of hunger, he'll cut your wages in half."

"You're just joking, Mom, but it's true we're constantly short of funds and keeping the lab open much longer might not be possible."

"Really bad, huh, dearie?"

"Who knows? But it's what he says and I have heard donations have slowed down to a trickle. When he runs out of money to pay his assistants, I'll be the first to go; Millie has been there longer than I have. Somehow, he'll manage to pay for animal treatments, though, even if he has to care for them using his own money."

"Then he'll find a way to keep you on, also. Stop worrying so much; finish your breakfast and be on your way."

Angela spooned the remaining cereal into her mouth, leaving what was left of the sugary milk in the bottom of the bowl. Her mother was right. Going to work late was frowned upon by her employer even though he, himself, was sometimes tardy or even truant from his position. She swallowed what was left of her orange juice, took the last swig of coffee and pushed herself away from the table. She finished dressing and primping and five minutes later was backing her decrepit Piquet out of the garage.

* * * *

"Morning, Ang," greeted Professor Millard, as she pulled the door open and swept into the lab.

"Good morning, Professor," she returned, her voice lacking its usual warmth and vitality.

She stopped at the coat rack as his next words reached her, "Another bad night?"

"What are you, some kind of mind reader?" she guessed.

"No, but it's not difficult to see your puffy eyes and make a shrewd deduction. Those dark shadows and hang-dog look on your sour puss are also a giveaway. Had those dreams again, did you?"

"Uh huh," she admitted, hanging her thin jacket on the hook. "Guess you didn't need to use extra sensory perception, after all."

"Not a bit," he said. "Scientists don't believe in mumbo-jumbo, anyway."

"Mumbo-jumbo, is it?" she scoffed, joining in with the banter, offering her own repartee, her lips stretched to form a faint smile. "You researchers should open your minds, sweep the cobwebs out and realize not everything reported to the senses can be judged by scientific measurement."

"Oh, yeah?" he said, somewhat defensively, but not angered by his favorite employee.

"Yes. There are things other people believe in you do not," she persisted, crossing the room to sit down at her desk, much smaller than his.

"You mean like extra-terrestrials and flying saucers, right?"

"No, not a good example, but something similar. There are things people believe but can't quite prove—but you can't disprove them, either."

"Okay, Ang, I'll let you win this round; you believe as you want. And I'll believe in what common sense, along with what scientific testing, tells me is true."

Angela had mentioned to him the sleep problems she was having. He liked her, even though she had lost some of her zestful glow of happiness, vibrancy and keen desire to please during the last two weeks, gradually turning into a drab, uninspired assistant doing some of his lab work. Fortunately for her, he was not of an inflexible temperament, quite able to take her change of behavior in stride. Eventually, he believed, she would revert to the feisty, exuberant person he had hired nearly a year ago. She was the sort of person he needed to assist in his labors, blessed with an insightful mind attending to minutiae and able to work part time for the money needed to put herself through community college. Further, she was a close-mouthed person who would not betray the results of his work to competitors before he was ready to announce them.

Millard leaned over the slide he was holding, an orange stain smeared over the glass he had prepared for study under his high powered microscope.

He looked up from the slide he was scrutinizing to find her staring at him. Apparently, she wanted to talk and he was a good listener.

"Yes?" he queried.

"I had the dream again," she said, hoping her problems would not seriously interfere with his work but, at the same time, encourage him to talk and listen to her.

"About the spider?"

"Yes. Again. Do you remember telling me about the shipment of arachnids you ordered from the supply house?"

"I do—but I only mentioned one."

"One is enough, but as you know, I've had an enormous fear of those creepy creatures as long as I can remember. Can't think of a time, even in my infancy, when they didn't occupy my thoughts in obsessive and unhealthy ways."

He lay the slide on his desk, giving her his full attention. "I also told you having one of those "weird creatures" around, locked up and harmless until you became used to it, might help to dispel your fears. "

"And I agreed to it, so I can't fault you for planning to bring one of them into the lab. But I'm thinking…now…I made a big mistake because I can't stop thinking about them when I should be taking lecture notes as my instructors are teaching. It's about all I dream about now and it's worse than it's ever been."

"Sorry, Ang. Maybe we should abandon the experiment before it makes matters worse."

"I would appreciate it. It's even worse since you told me you actually ordered one of those invidious, eight leggers! I can't keep them out my dreams. I toss and turn in bed, trying to shake them off, imagining they're scampering all over me while I'm sleeping. Sometimes it gets so bad I'm afraid to shut my eyes for fear they'll creep into my mind and dreams and then…and then…"

"And then what?"

"I don't *know*…probably do something horrible. Maybe eat me. Please don't laugh. Have you ever dreamed of a spider eating you, Professor? Ever known of a phobia in which one is dining on people?"

"No."

"It's a totally irrational notion, but I can't help it. My night visions are turning into a reality.

"It would be best for you to overcome this senseless fear."

"I know. I know."

The professor, sensitive to her susceptibilities, did not mention the shipment had *already arrived* and was, even now, stored away in the next room where Angela took care of the animals he used in his experiments. The spider was secured in a container, hidden on a high shelf where she would not find it.

"I'm out of ideas, Ang. I thought having a spider around was the simplest way to extinguish your fears—to confront them—but apparently I was wrong."

"It's what I've always heard, also. But now I dread being actually assaulted by an eight-legger with a black hairy body, outlandishly bloated, maybe filled with obscene poisons, gorging on the blood of its victims. I'm afraid the very thought might drive me over the edge and into an uncontrollable state of lunacy!"

"If it's so bad, I'll think of something else."

"Thank you."

"We'll find another way to conquer this anxiety you have. In the meantime, Ang, the animals you care for must be ravenously hungry, waiting for you to give them their first meal of the day. Hop to it and I'll consider your qualms again once I've finished studying this sample."

Angela nodded, saying, "Of course," and made her way into the inner room where the experimental creatures were lodged. Professor Millard had not suggested psychiatry, a course of action perhaps taking years of treatment, although he believed it might eventually be necessary. He did not believe she was crazy, just unusually emotional and at times overwrought, a young woman focused on things to which most people would not pay undue attention.

The door closed behind her and Angela stood there momentarily. Her eyes darting over to the long wall of cages where the animals were kept. They focused first upon Misty, a small Pomeranian with a tail wagging happily like a windshield wiper as it caught the trace of someone else in the room. The dog, unable to see, had her snout shoved against the wire enclosure, sniffing eagerly, its pink eyes squinting as it gazed in the direction of the visitor. It recognized Angela by her scent, gave a few joyful yips, and moved its tail back and forth even more rapidly.

Of all the animals she tended, Misty was her favorite. There was something infectious in the dog's jubilant behavior reaching the lab attendant's inner core, making her feel good all over as she responded to its intense joyfulness. Since its arrival, Misty had been the specimen Angela attended to first, holding the animal and stroking its satiny fur, whispering gently and cuddling it as though it were a newborn baby.

"And how have you been, Misty?" she cooed to it. "Did you have a pleasant night? Did you dream about eating a pile of bones?"

Misty looked up into Angela's face as though she understood every word, squirming as she tried to lick it. She had been blind since an unfortunate accident robbed her of normal vision, making her a good candidate for Millard's study. Both the professor and Angela were hopeful the Pomeranian would eventually be able to join the ranks of the sighted, her vision restored enough to share life with others of her kind on the outside. No matter how long it took, Millard would see to it she was well cared for, protected and encouraged to live a canine-oriented life as he continued in his search for a serum to eventually restore her sight.

Angela cleaned the cage, fed and groomed her, scratched between her ears and returned her to her pen before moving on to her next charge. Later, she would take Misty and some of the other animals for one of their daily walks.

Next on her list was a soft and gentle but easily agitated rabbit named Chester. It had been born two months prematurely without its two front legs. Dr. Millard's treatment was tailored to grow them to their proper size, as were the two hind ones. Millard had been challenged by this seemingly impossible task by a veterinarian who had known of his miraculous accomplishments on other creatures. Would he be able to restore the legs of this shy and timid creature? He would try. As yet, he had been unable to develop the combination which would stimulate growth of the missing limbs, but he was willing to continue the attempt, hopeful he would succeed, in time.

Angela fed the hungry bunny, talking tenderly to it and massaging the miniscule stumps, as directed by Millard, to encourage their extension. She was confident the professor would be able to discover something to aid the creature. What it might be, she had no idea, but she was encouraged knowing he had made cures in other animals to relieve pain, restore mobility and encourage the growth of different organs and assorted body parts. She finished stroking Chester's fur and plugged in the 'probe', a marvelous device invented by Millard to stimulate natural cellular regeneration.

Her attention next moved to Mondo, the unscaled rock python, and from him to Alexander, the rooster without a backbone and finally to Felix, the mouse born with two heads and a purplish antler growing between them.

She gave to all her devoted care along with the specialized attention they craved, happy to spend time with them as it distracted her from thinking about her own problems.

In the meantime, Professor Millard was lost in thought as he dissected the remains of a night crawler someone had brought to him, knowing of his special interests. He prepared slide after slide of various segments and finally gave up for the morning, planning to make another attempt the next day.

He was beginning to work on his next task of the morning when he heard a loud shriek from the specimen room. It was repeated over and over again, sounding as though someone had been caught in a log grinder! The glass he was holding slipped from his fingers and he mildly cursed as what was left of the crawler slid off the slide and onto the table. Thoughts of his examination were gone as he raced into the next room from where the unabated screams were coming.

"What happened?" he cried, rushing into the room.

Angela glanced down as she backed away from a large, swollen spider sitting on the floor next to the overturned box in which it had been encased. A look of wretched horror stretched the lines of her face,

"What happened?" he exclaimed again, lowering his voice and moving toward his assistant, his gaze fixated on the dime-sized orbs next to her staring up at him. It was an enormous arachnid, black as anthracite and nearly the size of a mouse, standing defiantly on eight stilt-like legs.

"Stop shrieking!" he demanded.

Angela stopped, but continued to shiver, and it took long seconds for her to catch her breath and settle her nerves. She backed up even further.

At last she pointed and waved her finger unsteadily at the creature.

"That's what terrified me. I was putting some pellets back on the top shelf and the cage up there moved *all by itself,* right to the edge, and then toppled over to the floor. I didn't touch it! The top of the crate sprang open and *that* crawled out."

"Now, now, nothing to be alarmed about," he said, attempting to placate her.

"But I didn't *touch* it. I was five feet away from it when the cage *moved itself*!"

"Don't worry about it, Ang. It will be all right."

His words were reassuring and comforting, but she sensed he did not believe her.

"Really!" she insisted, stamping her foot. "It moved by itself, or maybe the thing was jumping around inside and that caused it to fall."

"There, there. No one is saying you did anything wrong."

He retrieved the crate and its top, perforated with air holes, and moved to scoop the offending creature back into the container.

Let Angela have her fantasy if it helps to relieve her anxiety, Mallard thought. He did not accept her explanation of the receptacle moving without outside help, but he had no intention of refuting her claim. It did not matter. The spider was out and would have to be returned—and the sooner the better.

He put the box over it, restricting its attempt to scuttle away.

"Did it bite you?" he asked.

"No, no, but I was afraid if it reached me..."

"Well, it does bite, but its venom has been removed so it wouldn't have harmed you. Nature will not renew it for another month,"

"Oh, no? Only scare me out of another ten years of my life and turn my hair instantly white!"

"I hope it wasn't quite so bad, Ang and actually your hair looks quite nice. But I do apologize. It's my fault. When I said I was thinking of ordering it, you made no objection—so I did. What I didn't mention was that the shipment had already arrived—yesterday. Didn't want to alarm you. I put it on the top shelf, waiting for a good opportunity to introduce the specimen to you, have you become accustomed to it and reduce your fear of its species."

"*This* is what you were going to use to cure my phobia?"

"It's what I had in mind, yes. I thought the therapy would succeed, but I've had second thoughts since our talk this morning. I didn't want to dispose of it while you were in here working so I didn't mention it. It won't bother you again, Ang. I promise."

"I should hope not. Since it escaped once, I'd be in constant anxiety it would again."

"No, it couldn't get away again, Ang. This was an accident of some kind. I don't want to increase your concerns, so I'll abandon the idea and ship it back later today."

Angela nodded in understanding. Her sobs subsided. She reached into her purse for a tissue and dried her eyes.

"Well, thank you for your assurance, Professor. I'm finished with my work now and it's time for me to go to class."

"Then you run along. Mildred will be here in a few minutes to relieve you, anyway."

Angela turned and left without saying goodbye. She was uncommonly upset and still annoyed by his deception as she walked to the early model Piquet she referred to as 'My Piggy' and slid behind the wheel. It was scrapped and dented, abused and rusted, but it had been priced right and all she could afford; but she did not care as long as it started each time and got her to where she wanted to go. She turned the key in the ignition and drove toward the university.

* * * *

Millard shook his head. It was silly for Angela to be so upset over such a trivial matter. However, she was an ideal assistant, and suggesting her fear was unreal and should not result in an overwrought condition, would not end her troubles. It was unfortunate the accident happened but since it had, and there was nothing, he could do about it, he could only apologize.

The problem was, he did not want to return the sampling to the supply house, as he had promised. He wanted to keep it. He had already extracted the poison from its venom sac, but knew it would be replenished within a month or so. The properties of the toxin fascinated him, both the known and the unknown, and he wanted to add it to one of the formulas he was planning to use in the treatment of Misty.

"What should I do?" he wondered aloud, preparing a new slide. "Continue with the experiment and hope Angela's fear dissipates on its own? Keep the creature and drain its poison, as needed?" Millard decided to continue the deception and hope for the best. The worst that might happen, if found out, Angela might resign from her position with him.

It was shortly before noon when, his work for the morning completed, Professor Millard went to the specimen room and took down the crate containing the spider. He had changed his mind—again. It was more important to keep his promise to the young aide than acquire the scientific knowledge he might gain by using the spider's venom. He removed the lid for one last look before wrapping it up and mailing it back to the supply house.

The crate, he was bewildered to discover, was empty.

* * * *

Angela pulled into the McDonald's drive-through lane and ordered a cheeseburger and French fries. They came with a thank you and a smile from the attendant. She left the lot, turned right and drove two blocks to City Park where she left her car beneath a spreading maple tree. Stepping out, she proceeded to an unoccupied bench where she opened the bag and began to eat her frugal lunch. The sun was overhead, fighting its way through sparse cloud cover and then through a canopy of greenery to reach the ground in a patchwork-quilt design. She smiled as a squirrel ran up to within a few feet to stare at her, sitting on its haunches, looking at her expectantly. When she did not quickly offer a tidbit of food, it dashed away, arching its back, lurching up and down like a sea serpent parting the waves.

"Should have stayed around," she yelled at it, as the creature disappeared up a tree. "I would have shared this with you."

She was familiar with this particular animal and knew it would come back within the next few minutes—it always did—subduing its natural fear and overcoming its reluctance to associate with anything larger than itself and partake of whatever food was tossed its way.

The appearance of the spider must have been a coincidence, arriving when she least expected one, or perhaps it was something that indicated greater import. She believed such incidences did not just happened and there was intelligent direction of some sort behind them.

She opened her eyes wider at the sound of a scurrying rustle only to see an unknown creature scooting down the tree, one with the head of the squirrel and the body of a gigantic spider. It wobbled to the bench where Angela was so paralyzed, she was unable to move! It grabbed a large portion of burger from her grasp, the rest dropping to her lap, and returned to the tree where it disappeared a moment later.

"Isn't nature wonderful?" she thought with unusual sarcasm, slowly munching a morsel of french-fry removed from its container, following it with a sip of Coke to wash it down, alternating from one delicious taste to the other.

Sudden, she felt the sensation of tiny feet scuttling up the side of her leg and, looking down, spied a hairy body advancing upward.

"Eeek!" she gasped, compulsively, dropping what remained of her cheeseburger and sack to her lap. She controlled her momentary outburst, but not in time to prevent those who sat at nearby benches from hearing and turning her way. There being no further outcry, however, they lost interest and returned to their individual thoughts. Fortunately, her cup of Coke sat on the bench next to her, intact.

"Yuck," she said more softly, her voice under control and not reaching the others. It was a tiny creature, so small she was not certain it had the qualifying eight legs, but she still wanted to have nothing to do with it. She flicked it off, watched it fall, and with the same motion accidentally brushed the rim of the cup, sending it also to the ground. Quickly, she stood up as a few drops of soda splattered her dress. The remainder of her sandwich slipped from her lap and followed her drink to the ground.

Angela sighed. She was sated anyway, but would have finished her meal if it had not happened. She left the remaining food where it was, knowing some animal, more than likely her bushy-tailed friend, would be along and enjoy an unexpected repast.

She closed her eyes, momentarily enjoying the cool breeze sweeping through the leaves, wondering factiously if the sudden appearance had some inner meaning.

Angela picked up the empty bag, the wrapping and the cup, and carried the litter to a nearby trash basket where she disposed it. She had a few minutes before going to her one o'clock class, but was so unnerved decided to leave without delay. She would get there early and sit in the classroom, reviewing her notes of the previous day, waiting for her instructor and fellow classmates to arrive.

* * * *

It was late afternoon when, her classes ended for the day. Angela put her books into her briefcase and drove to the little house she shared with her mother. She parked in the driveway, closed her eyes for just a moment to collect her thoughts before going inside, and reflected upon the incidents of her day. She left the vehicle and was about to make her way to the front door when she heard a sharp and penetrating animal sound coming from the house across the street. She looked around and froze at what she saw! Despite the shadows of thickening twilight, her eyes fixated on an animal scuttling out from under the porch, large and hairy enough to cause the primal instincts of anyone to leap to instant alert.

Down the lawn towards her the massive spider charged! Angela's mouth opened wide with an astonished gasp as she saw the hairs on the creature's body elevated like needles. It was as big as a large dog, with shark-like teeth flashing wickedly at her, ready to impale anything with which they came in contact. Dripping from them was a greenish, lecherous-looking substance.

Angela, unable to move, began to sob. Had she not suffered enough for the day?

At the rate it was traveling, it would reach the edge of the front lawn in another moment, cross the sidewalk, then the street, and within another second have her in its jaws, grinding her into tiny pieces. There was no time to run and evade it and Angela could only hope it was an illusion that would vanish if she did not stare directly at it. She shifted her gaze for a moment and when she looked again was able to see a large chain, one end tied to a stake in the ground, the other attached to a collar encircling the hound's neck, bringing the charging beast to a halt at the edge of the grass. She blinked her eyes and when she looked again, what she saw was so reassuring she wanted to applaud. As she stared, it melded into the familiar shape of her neighbor's mastiff, a young one, still adding height and bulk to its frame. It stood there across the street, wagging its tail at her.

Angela released the breath she had been unconsciously holding and drew in another, this one more slowly and relaxing. Like the air from a pricked balloon, her anxiety dispersed and soon disappeared.

"My gawd!" she thought, "is my mind turning everything I see, no matter what, into a disgusting spider? It's going to drive me batty until I end up in a mad house, completely unable to function."

The dog, a friendly one she had often seen across the street, enjoyed the freedom of the yard and the passers-by who acknowledged it with a smile and cheery word.

Angela rushed inside the house where her mother greeted her from the kitchen and asked how her day was going. "Dinner will be ready soon," she added. "You have time to change and wash up."

Asking how her day had gone was a rhetorical question Angela did not bother to answer. She ran upstairs to her bedroom where she slipped into more informal, lounging attire, washed her hands and face and descended downstairs to the living room where she watched TV for the next few minutes.

With feet resting on a hassock, she concentrated on a journalist broadcasting the news of the day and the tension slowly seemed to seep from her pores. Soon she was comfortable and somewhat relaxed, much of her anxiety lessened; there she would stay until called into the kitchen for her evening repast.

Her mother, knowing something of her daughter's current fears, was unaware of the new ones occurring during the day, and Angela wondered if her activities should be kept to herself and treated as unmentionable secrets, locked in her mind, imprisoned in a dark vault and not to be shared. On the other hand, perhaps she should at least mention the delusions attacking her during the daylight hours. She considered doing so and then decided it would be just one more burden for a solitary mother to assume. Raising her young daughter, and at the same time contending with the adversities besetting a single parent, was enough of a struggle with which to contend.

* * * *

Angela fearfully crawled into bed, settling herself between the cool sheets, and tentatively closed her eyes, almost certain the horrors of the night would begin from where they had left off, vicious visions of being trapped in a steaming jungle environment where wild animals ranged freely and devoured each other, predators chasing their prey and avoiding the larger meat eaters who plotted to kill and devour *them!*

She slept fitfully, awaking nearly every hour drenched in muggy sweat, shuddering as though the apparitions invading her consciousness were real. Toward morning, the spiders made their appearance again, appraising her with dime-sized eyes. There was no way to halt their advance as they crawled onto her head and burrowed amidst the nest of follicles. The young woman was unable to waken, although she tried in vain. She could only lie there as though paralyzed, believing herself to be awake, but uncertain as to where or when the dream state ended and wakefulness began.

At one point in her nightmares, she felt the bites of countless needles jabbing into and using her scalp as a pin cushion, and before she knew it the burrowing began as countless devils sought to invade her brain, tunneling in and out of the furrows of her cranium, nibbling here, biting there, until she feared her cell structure was being chewed away.

She awoke with a groaning squawk with the heat of the morning sun creeping over her bedclothes on its way to her face, bathed with dried perspiration.

* * * *

The followed day was one of inexpressible horror. Breakfast time failed to satisfy her needs as it nearly always did, and she went about her daily routine, distraught, unresponsive and unhappy.

Arriving at her place of work, she experienced an abysmal repulsion when she opened the door to the lab to begin her duties. There at the table, its body swollen like a balloon, its hairs twitching as though in response to a concerto, was the largest spider she had ever seen. Four of its legs were below the professor's table, another three rested on the top and the eighth held a glass vial up to the light.

Angela wanted to scream, but her vocal cords seemed frozen. Moments later, she was glad she had made no outburst of revulsion, when the calming words of, "Good morning, Ang. How's tricks today?" came to her.

When she looked again, she saw it was Professor Millard sitting there, holding a phial and grinning at her.

"Angela!" he cried, his smile wilting fading from his face. *"What is it? You're as white as a lab rat!"*

Hesitantly, he came to his feet and went to her, his face etched in deep concern. She was so distraught, unhappy and deeply concerned the only words for her to say were, "Not a thing...nothing is wrong. I thought...I thought...I'll be fine in a moment."

She did not tell him what she imagined she had seen and despite her denial she was certain it would be a long time before she was fine again... perhaps, never.

"Nonsense," he said, putting his arm around her shoulders and leading her to a chair. "You're as white as a mound of snow and look as though you've seen a ghost. Something happened and I want you to tell me about it.

"Can I get you a glass of water? Brew some tea for you?"

"No, thanks," she declined. "I'll be all right in a minute."

How could she possibly tell him he had looked like a gigantic spider when she first walked into the room? She was tempted to tell him—he was such a gentle and understanding person—but she simply could not. Instead, she asked:

"Did you send the monstrosity back to the supply house?"

"Monst...you mean the spider I had ordered?"

She stared at him, unable to confirm for a moment it was precisely what she meant. She merely nodded, restraining her response, hoping he did not answer in the negative.

"Why, yes," he lied.

He had honestly planned to return it and keep his promise to her. But when he had gone to box it up, it was no longer there. He had searched the room without finding it and eventually decided it had managed to somehow escape and was now outside the building. A large bird or other animal would eventually find it, he assumed, and take care of the problem for him.

Fear of the spider must be what was troubling her, making her shoulders continue to shudder, but he could not bring himself to tell the truth which would only increase her anxiety. Nature would eliminate the spider for him.

Angela went straight to her work room without saying further words to Millard and began her desultory tasks. Did she imagine it, or did Misty actually snarl at her as she moved it to a temporary cage before cleaning its quarters. It sat there with an unfocused look on its face as she prepared its morning meal. The dog must also be having a difficult morning, she decided, for it bared its teeth as she reached to scratch between its ears.

"Suit yourself," she said, jerking her hand away. Animals, like people, had their temperamental times also, she decided. She was not in the best of spirits herself. Hopefully, both she and Misty would be feeling more congenial tomorrow.

The rock python, Mondo, wasn't doing any better, tightly wrapping its coils around her arm and squeezing so tightly it hurt, determined not to let her go. In fact, all of the creatures she tended seemed to be quite different in their individual ways. Felix, like Mondo, was overtly hostile, quite different from its usual behavior. And Chester seemed to be exceedingly fearful, more so than usual, trembling uncontrollably when she reached into its container, cringing when she attempted to move it into a temporary unit. The pleasant, usually timid and passive creature showed unusual aggression and a complete disdain for her attentions. All the others noticeably displayed a unique change in their temperaments.

Angela halted her scheduled tasks for a spell, wondering if the professor had looked in on them earlier in the day. Had he noticed the sudden change in the comportment of the animals? She considered talking with him about it, but changed her mind. He was not the type to notice such trivia.

It was shortly before noon time when Angela gathered her purse and prepared to leave for the day. The animals had all been attended to and this time she had no regrets about leaving them for another day. They, in turn, indicated no sense of sadness in her departure. They retreated into their own malaise and ignored her absence.

In the next room she found Millard staring absently at the wall, his work pushed aside, not engaged in his usual tasks and apparently deep in thought. He had been considering Angela's problem and steps he might take to help her. She had been an almost entirely different person this morning, quite distracted, barely greeting him, a sour look on her countenance and her step hesitant and uncertain. Quite likely, it was her phobia of the leggy critters weighing her down again, changing her usually happy and friendly demeanor to one of abstracted glumness.

He looked up as she approached and offered her a faint smile.

"Can you spare me a few moments before leaving for lunch, Ang?" the professor asked as she passed his desk.

"Certainly," she said, glancing at the wall clock and giving a nod of her head.

"Have a seat, please," he requested. He could tell by her slow response and indecisive movements she really did not want to. He would be quick and not take up too much of her time if it made her uncomfortable.

"I noticed a considerable change in the animals earlier today," he began. "Somehow they seem to be quite different in their behavior. Their friskiness is gone and their attention span is close to zero. They seem to be very tired and not nearly as responsive."

"I've noticed it, too," she replied. "They seem to be worse this morning."

A look of sudden interest appeared in her eyes and quickly faded.

"Do you have any idea what might be going on?" he asked, shuffling his papers around, nervously. "I've thought about it extensively and can't come up with any reason for the change."

"I have no idea, Professor," she said, her response terse and detached.

The tall, blond scientist, threads of grey growing between the strands of his hair, pursed his lips and shook his head.

"I wondered, at times, if it was my imagination."

"I don't think so, unless it's mine, also."

Millard stopped moving his papers about and looked at her keenly. "You've changed, also, Ang. Are you getting enough sleep?"

The young student laughed shortly, an edgy laugh, not a response to something amusing he had said.

"Since you mention it, Professor, my sleep pattern has undergone a change. I'm getting enough of it, I guess, but it's not 'good' sleep. I awake during the night with tremors draining the vitality from me and sometimes I'm able to remember isolated incidences of *things* in my dream more than disturbing—things outright frightening."

"Anything special you can recall now?"

"Spiders. Big ones, little ones, creepy crawlers with gnashing teeth, squirming through the tendrils of my hair and then burrowing through my scalp!"

Angela could not believe she was telling him all of this, intending to keep most of it secret. Even her mother did not know this much about her awful sleeping fantasies.

"Yuck! It's no wonder you're feeling as you do. Besides your sleep deprivation, are there other physical symptoms?"

There were, but she was certainly not going to mention the alteration of her monthly menstrual cycle or her uncanny craving for the taste of peppermint sticks. It was not something he needed to know.

"Just listlessness—a degree of weakness. I remember feeling the same way during a condition I had a few years ago when something drained my white blood corpuscles—at least it's how it was described to me. I forget the technical terms the doctor used. But I felt nearly the same way then as I do now. It lasted for a week or so until a prescription the doctor gave to me began to work. The conditions are similar, but it's not the same disorder. It's just the same lethargic feeling."

"Could be due to lots of things," Millard said, thoughtfully. "But these leggy brutes you mention, crawling in your hair...you didn't experience *them* months ago, did you?"

"Not a bit! I've always been afraid of the critters, but it's normal for many people, isn't it?

"Of course. It's a common dread."

"Another thing—maybe I shouldn't mention this, Professor—you'll think me crazy..."

"Yes?"

"When I got here this morning, I didn't see you at first. What I saw was a humongous arachnid sitting in your chair, working at your desk!

"I wanted to scream, but my lungs seemed petrified and nothing would come out! The monstrosity quickly changed into...*you*...and I was glad I hadn't said anything. You would have thought I was...well...buggy!"

Gawd! She had done it again—revealed those thoughts she should never have uttered to *anyone*. Her only excuse, she thought, as she left his clinic, was he was so nice and calming to talk with, so serene and comforting, so accepting and nonjudgmental; nothing seemed to upset him.

Professor Millard, on his part, was stunned at her revelation and at a total loss for wordage of his own. What could account for her beliefs and the behavior of the animals? Maybe it was something in the water, or perhaps the air pressure was lower or higher; even a fluctuation in the heat might be responsible. All of this he judged to be quite unlikely, but without knowing the actual cause, he could only engage in wild speculations.

* * * *

School did not go as usual for Angela. The voice of her instructor, Roland Rodrigues, droned on and on like a lively hive of frenzied bees, with little variation.

"How boring can one person be?" she wondered, her eyelids lowering for the sixth time in the last five minutes. "He continues endlessly, repetitively, with little of substance to say. Doesn't he know many of his students skimped and sacrificed to pay for their schooling, to earn a diploma leading to a more secure future? Did he not..."

On and on he went; Angela's eyes closed again, the pen dropped onto her folder of notes and she nodded off into the pleasant dreamland which had evaded her the night before.

"Miss Daniels!" boomed an angry voice, followed by a sharp cracking sound as Rodrigues' pointer slapped his lectern. "Am I keeping you *awake?* Are you *with* us today, or off on some cosmic flight of your own?"

Angela's eyes snapped open, as did her mouth, with no verbal response as she stared at the frightful scene before her. The creepy crawler was there, standing behind the podium, one spidery leg clutching a stick and the other holding its bloated abdomen swelling out like a beach ball, its mouth curved in a crooked sneer, its red eyes focused directly upon her.

"Err, err, " she managed to enunciate as the gigantic arachnid flailed away and then suddenly faded to reveal the form of her angry teacher standing there, his lips set in an angry scowl.

"No, sir. Perhaps if..."

"Not now, Miss Daniels; the others are here to learn and are waiting. Please pay attention. You're here to be educated, not to catch up on sleep you obviously didn't have time for during your frivolous evening."

Members of the class nearby snickered as Angela's face turned from its usual pigmentation to a fiery rose in color. He sniffed and shifted his gaze to include more of the students.

"And the rest of you, please understand: I am not a standup comedian here to entertain you. Behave yourselves!"

Angela was now wide awake, humiliated, repentant and chastened, unable to raise her gaze to look him in the eyes.

This must stop! This must *absolutely* stop, she insisted to herself. What I saw was only a phantasm and was not real! Rodrigues is not a spider and in no way does he resemble one—even if his legs are a bit gangly.

Angela kept her eyes opened for the remainder of the session, afraid to even blink. She cut her next class and went home to continue the nap from which she had so abruptly been interrupted. Her mother was not at home and would not be for another couple of hours. She was still not there when the young student awakened from her nap, refreshed, but knowing it likely meant another night of apprehensive sleep.

She next went to her computer and began working on a difficult project she had been delaying. Unable to concentrate, she proceeded to the Internet and typed 'spiders' into the browser before realizing what she had done. She was quickly offered more than a hundred million pages giving her information, most of them she would not be unable to use. She went to Wikipedia, usually one her first sources to begin her research.

She learned something of the existing types, but none matched the description of the brute seen in Professor Millard's menagerie. Was it a newly discovered member of the phyla, so recently discovered it had not yet been studied and entered into the pages of her references? She ended her research for the day, tired and feeling she had been cramming for another exam. She knew a bit more about her eight-legged nemesis, but had come across nothing to explain how it was so able to affect her.

Later, her nightmares returned and were worse than ever. The massive spider across the street from her home and the one at Millard's desk were the featured players in all of them, along with the one morphing into her teacher. It was surrounded by hundreds of tiny ones having the faces of her classmates. When Rodrigues came towards her, furiously waving his pointer, the smaller ones followed after him like a trail of ants.

"Eew!" she exclaimed, moaning and turning over. "It was a female after all and now it's hatched a brood of *babies!*"

Angela awoke with her entire body sopping with moisture and made her way to the bathroom to shower and rinse off the offensive secretions. She was fully awake and reinvigorated when she went to the kitchen to greet her mother and partake of her first coffee of the day.

"How are you, my dear?" asked Joyce, concern mounting as she studied the countenance of her daughter, noting the redness of her eyes and the hollows beneath.

"Just fine, Mom," Angela answered.

"You're a terrible liar, Angie!" she exclaimed. "You didn't sleep at all, did you?"

"Actually, I got a lot of sleep," she disagreed, dumping a slip of saccharin into her cup. "It wasn't so bad."

"Then it was the dreams again. Right?"

"You're right, as usual," Angela affirmed, shrugging her shoulders.

* * * *

After finishing her tasks at the clinic, the lab assistant enjoyed a Mc-

Donald's luncheon of French fries and a fish sandwich at the park, then made her way to the University of Higher Learning, as she termed the community college she attended. She discovered her first class of the day had been cancelled and her next would not begin until three o'clock. She could either go home and wait, or use the next two hours to study at the library. She chose the latter and spent her time strolling about its corridors and shelves, finally selecting some books to use in her upcoming, midterm composition, along with a ponderous volume regarding spiders. Her hope was greater knowledge would give her some insight into their more unusual properties and, perhaps in turn, help her to resolve her own troubles with them. Armed with her reading material, paper for notes and pencil in purse, she located a desk in a quiet alcove of the cathedral-like building, sat down and spread her sources out before her.

Not more than five minutes had passed when the focus of her attention was interrupted by words of a greeting from one of her classmates.

She looked up to see Jimmy Dunst, a skinny runt of a kid, pulling out the chair opposite from her and sitting down.

"Don't see you around these hallowed halls very often, Angie," he said. "Aren't you supposed to be in Rodrigues' class now? Our trig session won't start for more than an hour or so."

"My one o'clock was cancelled, so I'm just killing time 'til my next," she explained.

"I'm usually here about this time on Thursdays," he said, conversationally, setting down the book he carried with him, in no hurry to open it up. "Seems like I spend half my life at the library—especially with my part-time job, shelving books.

"Say, what's this?" he asked, reaching for the top book on her stack. "Spiders, huh? You a fiend or friend of the monstrous maulers?"

"Neither," she retorted, reaching out, retrieving the volume and returning it to her pile.

"Well, I'm both. Have been, ever since I was a little kid, running around the neighborhood with an insect jar, scaring the girls with my bug collection."

"Yuck!" Angela asserted. "Why would you?"

"Don't know. Maybe because I was a little boy and enjoyed scaring little girls. Thought it was great fun! Called the bugs my Wriggling Rascals. When I was older, sometime in my teens, I specialized in arachnids, carrying them in a bottle and offering to let my friends put their hand inside to pet them."

"Yuck," exclaimed Angela, again. "You must have been the terror of your neighborhood. Glad I didn't know you then."

"No one, not even Butch Gentry, took me up on the offer—and he was the toughest kid in the neighborhood. 'Course, I wouldn't put *my* hand in the jar, *either*. Didn't know which of the beasts, if any, might bite me. Eventually, I stuck a pin in 'em and nailed 'em to a cork board where they squirmed around until they died. Then I sort of lost interest in them."

Angela wondered if she had known a boy like Jimmy while she was growing up, one who was reckless and callous, intent upon frightening girls with bugs and such. If she had, might that have caused her phobia? Would his ruthless tyranny rub off on her after all these years? Maybe yes, maybe no. She thought back to her childhood and remembered no incidences where insidious insects or spiders were even mentioned to her, let alone used to frighten her.

"Jimmy, you're terrible."

"I know it." A look of contrition colored his freckled cheeks. "But it was my collection, and I guess I was proud of it at the time."

"Did you move on and mutilate cats or birds you caught?"

The lad laughed, nervously. "No, nothing so terrible. I grew up and lost my earlier fascination with such things in high school. Don't know what happened to my captures—my mother probably tossed 'em in the trash one day when she got tired of looking at 'em. Haven't thought of the collection for a long time."

"Wouldn't take me any time at all to get rid of it," she vowed.

Jimmy nodded. "Well, gotta leave. Going outside, lie down on the lawn for a while and read—catch some rays, maybe a curious insect or two. Care to join me?"

"No thanks. See ya later."

"Later," returned Jimmy.

He was sort of a nice boy, she reflected, although a bit loquacious and clueless as far as reading a woman's temperament when she wanted to be left alone. He had invited her to join him at the coffee shop on several occasions and she had declined. She did not know why, but now, after hearing him describe his treatment of helpless creatures, she suspected she intuitively picked up on some instinctive knowledge warning her to tread carefully where he was concerned. She had heard of people who tortured animals in their boyhood growing up to be dangerous serial killers. She did not think Jimmy was one, but he made her flesh seem to creep at times when he came onto her as though he was able to read her mind.

She did not believe in spooks, or anything else having to do with the paranormal. Ghosts, apparitions, anything infesting the dark hours before sunsets generally bored her. And why not? Never had she experienced anything out of the normal except for the current spider manifestations, and she felt sorry for those who did, especially those misguided individuals who called in to the *Coast-to-Coast* radio program she sometimes heard in the middle of the night. She had listened to it the night before, staying awake much later than she usually did.

Angela glanced at the clock and noted she still had more than an hour to wait. Maybe she should have joined Jimmy on the lawn, but no, she was better off where she was. She yawned and closed her eyes, shutting out the gray walls of the library and countless stacks of books, and felt the comforting peace.

"Trust your instincts," advised a voice, sounding quite close to her ears. "You were right to recognize Jimmy as being the sort of person to avoid."

"You're absolutely correct," she agreed, raising her head and turning to see who had spoken.

There was no one within a dozen feet of her.

She gulped. Was she rapidly losing her mind?

Angela spent the next several minutes in what she later believed to be a dream state, moving into and out of an impossible reality

"Who said that?" she asked uneasily.

"Me…I did. I'm down here."

Angela lowered her eyes to behold, squeezing out from beneath her purse, a flattened form growing in length and roundness, expanding into the shape of a tennis ball. A moment later a creature, fully six inches long, stood there on its eight legs, looking up at her. Its mouth, a moderately-sized slash, was closed, but from it came further words of explanation.

"You see me now, don't you?

The words seemed to be audible, but not to her ears. It was thinking, not talking out loud, somehow transmitting its thoughts to her.

"I…I…I think I do!" she stammered.

"I'm tiny," the small creature said, raising one of its eight spindly legs and flexing it at the middle joint like a weightlifter, *"but very strong."*

"This cannot *BE*!" she thought and looked about the room to see if anyone nearby was hearing or seeing the same thing she was.

No one was paying any attention to her!

"But it's true and you should believe it," the creature assured her.

Angela gasped. It must be reading her thoughts, just as she had been reading the spider's.

"Why are you reading books about my species?" it asked. "I can tell you anything you'd like to know about it. I happen to be one, myself."

"Nonsense," Angela thought back. "You're nothing more than a poorly digested fish sandwich…or a tainted French fry—or something I had for breakfast this morning."

She still did not believe, insisting to herself she was undergoing a strange form of feverish, irrational thinking.

"Okay. Have it your way—if that's what you want to believe."

"This is not real...real...real!" The words echoed in her mind repeatedly, a constant refrain repeated over and over again until consciousness was returned to her. Angela did not know what to believe and finally said, "It's the way I must think, or check myself into a psych ward!"

"You would not be happy there."

Angela was becoming more flustered and frustrated and then her mind turned to thoughts of defense. She could grab one of the books and smash it down on the menacing uninvited one, flatten it and watch the blood squirt all over.

"I would not try it," the intruder thought. "I am quick...very quick... and, if necessary, I can teleport myself to any place I wish, even to other dimensions.

"What would you like to know about me?" it asked, changing the nature of their conversation. "For your essay, I mean."

Angela could think of a million different questions to ask of it. She tried to calm herself down and resist the temptation to flee the building away from this...this... evilness...whatever it was.

Or perhaps she should accept its invitation. Play along with it.

After further thought, it's precisely what she decided to do, although she had never heard of a sentient spider and did not believe for a moment one actually existed—at least, not in a sane world of reality.

"Tell me about yourself," she said, marveling at how easy it was to think the words instead of pronouncing them out loud.

The strange entity sat down, lowering its haunches so its rear rested on top of the desk, its front legs propping it up, sitting there like a puppy.

"To begin with, I am an arachnid *of the* Loxosceles genus, born in Santa Catarina, Brazil and referred to as a Santa Scrambler. As you can tell, I possess extraordinary properties."

"I certainly can."

Perhaps, by playing along with it, she could eliminate its influence and emerge from this dream state, or whatever condition she was in, unscathed. After all, this could be nothing but a hallucination,

"My name is Hairiet—you can call me Hairy. Can you guess why?"

"Because you're so...so..."

"Hairy? Is that what you want to say?"

"Well, yes. But I did not want to be rude...."

"That does not bother me in the least, Angela Daniels. I am what I am. My mate's name was Harry, also. He no longer exists. After impregnating me, I ate him! Finished him in three bites."

"You're pregnant? You don't look as though you are."

"Oh, but I am. "Shortly before my own birth, my mother was chosen to be the subject of a senseless experiment and was bombarded by gamma rays. Her altered genes were passed to me, giving me unusual properties, making me distinct from others of my kind."

"Resulting in your marvelous abilities?" the young student wanted to know, awed at the authenticity of what she believed to be the strangest dream ever experienced.

"It is. You see me now as I choose to appear. The real 'me' is a little larger, but not nearly as big as the dog you saw the other day. Yes, the pooch was me. One of my mental, acrobatic tricks, of course.

"You wonder about my attributes? One of them is an ability to shrink and expand at will. At this moment, I am the size I want to be without drawing excessive attention to myself."

"Very wise."

"I saw you first at Professor Millard's clinic. Remember? I was on the top shelf in his animal room. Deciding to know you better, I caused my cage to fall off the shelf and onto the floor."

"You did?"

"I did. I am an adept illusionist, among my other abilities, with the ability to create delusions; when I am around, you cannot be certain if your thoughts are your own or what I want you to believe. Telekinesis is another of my abilities."

"You're not actually talking out loud now, are you? You're in control of my mind?"

"I am. And you, in turn, are able to read mine, so we can exchange mental messages. Just another of my…"

"I know…attributes," Angela finished for it.

"Exactly! I know little of what happened before I was born. Perhaps one or both of my parents were extraterrestrials."

"Ooohhh," thought Angela, in feigned dismay and sarcasm, "That explains everything, doesn't it?"

Angela rubbed her eyes, uncertain if she were fantasizing again or actually in communication with a Santa Scrambler.

"I'm also able to change into different bodies and transport myself through space from one place to another, at will. I'm able to do many amazing things."

"Multi-talented," Angela thought. "What is it you want of me? Why pursue me as you do?"

"Because," and its thoughts became suddenly ominous, "I will be giving birth to my young quite soon and they will need a place in which to live."

Angela, not quite knowing why, was horrified at its words.

"You will be the nest, Angela—their refuge. I have explored your brain cavity and believe it the very best place to incubate my young."

Angela shuddered and gulped, dropped her head to the desk and began to sob. When she raised it, the creature was no longer there.

What was fantasy, she wondered, and what was reality? Had she really been sitting here, talking to a fearful arachnid in possession of extraordinary abilities? Or had she managed to blend in different thought patterns making everything seem so real?

She felt like Alice falling down the rabbit hole!

Was she in desperate need of psychiatric help?

* * * *

Angela left her last class and strolled along the campus path to her car, enjoying the cooling breeze caressing her face. Flowers and shrubs grew along the walkway, providing cleansing, untainted air laden with a floral fragrance. She saw a group of acquaintances sitting on a mound look up and motion for her to join them.

The perplexed student smiled, but shook her head, no. She held up one of her text books, mouthed the word 'homework' and continued to her car. With so much weighing on her mind, she was in no mood to socialize and was certain she would be poor company. Her time would be spent more productively if alone by herself.

Had she been attacked by another vision back at the library? And, if so, why at this time, when she was in a state bordering on helplessness and near hysteria, too mentally exhausted and vulnerable to study for the approaching exam coming in a couple of days. Hopefully, her mind would settle down and she would be able to adequately cram and then bluff enough to earn a passing grade.

* * * *

"Dearie," her mother said in distress, after hearing Angela's account of her day. "Relax!"

Her parent was tempted to scold her when hearing of the monstrous phobia tormenting her daughter. Ordinarily, she was able to provide practical and meaningful advice when asked, but this time she had little to say. What do you tell someone who might be in the process of losing total control of herself, caught in the throes of complete unreality? How could she, with no aptitude for psychiatry, attempt to probe her daughter's deliriums in a few minutes and offer her comfort of some sort? She obviously needed the treatment of a significantly experienced psychiatrist!

"If it was me, dearie, I would talk to Professor Millard and ask if he knew of someone he could refer, possibly at a reduced fee, or even gratis."

Angela looked at the anguish in her mother's face.

"What are you *saying*, Mom? I need psychiatric help? I'm ready for the loony hatch?"

"No, I'm not suggesting it at all!"

"Then just what *are* you saying? Perhaps I didn't hear you correctly."

Angela felt as though her life preserver was rapidly deflating and she was sinking into oblivion, drowning as one more causality in life's onward trek.

"I'm only suggesting you need help, Dearie. I don't know how much, but it's more than I can provide."

"You're right, Mom. You'd help me if you could. I thought...I thought..."

"You thought I had a Mommy Bag of tricks, didn't you? That I could open it up, reach in and pick out something to solve your dilemma. I'm sorry, dear. Life doesn't work the way you think. I have problems of my own with which to contend. Ever since your daddy left us..."

"Don't say it, Mom. I've heard it often enough!"

There she goes again, Angela thought. She could not leave it alone, like a scab demanding to be picked. It was true, though; she did have problems; but it was not Angela's place to resolve them, although she would, if she could. Not now, not when she...

She stood up abruptly, excused herself and went to her bedroom to think...to study, maybe get a little schoolwork done, even though she had no enthusiasm for either.

* * * *

At night, Angela dreamed vividly. Unexpectedly, Hairiet made a brief appearance. She was caught in its web, helplessly tangled in its sticky threads, fighting to gain her freedom, when she tumbled through and began to plunge into unknown and terrifying depths. Looking up, she spied Hairiet releasing another silken filament from her spinnerets, then plummet downward to wrap itself around her middle. Spidery hand, over spidery hand, it pulled the sleeping coed back up and into the tangled trap. She awoke and sat up in bed, fearful if she closed her eyes she would again be in the grasp of her black nemesis.

Her dreams seemed to be so tangible, so exceedingly real, as her fantasies blended into and out of what seemed to be such palpable authenticity, preventing her from telling which was real and which was not. The Blackness identifying itself as Hairiet seemed to be with her constantly, making unwanted intrusions into her world, whispering to and frightening her. The dark, hairy thing was polite at first, more reticent and restrained, but as the night wore on it became less friendly, colder, more *spidery*, displaying an absence of warmth as it became more invasive, demanding and controlling.

There was nothing Angela could do to resist its will. The time had come. Its eggs were ready to be deposited, incubated and hatched—and Angela was to be the host.

"*NO!*" she cried out loudly enough to wake her mother in another room but who continued to soundly sleep as though she, herself, was under an enchantment and unable to help even if there were something she could do. Angela must deal with the situation on her own. Professor Millard was not available, the college clinic was closed, nor was there anyone else from whom she could seek assistance.

Her mind drifted back to early youth when her parents had taken her to church and life was infinitely more pleasant and desirable. She thought of times when her mother said nightly prayers with her, and she would drift off to prepare for another day of normalcy. She had known then how to express her devotions, how to ask for the Lord's blessings and help in times of need, but now the words failed to materialize in her mind, as she could think of nothing but what was happening to her.

"*It's time!*" The thought came to her from Hairiet.

For the next half hour, it seemed as though a thousand legs crawled around the foliage of her hair, investigating every fractional inch, looking for—what? She did not know. What she did know was the exploration felt indescribably *dirty,* as though an unclean entity was thrashing about the thickly clustered strands of her tresses.

"Ouch!" she cried, repeatedly.

She attempted to sit up but found she could not. She tried to run her fingers through her locks, to grab the invader and yank it away. The action was denied her.

"Oowe!" she cried again. It *really* hurt—severely—as though some-one had jabbed a pin into her scalp and left it there. She could only lie in bed, helpless, and allow what was happening to continue, experiencing the horror of an exploratory probing of black feelers inspecting her scalp. Hairiet moved slowly, her enormous belly dragging through the follicles, seeking the weakest point of entry. Following the hard, painful jab, she felt another poke, this one so severe it felt as though a screwdriver had been driven into her skull.

Somehow, she raised her hand to run her fingers through her hair, finding a hole in her cranium into which she could insert two fingers. She withdrew them and, although the darkness was too intense for her to see, could feel something sticky and wet clinging to them.

Angela blacked out.

She did not know how long she had been unconscious when she opened her eyes and felt the sensation of thousands of tiny feet trespassing in the inner reaches of her skull and the thought came to her of countless miniature arachnids seeking a portal out of the interior and into the outer world.

Was the brood of the obscenity hatching, Angela wondered, retreating once again into the secure darkness to escape the terror, once again losing consciousness of everything to avoid the horror of tiny multitudes gestating?

Was hatching a good thing, she later wondered, as the incessant herd of miniscule feet scrambled about and infinitesimally small mouths sucked upon the nourishment so necessary to their new lives, threatening to send her screaming over the edge into a world of obscene insanity.

* * * *

When Angela awoke the next morning, blinking her eyes to avoid the morning rays of sun light, the first thing to grip her attention were the tiniest of insect-like creatures crawling about the bedding, hundreds, thousands of them, looking like print marks on her spread. She had never seen such a picturesque fabric before and, as some of them moved, ever so slightly, she was soon convinced they were *alive*.

"Bed bugs!" she immediately thought in disgust, opening her eyes more widely to study the visitants. Her head throbbed with unbearable intensity, as though she had undergone a major surgical operation involving a scalpel and a deranged surgeon. The pain was compounded by intense dizziness immobilizing her, preventing her from sitting up for fear of falling back in bed or rolling to the floor. The pain went on and on without surcease and then she felt the slightest movement in the inner recesses of her skull and the twitch of more little legs emerging through an open cavity at the top of her head, dropping to the blanket to begin a new reign on earth. At the same moment she noticed her pillow and sheets were soaked with blood.

"God, oh, God," she cried, seeing the swarming multitude of sisters and brothers scamper away, almost covering the bed. *"Help me!"*

Angela looked from her pillow to the surrounding blanket. It was also defiled, soaked with what she believed to be her own dried blood, brownish and still gummy.

On her second pillow, off to the side, sat Hairiet, much larger but considerably sleeker, with a wasp-like body no longer bloated and spherical.

The intense pain returned with even greater intensity, feeling as though her head had been slammed with a bat swung by a professional baseball player.

A satisfied smile was on Hairiet's thin lips. *"Do you like my children?"* came her happy thought just before Angela passed out again, wondering with sickish glee if she would be invited to the christening, unwilling to confront the infestation scrambling about.

She awoke minutes later, wondering if she had experienced the worst, or if what had occurred was merely the preamble with the most devastating of all to follow. She raised her hand and touched the back of her head which felt as though it had been struck with a shovel. Her hand felt what seemed to be an inverted bowl in her skull, wet and tacky, large enough to put four fingers into it. They returned smeared with the same substance, red and sticky and wet.

As though a silent signal had been given, each of the infants turned and faced in one direction, then formed into columns before scuttling down the spread to the floor as though they marched in cadence to an inner voice. Hairiet sauntered over to the edge and watched her descending brood.

Angela covered her eyes with trembling fingers, her trepidation of the harrowing sight crippling her with scream after scream.

"There they go," said Hairiet, with immense pride and affection, "my brood, ready to feed and grow and reproduce, my family, off to see the world."

MIRROR OF MEDUSA
Ashley Dioses

Her serpents cried in fair Medusa's ear,
For men encroached upon our lair inside
A cave of wonderments, so dark and drear;
My very surface cracked at Neptune's bride.
Her end was drawing near, and so she paced
Around her garden made of men of stone.
These men were enemies she never faced,
Yet would she live, or welcome Death alone?

As fair Medusa stood in front of me,
I watched her veil descend and fall away.
It drifted down—her eyes, I then could see,
Were emerald wells of pain and deep decay.
Her curse did not reflect, and it was known
Medusa's eyes were theirs, and I was stone.

SUMMER BREAK
Samson Stormcrow Hayes

Shiggy shuffled slowly down the dirt road that lead from the beach into the town of Innsmouth. He was weary after a long night working the kelp beds. His grandmother ran an online algae based Omega-3 vitamin business that was booming and he was spending the summer helping her out. Shiggy was so tired he didn't even notice when his friend Largo Dampworth appeared beside him.

"Good morning!" said Largo. He smiled at his friend, his large lips smacking with delight.

"You mean good night," Shiggy corrected. "I'm going to bed."

"Bed? But it's going to be a beautiful morning. I read that the sun won't be out until noon."

Shiggy shrugged his bulky shoulders, shook his head and said, "I want nothing but the darkness of my closed eyelids." He blinked his large bulbous eyes for emphasis.

"I was hoping you'd join me. It's the first day of summer. Festival will soon be here."

"Festival!" Shiggy spat. "More wasted offerings to Dagon. Perfectly good food wasted on eels and lobsters. Why else do you think they gather around Dagon's statue?"

"Even worse." Largo smiled. "Tourist season begins."

They laughed. Tourists never came to Innsmouth.

They heard a car approaching from behind, but didn't pay it any attention until it honked. Turning, they witnessed a trulky odd sight—a bright yellow convertible with California plates. Inside the car were two young men, early twenties, suntanned with blonde hair. Two long surf boards hung out the back. The driver leaned over the side and asked, "Hey, buddy. Is this the way to Innsmouth?"

Shiggy and Largo nodded slowly.

"Are there any good hostels in town? We're here for the surf."

Largo and Shiggy looked at each other, uncertain what to make of these strangers, these...tourists? Finally, Shiggy suggested, "Try Nelgoth's. He rents rooms during the summer."

Of course, most of the rooms Nelgoth rented were for those arriving for Festival.

"Thanks!" Before he popped the gear and drove off, the driver held out his hand in a strange gesture, his thumb and pinky extended.

Shiggy awkwardly tried to mimic the gesture with his stubby fingers. Unlike the tanned Californians, his skin was pale with a sickly green hue. Suddenly, Largo clapped his hands with a rubbery "thwak".

"I've got an idea," he announced.

"If it's as bad as your other ideas, I don't want to hear it," said Shiggy.

"Do you want to get out of Festival this summer?"

Shiggy nodded.

"Then let's get outta here," said Largo.

"What?"

"Let's leave Innsmouth for the summer."

"How?"

"We hitch a ride with those guys. We'll tell them we know where the best surf is."

"We *do* know where the best surf is."

"Exactly. They'll be so happy with us, they'll keep us around for the summer."

"And our parents?"

"We come back in the fall and say we were kidnapped."

"Kidnapped!? Who would kidnap us?"

"Whatever. We'll have two months to come up with a better excuse. Whaddaya say?"

"I'm in," Shiggy nodded. "Anything beats working the kelp fields all night."

They quickened their pace toward town, walking as fast as their stubby legs would carry them. When they arrived at Innsmouth, they went straight to Nelgoth's, but they didn't see the convertible anywhere.

"Where could they have gone?" asked Largo.

Shiggy thought for a moment, then suggested, "Borgwath's Hotel?"

"Oh Dags. If they went there, they'll be turned into fish feed. We'll have to get to them first."

"How do we do that?" asked Shiggy.

"We have to scare them away."

"How?"

"Have you seen us?"

Largo pointed to their reflection in a window. Although they were still teens, their bodies were quickly developing what outsiders called "The Innsmouth Look." In addition to their pale skin and bulging eyes, they were developing several long slits along their thick necks. In another decade these would turn into gills. A few years after that, their webbed feet would extend and they would eventually turn to the sea where their parents half-lived and their grandparents were already residing.

"Don't worry, I've got this all figured out," Largo continued. "We'll wait till nightfall, then we'll sneak into their rooms and—"

Shiggy pointed. "Too late!"

Borgwath Swaddlebottom, hotel proprietor and high priest of the Temple of Dagon, was coming down the steps of his hotel. He carried two buckets in his long arms. From one of them, the boys could see a dismembered hand with the golden brown hue of a suntan.

"Tonight, the deep ones feast," Largo sighed.

They both shrugged and turned away.

"Another wasted summer," said Shiggy. "All night in the kelp fields; all day at the temple. Why don't we ever get to have fun?"

Largo grabbed his friend's slippery shoulder. His eyes, already wide, were even wider, in delight.

"I've got it!"

* * * *

The convertible cruised down highway 95. Shiggy's hand clung to his head holding his new hairpiece in place.

"Do I look all right?" asked Shiggy.

"You look great!" said Largo. "Everyone will think we're from California."

While Borgwath was busy in the basement chumming up the bodies, Largo and Shiggy snuck into the room the Californians rented and grabbed the keys to their convertible. They stopped at Portsmouth and bought two blond wigs that hung awkwardly over their round faces. They sprayed bronzer over their skin turning it from pale green to pale gray.

"Where are we going?" asked Shiggy.

"Florida. I have a cousin there who works a gator farm. He'll take us in."

Shiggy waved at two teenage girls driving next to them. One of them covered her mouth as she choked back her nausea.

Largo smiled. "This is going to be the best summer ever."

THE CARPENTER
Ken Hueler

The children discovered his safehold on the first clear and cloudless Saturday of his fourth month of freedom. He felt the familiar letdown, the slap to his craftsmanship. Though forced to build with what he could scavenge—river debris, chunks from abandoned buildings, rubbish tip finds, garbage dump scrap—he had trusted the exterior blended seamlessly into the island of sawgrass and cattails. Perhaps the eight-ish, sharp-eyed girl had seen something too regular to be natural, or the glint of his wet eyes peering through the slatted window, or—who knows? But she had pointed, and the boys had diverted their feral attention to slide along the invisible wire from her finger to him.

The carpenter sighed. Unless he convinced them otherwise, they might tell adults, which would be worse. He left the house, uncovered his boat, and poled from behind the humped palisade of grasses. The children shrieked, so he stopped, safely far, to let them get used to him. He had an overlarge head, almost hydrocephalic, and giant, calloused hands. His big nose thrust out under sharp eyebrows, and his square jaw seemed to shove his lower lip into the upper one and then over into a flappy spill.

He was canny with children: how slowly to approach, what to say, what to do. He introduced himself. He promised to build them boats of their own so they could leave the squishy marsh trails and discover the vast hidden world beyond, perhaps all the way to the river. He secured their first promise not to betray his hideaway.

He fashioned the boats in one busy week. Both had room for four and a locker to store toys, lunches, and found treasures. The children were delighted. He led them, that first time, along a crimped channel, calling back to point out his previous discoveries: a muskrat push-up; the unbroken taillights of a sedan rising from the mud like the unblinking eyes of a crocodile, a mystery so many miles from any road; a clump of swamp cinquefoil with flowers like frozen splashes. They stopped on a small island, lightning-cleared and turning green again, for a picnic. He talked of many things he'd encountered from his travels, bowdlerized for the young children. He extracted the promise of secrecy twice more, and then he guided them back.

That very week they lied. On Saturday a larger group appeared, some dangerously older. They'd be more suspicious, more like adults. As he glided towards them across his pond he decided against a trip to the island with the strange bugs; the older kids looked too wary and might infect the younger with their fear.

He did get them to his home. They fell upon it with wide-eyed wonder. The narrowing hallway with its rising floor and dropping ceiling grew or shrunk them as they coursed through; circular stairs rose to a domed blind; one room had furniture built into the ceiling and all four walls, in case a great force tipped the house; another held boats too small for even the youngest, each ferrying two lidded boxes; and withal he'd carved designs and scrollwork inlaid with opalescent shell shards. He forbade them to enter his cluttered workshop. When they asked why he had no bedroom, he lied that he was too busy to sleep; in truth, he was terrified of being taken unawares. He wished he could show them the home he had built inside an abandoned warehouse, as elaborate outside as within. After a harmless afternoon he extracted the secrecy vow three times more, and he sent them on their way with the promise of the bug island next visit.

* * * *

Some children cannot keep secrets, and the carpenter could never tell which. A few always slipped. The number of companions increased. Oh, they had merry days, but he knew more meant greater risk. He began hoping they would forget him, but they wouldn't, and if he hunkered on his island, they would grow impatient and tattle.

One night he felt a shudder from something large striking a piling. He tried to pretend it had been an unmoored boat or some harmless river creature, but then came the repeated slap of thick flippers splintering a support post, the ripping and bending of floorboards diving, and weary, angry snuffling as something began scrabbling up the incline of wreckage. The carpenter bolted from his workbench. He was already dressed; he always was. When he was certain the creature had left the water, he slipped into his boat. Onshore, he fled through paths and animal trails.

At the road he had to duck twice into bushes. He chose an intersection a mile down, surrounded by fields of tall crops as concealing as the rushes and cattails. Dawn brought more cars driven by adults. Finally, one of his friends, an older girl, sleepy and cross, approached on foot. When the carpenter called out she jumped, but she had visited him often enough to relax. He told a lie—could she help track down the owner of a lost horse…did she want a jeweled necklace he'd discovered—and then forgot it. He promised she'd not be late to school and misplaced that memory, too. Whatever he'd said, she followed.

When her attention lapsed, he slung her limp and leaking over his shoulder. He hurried home. In the workshop he used his coping saw, gimlet, and cat's paw to card out and set aside the best. The remainder he minced to conceal his theft.

Timidly, for the scent of blood would awaken and excite the beast, he crept to the furniture room. The tusked, mound-like creature lay resting at the fold where floor had become ramp. The months had worn it flap-skinned and bony, but still much a danger. He shoved the platter forward and retreated as the monster cracked open its whiskered face. The carpenter returned to the bowl in his workshop; he wept aloud—he had liked the girl with the grand laugh and unashamed joy; he gobbled and licked the remains gone.

The missing girl made adults jumpy, but the next day one boy slipped away, greedy for fun. And he swore he had not told anyone. Tearfully, the carpenter divided him and afterwards mixed the bones with the girl's in one of the boxes. He placed it on one of the small boats, towed it to where the wetland joined the river, and let it drift. He watched until the current carried it around the bend. Then he went home.

* * * *

Now was hard: he had sent two more little boats a-drifting; grownups swarmed and guarded, and from desperation he had taken a few of those as well; and he had shed so much age his former playmates would barely recognize him. Meanwhile, though vivifying slower, that monster was making a shambles of the carpenter's work. Broken boards, gnawed timbers—his loving craft marred. He wandered the house, patching and shoring. Why did his creations have to end this way? Why did children always find him? How did the thing? He considered fleeing, but clung to the hope he could still salvage his creation, that this time he could bring enough food for his guest to become satisfied and calm, domesticated even.

Unbelievably, two tiny survivors of his group showed up to warn him about the disappearances. The carpenter hid his change with a tied handkerchief, poled across, and showed them some of the tools from his workshop.

As he worked at his bench, the monster burst in, cracking the doorjambs wide with its paddle-like limbs. Swinging its tusks, it chased the carpenter from the bodies. As it ate, the carpenter gathered his tools. Once sated, the thing would fall into a dazed stupor, but it would wake filled with might from consuming the raw life essences, and with wrath for being so long denied them. How much resentment it bore him the carpenter wanted never to discover. He slipped out and boarded his boat.

He navigated the streams to the river. Where had his friends floated to? He had not considered that until now. Perhaps they had found a place of safety, one where he could go to grow old and die in the beauty of one of his creations, somewhere the thing could not find him and destroy it all. He let the currents clasp and guide him.

A boat passed. He waved.

Regardless, he would, for at least a little while, be free again. He would build a new home, somewhere still close to a river, but drier this time—woods, where he could chop and plane fallen trees instead of cobbling together found boards. That would be simply grand. And the friends he might meet there would be so nice and smart and not come to his place when the monster did, and they would not force him to do all those terrible things and choke down their innards to keep them from the monster.

A tree! A stout tree. He would live in one. That would be difficult for the monster, with its lack of fingers, to get up to and to destroy, and what fun it would be. He could do a wraparound, or multilevel.

He started to whistle at the bend, wondering what magic lay beyond.

✗

BEESH GAH BEESH
Kenneth Bykerk

A Tale of the Bajazid

"Yii yaa xaa bááhádzid! Yii yaa xaa bááhádzid!" The words flew forth unbidden. "Yii yaa xaa bááhádzid!"

Blank looks, empty eyes on ugly, dirty faces. What was wrong with them? The old man, the bóhólníhígíí, spoke up, his words meaningless garble. Litso Gah spoke the bilagáana tongue, but only so well. The bóhólníhígíí, the man who hired him, was more difficult than most. He had a soft mouth with too many teeth missing to be understood well by even his own people. To Litso Gah, it was just noise.

"Yii yaa xaa bááhádzid!" Did he not know? Could he not feel it? Were they all blind? Litso Gah looked at the gathered faces in horror. They were doomed.

"What is it you're saying?" The old man was speaking loud, slow, but at least clearly.

Litso Gah had but one response, the same as before. He didn't know how to say it in the bilagáana's tongue, but he shouldn't need to. He could feel it, an understanding in every fiber of his being. He knew this place, knew it how he did not know but he knew it now and he knew it forbidden, cursed, monstrous...bááhádzid. This realization came with recognition, recognition of a place unseen and unknown but in whispered legends from the mouths of elders. This realization brought fear, stark and primal. He had to get out of here, he had to leave.

The old man with the white dághá covering his jowls was screaming still, his words devolved to incoherence.

"Yii yaa xaa bááhádzid!" How to make them understand? They were going to die if they stayed. They had to leave. They had to leave now before they woke it, before they brought it out of its slumber. Litso Gah had no love for these bilagáana, but no one deserved what was coming if they stayed. Some of them, the zhinii with his skin blacker than midnight, for example. The zhinii suffered abuse from nearly all the rest of the company in some way or another but he bore it with grace and treated Litso Gah with more respect than any of the others. Some of the bilagáana were decent men as well, but they looked mostly alike. The zhinii, Buck, he stood apart because of his obsidian skin. The two nakia in the party were distinct as well, distinct enough to avoid. Litso Gah had a long and deep distrust and hatred for Naakái Diné'i'. He could see that hatred returned, especially in the eyes of the one called Javier, but not even they deserved what waited here. How to make them understand? He didn't have their words, words they would understand, not even in the nakia tongue. All he had was, "Yii yaa xaa bááhádzid!"

The bóhólníhígíí swung his hand hard back across Litso Gah's face. Litso Gah stared into the old man's eyes. The leader of the party he'd been hired to guide was a cruel and arrogant man. He had been short and terse with Litso Gah the whole of this journey. Two whole moons he had been with them hunting and hiking through these mountains, guiding them while they searched the creeks and valleys for that yellow óona they coveted so much. Greedy fools! This was their doom. If they didn't want to listen, if they didn't understand, if they couldn't feel the evil, the doo yá'áshǫ da in the very air about them, then it was their doom to suffer. Litso Gah was not a dog to be treated such. He knew when to run.

It was a beautiful day. The sun was shining bright in a clear blue sky and a soft, gentle breeze blew through the pines to mitigate the summer heat. Birds were singing in the cottonwoods that lined the creek ahead and the chatter of the forest behind was little stressed by the presence of thirty men and their pack animals farting and belching. They stood at the edge of a meadow, yet Litso Gah remained beneath the canopy of trees. His recognition had held his step and he had refused to proceed, to set a single foot deeper into this ch'įįdiitah, this hell whispered of by elders on nights of ill omen. He was not to die here. This was not to be his doom. With one last shouted "Yii yaa xaa bááhádzid!", Litso Gah turned on his heel and fled.

Swift as a rabbit darting from danger, Litso Gah disappeared into the underbrush. This was a vibrant and thick forest choked in low brush and it took mere steps to reach such safety. He didn't want to be seen running, he was not a coward, but he had no choice. He wanted to live. He didn't want to die. He did not want to be consumed forever by a demon.

He could hear the old man shouting with rage behind him. Litso Gah didn't care. He heard the cruel bóhólníhígíí shout about his pay forfeited. He didn't care. He heard derision of his honor shouted at his back. He didn't care. He heard his name maligned in mockery as the old man called out, "Yellow Rabbit! Yellow Rabbit! Run away, Yellow Rabbit!". His pride would suffer not. Life was more important than the impressions and opinions of a bunch of dirty, smelly, doomed bilagáana. He ran and disappeared through a thicket of undergrowth. He ran not caring where he put his steps, escape his only thought. Panic had taken over.

The first explosion caused him to wince, to duck ever slightly as he raced through the brush, the bullet whizzing past his head and tearing through the leaves around. The second blast urged him ever onward, a blind, mad dash. Legends of blood spilt and the demon, the ch'įįdii that haunted this valley which the spilling of diL wakened, prodded his steps. The third crack he ignored, inured already to the lesser danger behind him. It was what waited all around, what lurked in the very soil and breathable air of this place that sent terror through him.

He wasn't watching where he was running, too intent on the act of fleeing to be careful where his feet landed as that third blast tore the air behind him. He blamed his fall on that, spitting a curse as he tumbled over a fallen log and rolled some distance down a short slope choked with brambles rife with thorns. He felt the spines tear at his flesh as he fell, felt the rocks hidden beneath the thick carpet of pine-needles scrape his skin as he slid down the slope. He landed rough, smashing up against a large stone covered in dried moss. Stars exploded in his eyes, pain shooting through him too quick, too sharp to contend. His world swam as darkness threatened his sight.

He stood as quick as he could, his balance wavering and his vision blurred. His head swam, a dull ache rising from the back of his skull. This did not matter, could not matter. He needed to go, to run, beesh! The first step failed and he dropped to his knees by that boulder. Pain raced through him, but damnation was worse than pain. Pushing harder, he made his feet again and placed one before the other. One step, two steps, three steps was all he allowed himself before launching again into a run. Pushing past the vertigo, he caught his balance and fled, heedless the scratches and bruises over his body and the burning pain in the center of his back.

He ran. He had to. If it was the last thing he ever did, he had to escape this place. There were legends, stories passed down of a valley damned and forbidden, cursed by a demon without a true face, a ch'įįdii of singular evil. It was but a myth forgot, one heard from other tribes in trade for his people generally did not travel so far south. His role in the expedition that brought him here was not for geological knowledge for he knew nothing about finding óona. Gold held little value for him. He was along for his knowledge of the people and the terrain, what was safe to eat and where to find water. Most importantly, he was along as an interpreter to help negotiate passage. Now he was in the land of this myth, these stories whispered, and he knew only one recourse. Beesh!

He ran blind for some distance, crashing through the brambles and underbrush as he fled, the sounds of the party he left lost behind him. He paused to check his path. While he wanted desperately to flee this place, he needed to be sure his path took him in a direction he could use, one that didn't separate him from the route home. He turned his gaze to the sky to catch his bearings and shook his head. The sky was darker than it should be, the blue in the sky fading to a duller shade. The sun stood high above, a summer sun, but it hid its location in the sky. Litso Gah could not tell its position, could not gain a focus on the cardinal points. The sun itself seemed to burn with a greater intensity, a heat which beat down from a shrunken orb.

Litso Gah shook his head, disoriented, and ran his hand to the back of his head. There was a bump, a large one. This did not bode well and Litso Gah knew it. He had hit his head and hard. On his hand, there was blood. It was bright red, brighter than it should be while the color of his hand was washed, faded as if seen in twilight. Surely, he thought, this was from striking his head. His vision was off, he was disoriented and the burning pain in his back was becoming a distraction. He tried scratching, tried reaching the abused spot, but no matter how he tried, he could not reach that elusive itch. No matter. He must run. Deciding which direction must be north, he started again on a steady run, one meant to carry him far if not fast.

He was Litso Gah, the swiftest sprinter in his clan, quick enough to rival a Hopi runner. He was his namesake, earned as a youth in contest. Like the rabbit, the gah, none other could match him in a dash. Born in the shadow of Dook'o'oosLííd, Litso Gah was restless and unready to settle yet for the life of a farmer. There was more to see in the world than the lands between the four sacred peaks. With the ever-increasing infestation of bilagáana from the east, opportunities for a life beyond the tilled field called him west and south into the lands of the Yavapai and the Apache. For one with an enterprising spirit, bold and seeking adventure, this was an age to be alive.

Now he ran. Through gullies and ravines, over hillocks and through brambles and forest glades, he ran. Fear, not adventure, carried his steps. Memories dim of barely recalled stories spurred him on. This was a valley of legend, of tales whispered about a land forbidden, a place held in collective memory and superstition safely distant from Litso Gah's homeland. The stories filtered into his tribe were ones garnered from beyond, brought in through trade with neighboring peoples. Still, they remained legend even though nearby Hopi claimed, as recent as his father's youth, to have encountered this dread place. There was a story told and retold in recent years, one from Hopi traders of an account near thirty years before. A mad bilagáana, one of the first to appear in these lands, stole some sacred relics, katsinas, from a Hopi village. The men of the tribe chased the thief for days until they caught up with him on this fabled creek. The four Hopi who returned swore the ch'įįdii of the valley rose from its slumber and took the ii' sizíinii, the souls of two of their number. They described the horror of the mad bilagáana transforming into a terrible white cloud and consuming two of their tribesmen.

Litso Gah wasn't a fool. That white smoke was the bilagáana's musket, obviously. There was no truth to those tales, just scared men failing at their duty to retrieve and avenge the insults against them. For this, Litso Gah had held in contempt his neighbors all these many years. Whatever respect and honor he held for them for the diverse reasons deserved, was tainted by his impression of what he saw as cowardice and failure. When he saw that meadow though, something touched him, and truth was realized in a cold sweat that broke his skin. He knew then that those tales, those legends were not just the passing whimsy of cowards. No, there was something deep and dark here, something that made its presence known to him and him alone for none of those he guided here seemed to sense anything wrong. For him, it was truth and revelation in a cold certainty, the hair on his nape standing up as if the ch'įįdii itself were whispering in his ear.

So he ran and he ran with the secrets of a demon haunting his every step. He sought the sky again yet could not place himself. The sun, burning white in a darkened sky, gray and dull, would not reveal his path. Each time he stopped to catch his breath, the sun hinted his path astray, beyond what confusion could correct. Frustration mounted, and his wits eluded him. He was afraid and acknowledgment of such increased his dread, his hóyéé'. He feared for his vision for colors were wan, their hues diminished in all but certain shades such as the color of the blood that stained his scratched and torn flesh. That stood out stark, brilliant. But the sky, the clear sky was without color and the fire of the sun blazed without glory. The forest and the trees were as well dimmed, stripped of their glory but plagued not by shadows. There were no such markers to help determine course.

The strike to the head worried him. It terrified him, but he could not feel the loss of color. He could, though, feel the burning pain between his shoulder blades. He felt each step rattle his spine, each step a barely perceptible increase. This scared him even more. If the fall had hurt his back, what damage was each step doing? Would it leave him lying helpless on the forest floor even after he escaped this place? What happened that his back got hurt? Did he hit more than his head when he tripped and rolled down that slope? He had no answer other than to escape this t'ááláʼígo ch'įįdiitah, this singular hell. So he ran, the pain centered in his back feeding his desperation. He ran and he ran but never did the sun stop lying. He ran until his steps carried him from beneath the cover of the forest and out into the open air of a meadow.

There was no clear blue sky, and he felt no gentle breeze. The sky was near black and the sun itself a feeble, cold, white ball in a firmament devoid of any bright, litso light. This left the meadow before him obscured to a distance. He could see a creek, lined by cottonwoods, ahead of him, but the trees themselves hid in their own depths and no bird songs wafted forth from their branches. It was the tents though that caused him pause. To his horror, Litso Gah realized that he had, in the whole of his flight, done naught but circle wide to come upon the same meadow he had fled. Awkwardly leaping back beneath the cover of trees, he dropped to the ground and surveyed the scene before him.

These were the very tents of the party he had abandoned. Now they were arranged in this meadow in ordered rows as the old bóhólníhígíí stringently required his camps be arrayed whenever possible. On this broad sward, there was more than enough room for a full display and the camp had been established to provide such. From his vantage hidden at the back of the camp, Litso Gah could hear conversations, but he could not see their source. Whether his flight took him north or south, east or west, he no longer cared. He needed to be free of this place and any disadvantage of position he would rectify once clear. His route he decided would be straight, direct across the meadow from where he now was and from there, a course unerring and unchanging. This in mind, he crept forth from his concealment and began sneaking between the rows of canvas.

He moved along the periphery, slipping as carefully and quietly as he could between the supporting guy-lines. As he neared the last row, he peeked around a tent to see three men. One was the zhinii Buck, another the nakia Pedro and the third, the camp cook, a robust man with a bush of red hair and dághá Litso Gah knew as Hamish. The three men were engaged around the mess tent, the cook directing the other two in their labors. Litso Gah waited, watching to see if others were around and wondering where they might be. As far as he could see through the indistinct blur his vision offered, the creek was clear. He did not want to be seen, did not want anyone to know he was here. They thought he had fled. The embarrassment of becoming lost, of being seen after he was hired as a tracker and guide, weighed on Litso Gah. He did have his pride.

Litso Gah waited until the three men all stepped around the mess tent together and then he broke cover, running from the safety of the tents toward the creek with all his speed. The creek itself was lower than the surrounding meadow, a slight depression through which the water was channeled, and lined thick with cottonwood trees. As Litso Gah reached the cover of the trees, ducking down into the creek, he came up short. Just before him, standing in the shallow stream, was a man.

Litso Gah had nowhere to go. The man before him was unexpected. His very presence brought Litso Gah to a halt even before he took in who was before him, before he saw the face of the man staring at him. It wasn't the face of a bilagáana or a nakia or even a zhinii. It was the face of a Hopi, general features Litso Gah recognized and identified immediately without focusing on their true aspect. When his eyes took in the details of the man's face, of his dress and appearance, fear choked the startled words in his throat. The man before him was straight from Litso Gah's nightmares, a náádadiilgąsh nílch'i of horrific design, a spirit of the dead brought to awful life. The vision wore a dirty, stained, dun tunic and trousers to match with simple turquoise patterns embellished into the seams of the collar and cuffs. His clothes were wet, dripping and stained with algae and scum. Centered in the chest of the apparition was a red stain, bright in contrast to the faded colors of the clothing. The face of the Hopi standing before him was puffed, bloated with sores of decay prominent and empty, black holes for eyes.

The vision raised its hand, pointing directly at Litso Gah. The horrible mouth opened and water tinged pink flowed forth in a choked rasp, "Sikyatavo! Sikyatavo! We must flee! We must run! Come!"

Litso Gah was taken aback. The fiend before him spoke directly to him. It spoke the Hopi tongue, a language Litso Gah knew, one he understood. It was the name given him that sent icy tremors up his spine to join the burning pain between his shoulder blades. Though the words wore Hopi, Litso Gah knew it to be his own. He was Yellow Rabbit, in the words of his people, his neighbors or in the words of the white men. How did this thing know him?

Yináldzid, stark, horrifying terror gripped Litso Gah. Desperation and a fear of what lay behind took Litso Gah in a frantic circle around the thing before him. The Hopi hataalii with the scarlet flower on his chest reached forth for Litso Gah with blistered and rotting hands, its pleas a refrain choked in blood and water.

Evading the apparition, Litso Gah ran some distance before turning to see if he was followed. The phantom was swallowed in the indistinct blur of distance, a relief to Litso Gah. Seeing the creek from this direction though centered him. He knew where he was now. He knew his position. From the treeline behind him was where he had first viewed this meadow. He must have circled fully around and now, knowing from whence he came, Litso Gah saw his opportunity. If he ran back along their original trail, if he followed the path he had led the company on, he could find his way back. His previous flight had been wild but now he knew. He just needed to escape this place, this accursed valley.

Litso Gah turned to proceed and stepped back in startled horror. Before him was a bare-chested man without a head, or so it at first appeared. The head of the man, a runner and a warrior by build, hung over its back by stretches of torn, tortured flesh. It, this thing of nightmarish design, reached for him, grasped, clutched. As its fingers raked Litso Gah's loose tunic, he shoved and pushed the thing away. He could feel the decay before him, soft and pliant, as his hands shoved, as he backed away and around. He had to run, to go back the way he came. He had to. Side-stepping the flailing fiend, Litso Gah dashed around it and doing so saw its head. The face was a raw, open monstrosity from the nose down and the pate was a ruin scalped clean.

The treeline was ahead and with it the promise of a path home. He ran, fast as a hare fleeing the jaws of a wolf, he ran. Fear of an unholy nature gripped him, that blind panic returning. Tears streamed from his eyes as he dashed beneath the cover of trees. A tight, choked wail built in his throat as he ran through the thickets and underbrush. The pain centered high in his back exploded in fury as his foot slipped on a limb long rotten on the forest floor. He fell, his body tumbling down a slope recently disturbed and he crashed hard against a rock at the bottom of the short grade.

He stood as quick as he could, his balance wavering and his vision blurred. He stood, his head aching and his back on fire, and looked down at his feet. There was a body, a body in clothes he recognized. It lay face down against a granite boulder sharp with hard angles. The back of the body's head was matted, thick with congealed blood and flies. In the very center of the back of that body, right between the shoulder blades, was a flower red as the one which graced the Hopi hataalii's chest. Dread, hopeless hóyéé gripped Litso Gah. This was ch'įįdiitah unimagined. He knew those bracelets, that belt. He knew the necklace visible beneath the dead man's hair. He could see the profile clear, aniné shrouding the unblinking eye. Dread realization washed over him.

Litso Gah ran. With dying certainty, he ran. There must be a way, there must! He ran with the ch'įįdii of this forbidden place haunting his steps. He ran with desperate fear in his heart and a burning pain in his back. He ran, his throat dry, his lungs on fire, his mind maddened and broken for every flight returned him again to that stone at the bottom of that slope and the bones lost there to time.

THE GRAND GUIGNOL
Christopher Doyle

I was in my library, smoking a small pipe of Perique tobacco over LaFe-vre's treatise on ancient eschatology. I was just parsing out a particularly abstruse sentence in an even more recondite paragraph when my house-keeper knocked, or more accurately, scraped.

"Yes, Hélène," I barked. "Can't you see I'm trying to concentrate? And if you're going to knock, knock. Don't scratch like a declawed cat!"

"Oui, Monsieur," the reedy woman whispered, so quiet as to stoke my annoyance even higher. She knocked somewhat louder to show that she understood. "There is a visitor. A Mlle. Lafitte."

"Lafitte? I puzzled it over, but the name was completely unfamiliar. "What does she want?"

"She is an actress, Monsieur. She is, eh, very attractive?"

It was no secret to anyone in New Orleans that I have certain connec-tions in the world of theater, having made substantial investments in a few notable productions.

"Very well, Hélène," I sighed, my concentration irretrievably broken, "send her in."

"Oui, Monsieur," muttered the housekeeper as she disappeared.

In a few moments Mlle. Lafitte appeared. She was, as described, quite beautiful. About nineteen, she had a look of worldliness for her years. Her dress was graceful, if a tad on the tawdry side, a long, bell-shaped dress with appliqués, topped with a tight-fitting fawn-colored jacket, open to reveal a gossamer shirt that did little to preserve her modesty. But for an actress in New Orleans on the cusp of the 20th century, that was not unexpected.

I tapped out my pipe, removed my pence nez, and stood, taking her gloved hand.

"Mlle. Lafitte."

"Mssr. DuVent."

"A pleasure to make your acquaintance. Please, have a seat, and tell me how I might help you."

She sat on the colorful cushions of the divan, and I behind my desk, as Hélène set down a tray with a pot of Chinese tea.

"Monsieur," she started, "as you may know, I am an actress and sing-er."

"I confess, no, but I concede that you have the necessary physical appeal."

"Thank you, Monsieur. I studied music and dance since I was a child, and am a fixture in the chorus at various local theaters, the Bijou, the Atlantic Gardens, the Club Theater..."

I recognized these names, being some of the smaller venues in the seedier sections of town. "Well, Mademoiselle," I said, "If you are looking for work, there is not much I can do. I am on the boards of the St. Charles Theater, and the Grand Opera, but casting is not in my purview."

"No, Monsieur. Nothing like that. I had occasion to see your production of Hamlet, with Madame Modjeska. "

She and thousands of others, as earlier in the year I had been able to persuade the great Helena Modjeska to perform her Ophelia, with Edwin Booth as Hamlet, for a limited engagement at the St. Charles, to resounding success both artistically and financially.

"What can I say?" I said after a sip of tea. "Modjeska is second to none, with the exception of perhaps Bernhardt herself. But what has this to do with your visit?"

"You see," said Mlle. Lafitte, "I style myself an actress. I always thought I was an actress. Until I saw Modjeska. And now I realize I am just a pretty girl who says words."

"I am sure you must have more merit than that."

"No, it is true. In the past six months I have auditioned for no fewer than twelve dramatic roles and have been rejected each time. They say I do not have the gravitas, the emotional depth, the ability to convey the character. And, voila, I am back in the chorus."

"Then perhaps you need to study."

"I have studied, Monsieur. With LeBlanc, with Braudel, with Duby."

I knew each of these reprobate "teachers" by reputation and I could only imagine the "lessons" they inflicted on this eager pupil.

"I would like to assist you, Mademoiselle," I said with a shrug, "but I am not sure what I can do. I am not a dramatist, or a director, or an instructor. "

"But you are," she said softly and deliberately, her doe eyes sweeping me into their murky depths, "Alexandre DuVent—the man who solves problems."

And it was there she had me. Not so much the piteousness of her eyes, although I must admit to my weakness in that regard. But I am a man who is able to study certain difficulties and obstacles and effectively mitigate them. Some call me a gangster, some a wizard, and some a devil. But in fact I am little more than an entrepreneur with perhaps a shade more education, creativity and resources than the average.

For example, persuading Modjeska and Booth to steamboat down the Mississippi despite torrential rains was in itself a minor miracle. And it is not uncommon for various persons to seek my services in the realms of business, health, law and other more obscure areas, even though I make no claim to expertise in any particular profession. That said, this was the first time anyone had come to my door seeking to be a better actress.

"Mademoiselle," I said, setting my cup onto its saucer, "I do not know why you think I can help you in what is traditionally a matter of talent combined with education, practice and application. However, I am flattered by your attention, and if I can, I will assist you. I will puzzle the matter over and if you return in three days I will advise if I can propose a remedy."

As I stood from my chair, Mlle. Lafitte clutched both my hands and tears welled in her bright brown eyes. "*Merci, merci beaucoup*, Monsieur."

"It is nothing. And for now, you must take your leave, as I have guests coming shortly and I must prepare."

With that, Hélène drifted in, handed Mlle. Lafitte her parasol, and escorted her out the door. When Hélène returned, I instructed her to prepare the formal dining table for Madame Broué, who would be presiding over a séance for eight of my acquaintances.

* * * *

Madame Broué was a spiritualist and medium of some renown, although to her credit she kept herself away from those social gatherings that had gained popularity, in which well-to-do invitees part with gold in exchange for being scared out of their wits. No, Madame Broué's séances were not performances, with raps on walls and under tables. Rather, she was a true medium, who would invite willing spirits to reveal themselves using the mechanism of her own voice.

The other attendees of the séance were local members of the intelligentsia with an elevated interest in the occult, and due to some of their high rank in various institutions, including the University and the Church, I will not name them here. To put in mildly, the evening was a resounding success. Madame Broué channeled several willing spirits quite convincingly, and revealed facts about many of the attendees that proved themselves true if only by the gasps of those whose intimate secrets were laid bare in the darkened room

When the final spirit had departed the vessel of Madame Broué's body, and she had resumed control of herself, the lamps were re-lit, and there was a question-and-answer period for Madame. As she was a woman of some years and was understandably tired by her interaction with the spirits, this was kept to one question per guest.

"Madame," asked the wife of a prominent banker, "when you are in the trance, and the spirit has taken up residence, do you feel like yourself with a visitor, or do you feel like someone else entirely?"

Madame, her face crinkling with concentration, considered the question. "I feel at one, if I may say so, with the spirit. If the spirit is youthful, I feel youthful. If the spirit is angry, I feel angry. If the spirit is lost and morose, I feel lost and morose."

"And," asked a gentleman in the logging trade, "do you feel more or less intelligent, depending on the spirit?"

"Yes, indeed," she answered. "And my posture, the way I use my hands, the tone of my voice, are all dictated by the spirit."

After a few more questions, Madame was quite exhausted, and it being well past midnight, the party departed for their various carriages.

* * * *

The next day I sent a short note to Mlle. Lafitte by one of my servants and requested that she bring with her an audition piece at the time of our appointment. When Hélène brought her into my library the day after the next, she appeared surprised as she greeted me at my desk, Madame Broué sitting on the far side of the divan. The two women could not have been more different, Mlle. Lafitte in the absolute flower of beauty, and Madame Broué in marcescent old age.

"Mlle. Lafitte, this is Madame Broué. Madame, this is the young actress I spoke to you about."

Madame took the hand of the younger woman and read her face with a penetrating stare. "A pleasure, Mademoiselle."

"For me as well," said Mlle. Lafitte. "But please, you may both call me Odette, as I feel that we know each other already."

Hélène served the tea, a smoky oolong, and we each took our cup.

"Madame," I said, "is a very well regarded medium, Odette."

"Medium?"

"Yes, " I continued, "one who summons spirits."

Odette fumbled her fingers in a hasty sign of the cross, and exhaled, "Spirits?"

Madame smiled. "Your innocence is refreshing, child. But it is nothing sinister."

"I am sorry," said Odette, "but Monsieur, I thought we had an appointment for a meeting, in private. If this is not a convenient time —"

"But Odette, I asked Madame here specifically to help with your problem. Now, can you read us the audition piece you have brought?"

Odette produced it, the death scene of Annabella in John Ford's 17th century tragedy, 'Tis a Pity She's a Whore, in which the character, pregnant with her own brother's child, is murdered by him with a dagger.

"I have an audition at the LeGrand Theater the day after tomorrow," she said. "The play is intended to run for six weeks."

"The LeGrand," I mused. "A respectable venue, 1200 seats I believe."

"Please proceed, dear," urged Madame.

Odette did her best, and after several minutes of dialogue, in which I read the part of Annabelle's murderous brother, Giovanni, she ended with the impassioned line, "Forgive him, Heaven—and me my sins! Farewell, Brother unkind, unkind—Mercy, great Heaven! O! O!" Odette collapsed on the floor to punctuate her death throes.

Madame quietly blew her nose, and I could see that she was raising her handkerchief to hide an amused smile. I was able to keep a more diplomatic face.

"Well?" said Odette, gasping, still on the floor.

"The problem is as you have related it," I said, extending a hand to help her up.

"It was just saying words," sighed Odette, looking as if she might cry. Madame nodded silently.

"But I think I may have puzzled a way out of this dilemma," I said.

"Oh?" said Odette.

"You see, " I continued, "a natural actress can take a character from the page and reconstruct it internally, so that she becomes her for a few hours on stage."

"And this is a talent I lack and cannot acquire."

"Not entirely correct," I said. "Madame, for example, is able to take on actual spirits for a limited time. The essences of departed souls."

"Is that true, Madame?" asked Odette.

"Yes, child," she said. "And often I am accused of acting, which in reality has nothing to do with it."

"So, my proposed solution," I said, "which I have discussed with Madame, is to see if you have the aptitude to be a medium, rather than an actress. Madame would find in the ether a spirit suitable for the role which you are called on to play. The spirit would inhabit you for the time required, and you would perform. Once the performance is finished, the spirit would depart."

"Monsieur," gasped Odette, "I have never heard of such a thing."

"As you have noted," I said, "I am one who solves problems. And not always in the traditional manner."

Odette looked at me with those brown, shining eyes. And then to Madame. After a few moments, it seemed as if she was resolved to trust us. "Very well," she sighed. "What do we do?"

* * * *

After a supper of game hens and _pâté chinois_, we retired to the drawing room, where Madame's séance table was still set up from earlier in the week. We extinguished the gas chandelier, lit a few candles, and held hands.

"Spirits," intoned Madame," I seek one of you who has known a violent death. A violent death at the hand of one close to you. A violent death from one you loved."

We sat silently as Madame gurgled and murmured, and eventually a frail, thin voice cracked from her throat.

"I am such a soul. In anger and lust was I killed. By one whom I loved."

I could barely see Madame, but I could see the shadows of her long fingers gently grasp the head of Odette, press her lips to her mouth, and exhale.

Then Madame motioned for me to turn up the lamp, which I did just enough to bathe us in a faint twilight.

"Child," Madame whispered in her own voice. "Can you hear me?"

"Oui," said Odette, in a voice that sounded not like her own.

"Now perform your piece again," said Madame.

Odette stood, slowly, gravely. She was herself, but not herself. He eyes gleamed with love, anger and terror as she groaned the character Annabella's words:

"Oh brother, by your hand! Forgive him Heaven, and me my sins! Farewell, brother unkind, unkind! Mercy, great Heaven! O, O!"

Odette died in the most realistic, tragic death throes I have ever seen, on stage or otherwise. I looked to Madame's face. She was horrified, and her eyes glistened. I felt a pounding in my chest, as if I had just watched my own daughter murdered.

Odette's head collapsed on the floor, motionless. My instinct was to shake her awake, but Madame raised her hand for me to wait. After a second or two I could just make out make out a thin, white wisp of ectoplasm escape from Odette's nostrils, drift toward the chandelier, and dissipate into nothingness. And then Odette rose, awkwardly, as if recovering from a dose of opium.

Madame sprang up, clapping. "Brava! Brava!" And I followed suit.

Odette looked around, unfocused, disoriented. It was as if she had little or no recollection of the fine performance she just gave.

"What devils are you?" she gasped. "What have you done to me?"

I had no ready answer, but Madame said, "Child, you have just given the most convincing dramatic performance I have ever had occasion to see."

"No! No! Not at this price!" she screamed, and ran sobbing from the room, muttering broken Latin prayers.

I got up to chase her, but Madame held me back. "Let her go," she said.

"Have we failed, Madame?"

"Not if I know ambitious young actresses," she replied. "Just make sure Hélène and your driver get her home safely."

* * * *

The LeGrand was an older theater, previously known as La Fontaine, having been rechristened under new ownership after a fire a few years before. Its bread and butter were musicals and follies, in which Odette had appeared with some regularity in the chorus. Why they were mounting a relatively obscure tragedy with a plot concerning incest, as opposed to the much more bankable Shakespeare, or even a new comedy, is a mystery. But it was a bold choice that one had to respect in its disregard of conformity.

Madame, Odette and myself arrived in our carriage, the windows darkened with curtains of black velvet, at four o'clock in the afternoon. Odette was wearing a hammered silver cross, which had been specifically blessed by a priest of my acquaintance, and presented to Odette with assurances of its efficacy, which she nervously fingered. Odette and I alit from the carriage, leaving Madame behind with a few small candles.

A gentle rain had just stopped, and I was obliged to summon the driver off his perch to unroll a strip of green carpet for Odette to step on rather than spoil her shoes in the muck of the street. This was of great amusement to her sister auditionees standing under the theater's eaves, apparently her acquaintances from the follies.

"And who is this, Odette" smirked one, as we walked along the carpet, "your father or your pimp?'

"Or both!" seconded another.

I stood tall, attached my pence nez, and addressed them in a stentorian voice. "Ladies. If you please, I am Alexandre DuVent." I finished with a bow and flourish of my scarf.

This quieted them, as my name is not unknown in theater circles, and, given that unemployed players will never knowingly offend anyone who may have anything to do with their getting a role, they muttered, half curtseying. "Begging your pardon, M'sieur."

Odette and I stepped off the green carpet and entered through the lobby and into the theater itself. It was dark except for the footlights on the stage, where another young woman was just finishing her audition with a young man who presumably had been cast as Annabella's brother, Giovanni. I did not recognize the actress, but she was not without talent, and her death scene was adequate by any standard.

"*Trés bien*," exclaimed a voice from the center row, amid sincere clapping. I recognized him as Alain Beauvois, a competent director of sound reputation, desperate for success after a few poorly-received comedies. "Mlle. LaVallee, very good. I may say that barring unforeseen circumstances, the part is yours." The young woman, with happy tears, blew the man kisses as she exited the stage.

"Is that everyone?" said Beauvois to an assistant, who squinted at a chart.

"Certainly not," I piped up from the shadows. "Odette Lafitte has yet to audition."

"And who is this speaking?"

"Her manager."

"A manager? Petite Odette is coming up in the world. Very well." Beauvois clapped his hands twice in succession, "At once. We have not all day."

"*Un moment*," I said. "Mademoiselle needs just a minute. To get in character."

Just then Madame Broué wandered into the darkened theater. Her gait was slow and measured, and I could tell that she had been able to summon and possess the spirit in the darkened sanctuary of the coach. In the shadow of the stage apron, unseen by anyone but myself, she gently pulled Odette into her arms, and locked her lips to hers. After a few seconds of mild delirium, Odette opened her eyes. This being only her second time inhabited by a spirit other than her own, she was disoriented, and I steered her up the steps to the backstage.

"Ready when you are!" shouted Beauvois, and I lightly pushed Odette through a side curtain onto the boards.

The young man appeared from the curtain opposite, and delivered Giovanni's line, "Look up, look here. What do you see in my face?"

Odette responded in her "other" voice, with perfect elocution and dark intonation, "Distraction and a troubled conscience."

Even with that first line, I could tell that Beauvois was taken much by surprise. This was not the flighty, silly coquette relegated to revealing her underthings in risqué reviews. This was a woman of perception, of gravitas, of substance.

By the time Odette performed Annabella's death, Beauvois and his assistant were transfixed. Even the young man playing Giovanni was clearly in awe of her talent, as he finally raised his pantomime knife, and stated, "Thus die, and die by me, and by my hand!"

Odette's death scene was glorious, graceful, and heartbreaking. She clutched her breast, collapsed to the floor, and with the final "O!" expired.

Beauvois and his assistant jumped to their feet, and applauded briskly and spontaneously, as did the young man playing Giovanni. This was no matter of a courteous applause, but an irrepressible urge to clap until their hands smarted.

"Odette! I had no idea," shouted Beauvois, as I helped Odette off the floor, again noticing the smoky line of ectoplasm escape her nostrils and vanish into the curtains above.

Then Beauvois excitedly exclaimed, "Odette, could we now do the opening scene, where we meet Annabella? I can hand you the pages —."

I interjected testily, "I beg your pardon. But Mlle. Lafitte has another audition across town, and given the weather, we cannot spare the time. "

"Audition? No. No, she was clearly born to play Annabella. Cancel the audition. She has the role, Monsieur, she has the role. Meet my in my office and we will do the paperwork immediately."

Odette clasped her thin, silver cross, and looked pleased, but bewildered, as I led her back into the arms of Madame.

* * * *

The LeGrand Theater's production of "Tis Pity She's A Whore" (changed on the marquee at the last minute to "Giovanni and Annabella" after a visit from the local constabulary) was a resounding success. Word spread quickly about Odette's performance, and every show after the first week was sold out well in advance. Prior to each performance, Madame summoned the same spirit, which seemed to have no objection to the arrangement, and transferred it to Odette, only to retreat in a wisp of ectoplasm after her death scene. Each night Odette's final curtain call was met with longer and more furious applause, and the initial run of six weeks was extended twice, after which time Odette refused to play another night due to exhaustion.

And she was truly exhausted. After the final performance, she fell in a heap into my arms, and Madame and I escorted her out through the throngs of admirers, well-wishers and theater critics hoping for an interview. We waved them all away, alighted the coach and instructed the driver to return to my home at his best speed.

* * * *

Odette said nothing for most of the trip, until at last she blurted out, "Madame, I don't know how you do it. The spirit you have summoned for me has become so familiar, so united with me that when she escapes, I feel only half myself. I did not used to feel this way. I felt content and complete."

Madame looked to me and after a few moments, I said, "Odette, you have very succinctly summed up the mental condition of the greatest actresses. Why do they keep doing difficult performances, journeying through muck, desert and storms to play before unwashed audiences in the most far-flung places on the map? It is not for money, for after a certain point they need no more. It is because they do not feel complete unless they are regularly turning themselves over to a character."

"Yes, but this is obviously that and more. Madame, do you not feel especially empty after a séance?"

Madame, not one to reveal too much about herself, cleared her throat. "Yes, child. I do feel hollow and empty. But only until the next one."

Odette looked sad and jittery. "I owe so much to you both, this is all I ever dreamed of. But I do not know if I am strong enough for a steady diet of this." Odette began to weep and pressed her face into my overcoat. Madame patted her shoulder, and we exchanged a look that accepted this as the end of our experiment, and Odette's retirement from the stage.

* * * *

Neither I nor Madame heard from Odette for over a week. She was staying with her mother, a widow, on the rue Dauphine, and we had no desire to disturb her rest. During that time I received on her behalf dozens upon dozens of letters, cables and bouquets, from smitten men pleading their hearts, curious admirers wondering when her next performance would commence, and theater owners and producers requesting her services for various productions.

After about ten days Odette came to pay me a visit. She thanked me for my services on her behalf, but the time she had spent with her devout mother had caused her to fully renounce the theater and all its trifles for a more grounded existence. I had no desire to sway her either way, since I was satisfied in my success and was happy to move on to the next challenge.

"Very well, Odette," I took her hand and kissed it. "You will always have the past few months to remember your success as a true actress. In my opinion you have outshone Modjeska and Bernhardt, and I should know as I have seen both on many occasions."

"Thank you for your understanding, Alex," she said kissing my cheek.

"Oh," I said, handing her a basket of letters, "and as I am no longer your manager, I cannot keep your correspondence. I have divided them into billets-doux, letters of platonic praise, and business matters."

She smiled, sat on the divan, and fingered through the basket with her gloved fingers. "So many!" she laughed. And then a telegram caught her eye. "A cable from Paris?"

"Yes, Odette," I said.

"Paris!" she said, unfolding it and reading. "Alex, why did you not bring this to me?"

"I did not wish to disturb you," I said. "And given your decision I don't see —"

"Oh, Alex! This is a request from a theater in Paris—Paris!—for me to play a three week engagement!"

"Apparently a director of casting saw your performance as Annabella," I said, "and advised the producer."

"Alex!" She ran to me and threw her arms around me. "I could not live with myself if I knew I had an opportunity to play in Paris—the home of Bernhardt!—and did not take it! Alex, you must cable them back immediately and accept, whatever the theater, whatever the role. I must play Paris! Then and only then will I retire from the stage!"

* * * *

I did as Odette instructed, and in a few weeks received a contract and the script pages. I summoned Odette and Madame, and we reviewed the parcel together.

"It is for a new theater, Odette," I said, handing her the play. "Le Théâtre du Grand-Guignol."

"Strange name for a theater," said Odette. "Is it a puppet show?"

"Apparently not," I said, scrutinizing the contract. "You are asked to perform the part of Rachel in a play called *Mademoiselle Fifi.*"

"And why am I not to play the title role?" pouted Odette.

"Because that is a man's role," I said. "I read the play and it is quite novel. Based on a story by De Maupassant."

"Oh," she said. "And who is this, Rachel?"

"She is a prostitute, who kills a Prussian officer in occupied Normandy. Stabs him in the neck."

"That will be a change from having my heart cut out on stage each night by my own brother," she said with a laugh.

"But you realize," said Madame, "that we cannot summon the spirit that we used for Annabella. That was a murder victim. It would not suit this role."

"Madame," I asked, "are you acquainted with any sprit who might fit this description?"

"A prostitute and murderess? Not within the cohort of spirits I would call familiar. But I will do my best."

"The play starts in November," I said. That gives us three weeks. With preparations, travel, arranging lodgings, etc., is everyone comfortable with this excursion to Paris?"

Odette placed the contract on the table, pulled my pen from its inkpot and signed her name in grand letters, with a flourish.

"To Paris," she exclaimed, "come hell or damnation!"

I had Hélène prepare three Pontarlier glasses of absinthe and water and we all three toasted, "To Paris!"

While Madame and I each took a cautious sip, poor Odette bolted hers down in a gulp. Madame and I exchanged an amused glance. Odette seemed quite eager to sample a little bit more of the world before retiring to a life more ordinary.

* * * *

The steam ship passage from New Orleans to LeHavre was relatively uneventful. The weather was fine and in the eight days we spent aboard, word got out that Odette was an actress of no small reputation in New Orleans, and she became the toast of the voyage. It never ceases to amaze me the superior wine and delicacies that a hint of celebrity can coax from the barest larders. The captain even offered us improved accommodations, since a wealthy family had paid for three of the best state rooms but never boarded. Odette was lapping up this royal treatment like a cat with heavy cream, and she seemed to have completely forgotten her reservations about the player's life.

Madame, on the other hand, was less enthusiastic. She complained of her joints creaking in the humid air, and her breathing was labored and wheezy. Further, travel on the sea rendered her powerless to practice her art. "If there are spirits at sea," she said to me as we watched Odette play the coquette with a group of fashionable young men near the deck rail, "they are few and far between. Besides, how can I concentrate with the constant noise of the machinery and the lurching of the ship?"

I estimated the time we had left in my head. "If we arrive in Paris in four days, do you think you can settle in and be your normal self?"

"My normal self does not exist, Alex," she shrugged. "But I should be composed enough after a day or two on dry land to be as I usually am. And look, two more young admirers are paying their respects to our charge."

I glanced over and smiled. There was little doubt that Odette was, at that moment, the brightest young thing on the entire Atlantic.

* * * *

From Le Havre we traveled by rail to Paris and checked in at our lodgings in the Quartier Pigalle. Our rooms were modest, but serviceable, and we were greeted at the front desk with a pleasant bouquet of roses and a bottle of Champagne from Mssr. Méténier, the theater's director, to Odette's delight.

The ladies, weary from travel on sea, rail and cobblestone, immediately retired to their shared suite to collapse on the first non-shifting beds they had seen in weeks, while I, desperate to move my legs for a bit on solid ground, ventured out into the Place Pigalle. It was just after sunset, and

I shall never forget the army of smartly dressed young men and women mixed with artists, bohemians, urchins and yes, prostitutes, promenading in the streets and drinking in the smoke-laden sidewalk cafes. Certainly, I thought, with this variety of people alive, Madame should have no trouble conjuring up the soul of a suitable person not so fortunate.

The next day was our last before Odette was to report to the theater, and after settling ourselves in, dining and seeing a few sights in the city, we returned to the suite, and began the séance at about nine p.m.. Madame lit a few small candles, and we all held hands as she opened herself to those spirits and forces imperceptible to typical mortals.

"Spirits," intoned Madame, "I seek one of you who has fallen into a sordid life. One who has taken a life with her own hand. A violent death of one despised."

We sat silently among the flickering flames as Madame murmured, and eventually a wheeze gave way to a raspy, angry voice. "I am such a soul. My fortunes never rose above the street. And bloodletting is an unwashed stain upon me."

Odette's brown eyes glanced at me with a hint of worry, but then a bright ambition shone in them as she leaned over to Madame and pressed her lips against hers.

After a few moments, Odette rose, and delivered the seminal part of the play, in which the occupying Prussian officer balances a Champagne glass on her head, spills it and laughs at her.

I fed her the officer's line, "The women of France belong to us!"

"That, that is not true! you shall never have the women of France!" Odette sputtered, seething with rage. " I—I am not a woman! I am a prostitute! and that is all a Prussian deserves!" She made a very convincing stabbing motion to my neck, which took me by surprise such that I had to restrain her.

Madame turned up the gas lamp and slapped Odette sharply across the face. The ectoplasm, darker than that of the Annabella spirit, almost like Russian cigar smoke, roared from her nostrils and vanished into the darkness of the ceiling.

In a few moments, Odette was herself, her eyes shining.

"Was I good?" she asked.

"Almost too good," I said, and blew out the candles.

Madame looked concerned. "I am not sure I like this spirit, Odette. I felt an anger far beyond what I am used to."

"But that is what the role calls for, Madame," said Odette. "And I am none the worse for wear. Besides, it is late, and rehearsal is at ten o'clock tomorrow. That is the spirit we shall use."

Madame looked unsure, but she was clearly too tired to argue, and

Odette's bright confidence won the argument.

* * * *

The Théâtre du Grand-Guignol was on the rue Chaptal, and its tall arched doorway gave away its former life as a chapel. As we entered, we noted its tiny size, only about 300 seats, and its unusual decor, with confessionals to one side and large statues of angels hanging over the orchestra pit. It was nowhere near as large or as nicely appointed as even the most third-rate theater in New Orleans, but it did have an undeniable atmosphere that could not be recreated with new paint, plaster and velvet. I looked over to Madame for her read on the premises, but she was carrying herself and the recently engaged spirit in her tired body, and I did not wish to distract her with mundane questions.

Apparently, we arrived just on time, as a young, handlebar-moustached gentleman came out to greet us.

"Ah, the esteemed Mlle. Lafitte!" he exclaimed, taking her hand and kissing it. "I am Oscar Méténier. I cannot tell you how glad we are to have you to play our Rachel. When my agent Henri wrote to me of your talent, I could not help but put my line in the water, but I did not dare hope that you would actually come. I am ecstatic."

"*Merci*." Odette smiled. "I am honored that you asked me."

I introduced myself and Madame, cautioning that Madame had a tincture of opium each morning for her asthma, and she would not be herself for an hour or so. Thus she could host the spirit without distraction. In a few minutes the rest of the cast entered the theater, and after a few minutes of introductions and pleasantries, Méténier brought the rehearsal to order. I sat with Madame in the first row and waited for the appropriate moment.

"Everyone!" said Méténier, "Thank you for coming at this early hour, and thank you especially to Mlle. Lafitte, her agent and manager, for coming 5,000 miles and arriving before the rest of you layabeds, who had to walk only four city blocks."

I watched Odette's face brighten. She liked this director, and she was obviously thrilled to be actually rehearsing a play in the center of the Quartier Pigalle in her dream city.

"Now," said Méténier, "I would like to start with the orgy scene, simply because it is the showpiece and it must be perfect. And I must confess I am dying to see Mlle. Lafitte play it." The cast rustled their pages to the appropriate place, and the four men playing the Prussian soldiers, and three other women playing Rachel's companion prostitutes, took their places on stage.

At this point I helped Odette along by saying, "Please Odette, a kiss for Madame for luck."

Odette knelt in front of Madame as I placed myself between them and the stage, and in the shadows the spirit was exchanged. Madame looked somewhat relieved, and Odette's eyes became piercingly focused as she mounted the stairs and joined her comrades.

The props had all been laid out, the glass, the knife, the Champagne and cigars, and the scene started as I had read it, the Prussians dining lasciviously with the prostitutes, until one of them, the Madame Fifi of the title, bit Rachel's lip so hard she bled.

"And here, Odette," said Méténier , "you will bite on a capsule of artificial blood that will trickle down your face, and onto your costume. Continue."

Odette's dark eyes stared at the soldier as she spat her first line with absolute menace, "You will pay for that."

The young man playing the officer placed the filled champagne glass on Odette's head, and said "The women of France belong to us!"

Odette jumped up, spilling the glass, and sneered, "No! You shall never have the women of France!"

"Then what are you doing here?"

"I am not a woman! I am a prostitute!" Odette's eyes flamed brighter than I have ever seen them. She grabbed the knife, which was as real as any blade, and lunged toward the actor, slitting his throat from ear to ear, as blood gushed down onto the stage. Then, off script, in a wild frenzy she attacked the other three actors, who had not quite realized what was happening as she slashed at the eyes of one, ripped open the belly of another, and it was only the fourth, a large, bear-like man who played the soldier known as Otto, who was able to grab her by the arm and wrest the knife from her.

The attack had begun and ended in less than thirty seconds, but the damage was horrific. A small lake of blood welled up under the three victims, laid out at twisted angles on the stage floor, gasping like beached fish. The three other women screamed like dying cats as they fled the stage, their shoes tracking blood behind them.

A terrified stagehand, shouting "Police! Murder! Police!" bolted out of the rear exit, and shortly after four policemen in brass-buttoned tunics rushed in. Having determined that the three victims were beyond hope, they efficiently placed Odette in irons, and led her away as she rabidly screeched the most wicked profanities.

* * * *

Outside, as a crowd of onlookers grew, Odette was caged up like an animal in the back of a Black Maria led by two horses, and the three corpses, draped in black crepe from the theater, were deposited in a nondescript hearse. At the police captain's orders, Madame and I followed the rolling cage on foot, and I could not help but note to Madame that I had not noticed the wisp of ectoplasm escape Odette's nostrils.

'It has not", muttered Madame. "There is only one hope for her, and that is to have a priest perform an exorcism."

"And then what? She is a murderess with half a dozen witnesses."

Neither Madame nor I had a good answer to that question, but once we arrived at the police station we produced our passports and answered endless questions, while the muffled grunts and screams of Odette echoed from a remote basement cell. We confirmed that Odette was our charge, and we her managers. No, she never displayed behavior like this before. It was totally out of character.

There was no point in revealing more.

A doctor was called, and he returned, signing a paper to have her transferred to a local asylum. Once we were released, Madame and I hastily made our way in a hired coach to Notre Dame, to fetch a suitable priest to perform the exorcism.

But these last efforts were for naught. As we rushed into the asylum with the bewildered priest, we learned that petite Odette, the innocent girl who only wanted to be a convincing actress, had managed to rip open her straight jacket.

She had then hanged herself with the sleeves.

WHEN DEAD IS DEAD
Cindy O'Quinn

I feel the weight of life pressing against me, wrapped in a caul of sorrow.

The hum that leads to all the right choices falls silent. A soundtrack playing to the tune of life skips a beat and falls flat. Gone.

When words are lost to me, I seek shelter elsewhere. Far beyond the stars, circling above the night. Where darkness kisses gentle regret before reaching the unpromised light.

Shadows of the past are the ghosts that haunt me. Tears succeed only to strengthen my monsters, but my heartfelt laughter will eventually annihilate them.

Stark emptiness fills their eyes. That's what happens to eyes—those windows that lead to other places. They go empty when the loss is deep enough.

Dead and gone. Always dead, but

DAY OF REMEMBRANCE
Matt Spencer

A lone covered wagon rolled along the winding dirt road, surrounded by miles of windy pasture, under a heavy midday sky that made the air taste like rain. The slouched, hooded driver reigned the sleeshkill to a halt, in front of the road sign announcing arrival in the township of Recompense. The half reptilian, half insectile beast snorted through its long, exoskeletal snout and clawed the ground with its sharpened hooves. In the distance, maybe a mile off, the town's rooftops stabbed the gloomy sky, from behind a thin smattering of twisty trees. The sign was nailed to the top of a crooked, leaning post, shoved deep into the mud.

"Why'd we stop?" said Tia, who sat in the back of the wagon, across from her twin brother Ketz.

"None of those assholes said this was supposed to be here," said Gurgi, the hooded driver, in his nasal, squawking voice, not quite by way of answer.

He jumped down and crouched squinting in front of the signpost. Halfway down the post, a smaller, newer-looking sign hung by a cord on a nail.

Tia and Ketz climbed out and joined his investigation. "What's the matter, stud?" said Tia, one hand in the pocket of the long brown coat she'd filched in the last town they'd passed through, the other adjusting her slouching, wide-brimmed hat. "You're the one said you knew all about this town, that we were sure to hit pay-dirt here."

Gurgi twisted around jerkily. His fleshy, snaggletooth face looked even uglier in the shadow of his hood. He was a couple years younger than the twins, but you'd never guess by his face, which looked like boiled meat. "Never said I knew *everything* about it, bitch! I just said I'd heard all the stories, from reliable sources. Today's the day."

Ketz's long coat hung open, in case he felt like reaching for the Ghestru blade that hung from his left hip. "*Reliable sources*, huh?"

"Hey, fuck you, man!" Gurgi's hand already drifted towards his own blade, under his own coat, probably not even realizing it. "What about it, you little Nagga Mountains blend-boy punk, huh? You supposed to know so much, about different scrawlings from all over the world, right? What's the sign say?"

Ketz looked up. "Says we're enterin' the town of Recompence. Ain't that what it's supposed to say?"

"Oh, *har har!* I meant the little sign, asshole." Gurgi stabbed his finger at it.

"You're the one from this side of the Great River. You tell me."

Something caught in Gurgi's throat, like Ketz had hit a nerve. "Fuck you, man," he repeated.

"I hate to say it, brother dear," said Tia, "but he's got a point. So if you two could maybe quit suckin' each other's dicks for a second, let's see if all that learnin' from Silisha can help us out right now."

Ketz shrugged and crouched in front of the sign. "Says...huh...It's a weird dialect, even for these parts. Somethin' like, *Today's the dead's day. Any travelers passin' through, show proper respect, please and thank you. If you don't, that's on you.* More or less, anyhow."

Gurgi's face lit up. "See, guys, what I tell you? That's what I been hearin' about, why it's the best score around...but only today, once a year."

Ketz peered down the road. The town looked tiny and quaint. "You call *that* the best score around?"

"Shit yeah. Some battle fought here a couple hundred years back. Every year on the anniversary of it, from midnight to midnight, the local yucksters all shut themselves indoors, don't cook anything, don't light any candles, don't go outside for nothin', just eat bland food they prepared the day before. Place don't even sound developed to have indoor plumbing, so I guess they shit in the corners all day." Gurgi snorkeled laughter. "Supposed to be in honor of everyone who fought or died in that battle, to give all their ghosts a day to themselves or somethin' dumb like that. They call it a *holy day.*"

Ketz nodded. "Yeah, I heard of places in Deschemb that practice weird shit like that...Wait, this is *that* Recompence? As in, where *the Battle of Recompense* happened?"

Gurgi shrugged and snorted a big snot-rocket out of his nose into the dirt. "I only ever heard of one town called Recompence, so sure, I guess. Why, what have you heard?"

"Since crossin' the river? Just folklore, really, from different folks. None of them mentioned the holy day."

"That's all real fascinatin'," said Tia. "What's it got to do with why we're here?"

"Don't you guys get it?" said Gurgi. "Even the town watch ain't allowed outdoors today. That means all their shops, everything, it's free pickin's!"

Ketz sniffed the wet air and glanced at the clumps of tall grass on the roadside. They swayed in the soft wind, away from the town. "I don't like it," he said. "C'mon, man, look at that little place. How much plunder you expect to get out of these backwater yucksters anyhow?"

"What's the matter, Nagga Mountain Boy, you picked now to grow a conscience?"

"Maybe so," Ketz growled low. "Or maybe you just didn't read me so good. But then, you don't *read so good* in general, do you, boy?"

Gurgi's fleshy face tightened. "And here I heard you two was supposed to be a couple'a hot-shit, bloodthirsty outlaws."

"Keep flappin' that big mouth of yours and find out," said Ketz. His hand slipped beneath the flap of his coat for his blade.

Tia's hand shot sideways and fastened on Ketz's wrist. "Pour ice water on it, Ketz. You wanna rustle up the coin to get us back across the river and on our way home, or what?"

Ketz's grip relaxed, but he still glared at Gurgi. "Still just strikes me, we might'a found a less dumb way...like one that didn't drag us all the way out here to the middle of nowhere, stuck in that damn cart for three days on the road with this asshole. So Gurgi, these *reliable sources*, they told you what kinda *big score* they make out here every year, huh?"

Gurgi's mouth, which was freakishly big both literally and figuratively, hung open. "Well...no, they never said nothin' specific about it...Look, man, that's the beauty of it! No one's ever thought of this before, because here it is, out in the windy, gloomy asshole of the country. No one lives here 'cept these yucksters, and here's us to pick 'em clean. You got somethin' better to do, you're welcome to walk right on out of here to wherever you wanna go. That goes for you, too, Tia...except maybe without your asshole brother around to cramp our style, we might finally get better acquainted."

"Oh Gurgi," she said, "I don't need my asshole brother around to keep me from puttin' my boot up your ass. He's got a point, though, Ketz, We come this far. No sense havin' wasted the time."

"Fine," Ketz said at last. "Let's get this shit over with."

They all climbed back into the wagon and rolled on towards Recompense.

* * * *

"There's a wagon coming, Mama," said Stili as she peered through the slatted windows.

"Remember to whisper, dear," said Stili's mother, from deep in the gloom, "especially when you're that close to the window. What happens beyond the slats is for them, not us."

Stili mouthed that last part in time with her mother's speech. She already saw quite a bit outside in the streets...shadows with nothing there to cast them, that split from the ground and moved about like mingling vapors. Some of those shadows had already taken on color and shape, the illusion of dimension even, all while staying translucent. Stili loved to watch them. Sometimes she fancied she could hear them, too. Despite the gloom and confinement, she'd always loved this day since she'd been a little girl. For the longest time, Mama had tried to keep her from watching, but by the time Stili became a young woman, her mother had accepted the futility of it.

It wasn't like there was any disrespect in watching the spirits. Occasionally, over the years, she swore, some of them had smiled right at her. Plenty of phantom wagons always rolled into town…of people who'd gotten caught in the stampede of combat, who'd never completed their journeys home 'til now, or of the fallen horn-devil people, who came to revel with their former foes, who now embraced them lovingly like old friends. They were dead, and after all this time, so was anyone they'd been protecting or taking orders from, so what was there to fight about anymore? The peacefulness of it, the joy where there'd once been bloodlust and hatred, was the most beautiful thing Stili had ever seen.

This wagon, coming along the main road, wasn't one of the phantoms. She felt its rumbling approach, heard its wheels rattling, heard the sleeshkill's clawed feet clicking as it trotted. It rolled out of sight before she could get a better look, so she hurried through the dark house, nearly running right into the kitchen table, to another window.

"Careful, there, dear," Ma whispered from over by the stove. "It's just some travelers passing through. Even this day sees its share of those. You know that."

"'Cept this one's stopping, in the village square, right in front of the monument…Looks like three people getting out…There's a short, fat one and two tall, skinny ones…I can't tell where they're from…The short one's got on a big hood, and the tall ones have on long trail-coats and big trail-hats…I think they're some kind of foreigners, well, the tall ones, anyway."

Mama turned up the tiny flames, beneath the two cooking pots on the stove. It was true, lighting flames inside was forbidden on this day… but her duties were such that she required special allowance. Still, she always kept the flames cautiously low. She'd been at it all morning, and the thick, white liquid in the left pot had just now started bubbling. She lifted it slowly by the handle and poured half of the contents into the pot on the right, over a thick, deep red, paste-like substance. When she stirred the contents together, it took on a dark pink texture. Only eyes so long accustomed to working in the low light could tell when it looked just right. She plucked some dried leaves from some of the hanging parcels above the stove, crumbled them, and stirred them into both pots.

"Whoever they are," said Mama, "they'll soon enough figure out that today ain't the day for a warm reception in Recompence, and they'll be on their way. At least I hope so. I do hate having to see to those who don't... to make the peace anew."

Stili hoped so too. She didn't want to see the spirits stop being peaceful. If that happened, Mama would force her to take part in what happened next. That had only happened a few times in Stili's lifetime, and she hated that part worst of all. Outside, the shadows had already moved in curiously around the three visitors, who still didn't seem to notice.

* * * *

The bed of the wagon was empty, except for their three travel bags. If you believed Gurgi, they'd soon change that, by filling it with as much plunder as their one Sleeshkill could pull. Then again, not much of what came out of Gurgi's mouth was believable, as they'd figured out since taking up with him. How the fuck had he ever seemed trustworthy? Because desperation made bad ideas look good sometimes, Tia guessed.

She and Ketz had strayed far from home, further down the Great River than they'd ever intended, so they'd hitched a ride upriver on keel-boat, to find a quicker trail home. A big storm had come in and washed them ashore on the western bank. So far, what humanoid population they'd found was almost completely Schomite, though of a strange, squat, ashy-skinned breed, who didn't trust the sight of their swirling, mountain-shaded complexions, or tall, lanky frames. Where the twins came from, they were a little shorter than average, so it was funny to find themselves someplace where they practically towered over most people. They needed a lift back across the river. No one was inviting them onboard for free, and no one would hire them for work...nothing honest, anyhow. They were good enough at sneak-thievery to get unruined clothes and keep enough food in their guts to keep on their feet, but wholesale banditry was out of the question, in these lands they didn't know, where whatever enemies they made did...at least on their own. So when Gurgi had talked himself up like some hot-shit bandit, who could get them in on a big score, it sounded like as good an option as anything.

"Too bad it's just us three," Gurgi said excitedly. "I mean...I *almost* had a full crew put together, with more wagons and bigger ones...but...that all fell through at the last minute."

"Who was that," said Ketz, "more of your *reliable sources?*"

Tia sighed. Ketz just wouldn't lay off. She got it. She'd spent the same days he had, traveling with this conniving ratfuck who wouldn't shut up, but the guy still sounded like he might be useful to them. He just *really* rubbed Ketz the wrong way, though.

They all climbed down and looked around. Gurgi tethered the Sleeshkill to a nearby post. The road into town led right to the village square, with a thirty-foot-tall monolith carved smoothly out of some shiny, bright-green stone, with tiny scrawlings chiseled on it from top to bottom. The thing stuck out, surrounded by all these plain cottages and other clean, simple buildings. In the square, the main road intersected with three others, like an eight-pointed star with the monolith at the center. Ketz went and looked the monolith over in awestruck curiosity.

Tia clapped sharply. "Okay, let's keep this show movin', boys. I say we each strike out in a different direction, get the lay of the land, meet back here in twenty minutes, swap stories, figure out where the most valuable goods are, that our rig'll carry." Ketz kept looking at the monolith, but shrugged in a way only she'd recognize, signaling that he agreed with her. She still shouted, "Hey Ketz! You can curiosity-seek later. Pick a road and get to work!"

Ketz turned and sneered, but also twitched one eye, in their special silent twin language. She gave him another quick wink. "Fine, whatever," he said, flexing his left shoulder while shuffling his right bootheel. He turned and darted past the monolith, up the road that swerved off to the right.

Once Ketz was out of sight, Gurgi gave Tia his biggest smile yet. "I can tell which of you two calls all the shots, honey. We get this spot's plunder to where we can sell it, maybe I know some guys be interested in what a gal like you could bring to a crew…if maybe I tell 'em how sweet you've been to me…hear?"

"Sure, I hear you," she said. "Before we talk business, though, I wanna see what you got on the job." Her voice dropped. "You heard me tell my brother to meet back here in twenty minutes. Why don't we make it fifteen, big boy, huh? Just you and me?"

His big, rotting mouth grinned giddily. "Oh yeah, honey, I hear you. So which way do we go?"

"I'll go that way." She thumbed over her shoulder. "You take the opposite direction. Looks like some houses with stables that way. Sturdy tools make for good trade, I've found." She pointed over his shoulder.

Gurgi nodded swiftly, then turned and trotted off. Tia sighed heavily. At long last, a little solitude! She breathed it in and out slowly, then turned and headed down her road of choice…the one Ketz's shuffling foot had suggested. Maybe Ketz had his wits about him after all. If Tia knew her brother, he'd head far enough up his road 'til he was sure he was out of sight, then he'd double back, cut between some buildings, and meet her at the end of her road. It was time for a serious talk about their partnership with Gurgi. As she saw it, things didn't look good for the boastful, leering prick. Somehow, she doubted Ketz would object.

Tia walked along the still, silent thoroughfare. She'd have sworn the village was deserted, except all the buildings looked to be in decent repair.

Everything looked so *clean*, with trimmed shrubs lining the dwellings and places of business and bountiful crops growing in yards. It wasn't what you'd expect from such a remote village, in this gloomy countryside, but then, there was a lot about the lands west of the Great River that didn't make sense to Tia. Maybe there *was* wealth here worth plundering. That didn't warm her to the idea of staying in business with Gurgi. What had she been thinking, taking up with that fishmonger runt, talking himself up like some master thief? Had her and Ketz's options really been that rotten?

The more Tia looked at the dark windows and doorways, the less she liked the idea of going inside to look for valuables. Her hand slipped within her coat and settled on the pommel of her long, curved knife. Somehow, she didn't find the usual comfort from it.

What had that sign said, according to Ketz? *Today belongs to the dead, so please respect that, and if you don't, that's on you.* Tia ambled to a stop at the end of the street. She tugged her coat shut against the shivers. Ketz had said something else, about *a bunch of local folklore.*

Keep it together. How long did it take you to walk to the end of this street? She glanced up at the clouds. Just a few minutes. Ketz should be along in another few. Why are you letting all that crap get to you? People are just hiding in their holes like scared little rabbits, over some local superstition. Now here you are jumping at shadows, like you're no better!

To her left, there rose a long porch with a pair of batwing doors flapping at the center, against the looming entrance into the local saloon. Thank fuck these shut-ins at least had one of those! She glanced at the sky again. Ketz would be a while yet. In the meantime, she might as well settle her nerves with a drink. It was on the house, after all.

She climbed the porch. The front door loomed before her like a black hole into which she might tumble. Once she went inside, it was just a big, unlit room. Her eyes adjusted, so she found her way to the bar without tripping over the tables and chairs. What kind of booze did a town like this stock its saloon with? If they had anything good, she might have to snatch a few bottles for the wagon. She felt her way along the bar, found a small lamp, dug out a match, and lifted the glass from around the wick.

She was about to strike the match on the countertop, when a deep, crusty voice echoed from the shadows, "Bold move, miss...especially today."

Something about the voice flooded Tia's veins with ice water. She spun and crouched. She brushed her coat back and found her sword-grip. "So is startlin' me in the dark with a threat, asshole!" Her blade shrieked partway out of the scabbard.

"I didn't mean to sound threatening, Miss Tia," said the voice. "My apologies. I confess, I wouldn't mind a little illumination. Aw hell, go ahead, I don't see the harm, not in here anyway…all depending on what you do next, of course."

"How the fuck you know my name?"

"You'll wanna light that lamp before we discuss it further."

A moment later, the orange glow spilled over a sturdy figure, seated in a rocking chair behind the bar, clad in black from head to toe. His pale, shrunken, leathery skin reminded Tia of a mummified corpse come to life.

"So you seem to know who I am…"

"Not really. Just your name. And your brother Ketz's name. The spirits you passed on your way into town came here to tell me about you. I do not recall the other one's name."

"So you mind tellin' me yours, Mister?"

"I don't see the harm. Call me Kallar."

"Huh. Kallar…That don't sound like any of the local names I've heard in these parts."

He smirked strangely. "No, I guess it wouldn't." His accent sounded local enough, she noticed…yet somehow, not quite.

"Thought all the local livin' folks was supposed to be shut up in your homes today," she said. "Or is this your place of business *and* your home?"

"Not exactly, but I have a special arrangement, you see…both from the business owners and…well, from *them*. I suppose they take me for an honorary member…just waiting to step over there with them, honestly unsure myself as to why I haven't already…the only one left on this side who still shares their memories."

"Whose memories?"

"Why, those who were there, who died that day, of course."

"What, you mean the *Battle of Recompense?* Man, c'mon, that was…"

"Over two hundred years ago. Yes."

Tia peered through the candlelight, at the wall of bottles behind the bar. "Before we go on…Man, you want a drink? I'm havin' a drink!"

"You…had better let me get that for you." He pushed himself to his feet and grabbed a whiskey bottle, along with two glasses. He brought them to the bar and poured a drink for each of them. "First of all, you should know, Miss Tia, I think your brother's about to do a very foolish thing."

"Wouldn't be the first time." She lifted the glass, sipped, and grimaced at the unexpected sharpness.

"In a different way than usual, I mean. You two aren't on the playing field you're used to. You're on theirs." He gestured over her shoulder.

Tia spun and faced the whole barroom. It was no longer empty. Or rather, it never had been. Half of the patrons looked like the kind of pale, stocky farmers she'd seen in the other villages they'd passed through on their way here. The other half could only be described as humanoid demons carved out of some kind of red wood, except they moved like any fleshly bodies. They were all see-through. The first of the demons moved swiftly towards Tia, its yellow eyes blazing at her. Her blade shrieked free.

"That was a mistake," said the old man.

The shape rushed her. Her blade whistled in an upward-swooping cut. It passed through the figure's neck and shoulders as though through empty air.

"So was that," the old man added.

Tia took another swipe. The thing started shrieking. So did she.

* * * *

Ketz had caught Tia's signals fine, but he wasn't about to regroup with her just yet. What he really wanted to do, rather than plunder, was to take a leisurely stroll through Recompence, look for surviving landmarks from the all stories he'd heard, and see how much truth he could spot behind all the folktales. First, though, it was time to kill Gurgi. Keeping the moron around was just an invitation to get their heads on a chopping block somewhere. Besides, raiding Ghestru merchant caravans was one thing. Robbing docile farmers at their most vulnerable like this, that's where Ketz decided to draw the line. If Tia didn't like it, well, he'd let her call enough of the shots on this trip already.

He darted off the road, between some houses, and crept silently down towards the way Gurgi had taken. It wasn't long before he spotted the bastard, skulking along the center of the street, then towards one of the cottages not far from the village square. He might have been headed for the stable affixed to the place, but Ketz doubted it. Ketz moved silently up behind the stable, then around it, following the sounds Gurgi made. The guy was embarrassingly loud even when he wasn't talking…even louder when he was trying to be quiet. Ketz spread back his coat and loosened his sword in the scabbard.

A nob, then a whole door rattled, followed by a loud crash as someone kicked it in. "Ah, shit," Ketz muttered, though he wasn't particularly surprised. He darted around the stable, to the front door. It was dark inside, but Ketz made out the outlines of scuffling shapes just fine. He stepped inside and saw Gurgi dragging a thrashing girl out into the front room by the hair. An older woman—the girl's mother, Ketz guessed—ran at Gurgi with a frying pan clutched in both hands. Gurgi heard and saw her coming a mile away. He ducked the swing and backhanded her across the face, so she crashed into a counter and fell to the floor. He held onto the girl with his other hand, dragged her up, knocked some plates and cups off the kitchen table, and shoved her face-down over it.

Aside from the obvious, the most unnerving thing was that neither of the women screamed. The mother had put up a fight, and the daughter still squirmed plenty, but it was like they had it that deeply ingrained in them *not to make noise on this day*...like they were still more scared of their local ghosts than of Gurgi.

"Ketz," Gurgi shouted. "Shit, brother, you startled me. Hey, look what I found! Didn't I tell you? Easy pickings. I got this sweet little ripe one, though, so you're gonna have to wait your turn. Unless you don't mind the old bitch."

Ketz didn't say anything, just stalked forward, whipped out his blade, and lashed it at Gurgi's throat.

Gurgi let go of the girl and jumped backwards. Ketz's whistling tip barely missed his neck. "Hey, *whoa, whoa*, Ketz, what the hell you doin', man?"

"What's it look like?" Ketz stalked around the table and jabbed at Gurgi.

Gurgi managed to retreat just far enough so Ketz's sword-point only shallowly gouged his chest. By the time Ketz stabbed again, Gurgi's own blade was out, meeting his in a hard chime that echoed deafeningly in the small space. The girl, meanwhile, slumped off the table and landed on the floor. Ketz circled broadly, his blade leveled on Gurgi's neck.

"Okay, motherfucker," said Gurgi, "that's how you wanna play it? Fine!" He sprang forward, his blade glittering in the gloom as it lashed at Ketz's face.

Since they'd started traveling together, Ketz had watched Gurgi, knowing they'd eventually come to this moment. He sure as hell hadn't expected this much competent swordsmanship from the guy. Someone had taught Gurgi well. Their blades whistled and chimed as their feet danced and shifted tightly through the close quarters.

"*Yow*," Gurgi exclaimed, as Ketz's blade licked downward in a frenzied, desperate countermove. Gurgi's sword slipped from trembling fingers. "Man, you just...*Ow!*"

Gurgi shambled into the light that spilled through the front door. Ketz's sword had left a thin, dark red line across his foot. When he moved, the front half of the boot shifted unnaturally. Gurgi hunched forward, saw how he'd been mutilated, then vomited all over the place. He sank to one knee, then stood back up and swayed, drooling puke. His boot kept filling up with blood, which pulsed out of the slit. He fell over again and crawled backwards, leaving a smeared dark wake. "Nah, man, nah, man, *please! Man, stay away from me!*" He slithered outside, then vanished around the corner like a scuttling crab.

Ketz took a few slow, calming breaths, then turned and looked at the cottage's two occupants. "You gals okay?"

The daughter got up and shrieked in his face, *"What are you doing here? You're not dead!"*

"Not yet, anyhow, by some miracle," said Ketz. "You're welcome, by the —"

The older woman crept forward and joined her daughter in fawning all over Ketz. "This one, he…The blood that now leaks within our soil, it was he, not us, who spilled it. You know what that means, don't you, dear?"

"Of course, mother," said the young lady, suddenly calm.

She moved to a wall, where parcels of dried herbs hung from the ceiling. She tore off a chunk, crushed the leaves up in one palm, then walked back over to Ketz. She lifted her hand, palm up, and blew it in his face.

Ketz coughed and blinked, wiping frantically at his face. "The fuck! Girl, what the hell's wrong with…with…" He breathed in whatever she'd blown in her face. The fragrance was actually nice. His head swam. Before he knew it, he crashed to the floor and was out for a while.

* * * *

For a minute that felt like hours, Gurgi couldn't even figure out how he'd wound up like this. He couldn't even remember where he was. His surroundings spun by in a topsy-turvy blur. Raindrops pattered across his face. He should get out of the rain before it started pouring. He only ever managed to crawl a few paces before his foot dragged, sending fresh bright flashes of agony through him. Eventually, his hands landed against a wall. When he tried to pull himself up, his foot screamed at him again, so he fell back over on his side in the mud.

He lay still long enough for the pain to subside to a hot throbbing. His boot kept filling up with heavy liquid, like he'd just taken a wrong step through a marsh, except, he remembered nauseously, that wasn't swamp water. It was his blood. It spilled out of the slit and pooled in the grass. He breathed steadier, thinking, *Maybe that's the worst of it behind me.* He couldn't feel the front half of his foot, which sagged in a way it wasn't supposed to. *Maybe if I get up and only put my weight on the heel, the pain won't shock me so bad. I can hobble to somewhere safe and dry.*

When he made it to his feet like that, though, the front half flopped to the other side, so the severed bone edges slid against each other, which hurt worse than ever, so he screamed and fell back down. The bone-edges felt stuck on each other now, so the exposed nerves bit deeper through him. When he tried to crawl away from the pain, it only got worse. Eventually, his leg must have jostled just right, so one bone-shard slid off the other, allowing the nerves to quiet, so he breathed steadily again.

It was that asshole Ketz who'd done this to him. What the fuck had the guy thought Gurgi was talking about, about raiding this town on a day where there was no law at all, so they could do whatever they wanted? Sticking up for some pathetic little yucksters who'd left themselves wide open for it, over your own partner on the trail? What the hell was wrong with those Nagga Mountain freaks? They were even worse than he'd heard, or at least Ketz was!

What Gurgi saw next nearly sent him into another screaming fit. These streets weren't deserted anymore. The figures filling them weren't dressed like indigenous peasants, but rather like warriors...warriors who'd already been killed, by each other. Yet here they stood around like old chums, smiling and laughing. The blood from Gurgi's foot ran through the dirt and touched the foot of the closest one. That's when Gurgi first experienced the sensation of the land itself drinking the life from his veins. He saw it happen, saw his own blood run from the spreading pool and crawl up the man's legs, as well as those of the other figures carousing in the streets, one by one, though it couldn't have spread that far, even with the rain to mix with. It filled out the ghosts through the *inside*, so they drifted around like glowing phantom circulatory systems, with the rest of their shades still hovering amorphously around them. One by one, they turned and looked at Gurgi. They moved towards him, crouched over him, took hold of him, with hands that felt as real as anyone's. He rose up helplessly, too weak from blood loss to resist.

Before long, the glorious dead of Recompense gave him more reasons to scream.

* * * *

Axes, knives and clubs rained down on Tia, from all directions. The first blow knocked her to the floor. That must have been when she'd dropped her sword. At first, she couldn't tell how badly she'd been hurt. Then all those weapons split through her bones and organs. She tasted her own blood rise in her mouth. An axe chopped through her skull. That should have ended her, but then again, so should plenty of the wounds she'd already taken.

Sweet lands, just let it end already! Oh fuck, it hurts, it hurts, please, just let it —

It ended. She lay stretched out in pitch blackness and deathly silence, half-slumped, half-leaning against a hard clay wall, on a dirt floor. So far as she could tell, there wasn't a fresh scratch on her. So why did her nerves still coil and cringe, from everywhere those ghost-weapons had touched her? Her head hurt, like someone really had hit her with an axe. She shifted, groaned, and shut her eyes tighter.

"You awake yet, girl?"

She opened her eyes. Candlelight glared at her. She blinked. A narrow, rectangular cellar spread before her, with a small table in the far corner, next to a wall lined in bottles. The old man from the saloon—he'd said his name was Kallar—sat at the table, on a small stool.

Shit, that meant it hadn't all been just a nightmare. She bolted upright. "*Aw, fuck!*"

"Keep your voice down," said Kallar. "If they find us down here, I can't promise you'll stay in one piece this time...or that I will, for that matter. You certainly speak crudely for such a lovely young lady."

"Fuck you."

"Sadly, I'm far too old for that particular joy of life, along with most others...well, except one." He stood up and fetched one of the bottles. He sat down, uncorked it with his teeth, and swigged from it. He noticed Tia eyeing him thirstily. "Oh, what, you want a sup? Well, come right on over, pull up a stool, and help yourself...if you ever decide to move your skinny ass."

Tia rolled her eyes, shoved herself to her feet, came over and grabbed the bottle out of his hand. She sucked down a deep pull, then instantly lurched, gagged, and spat. "*The fuck's this shit?*"

"An older brew, one the owners here don't serve anymore." He grabbed the bottle back and sipped slowly.

"I can see why. Did a dragon piss in it or something?" She wiped her mouth. "So why the hell ain't I dead?"

"Because the ones who attacked you already were. If I hadn't gotten you out of there when I did, your mind would have shattered permanently by the time they were done with you. I don't think they'll bother us down here, but please don't tempt them."

"Who are they? Hell, *what* are they?"

"The ghosts of the Battle of Recompense."

"The what?"

The old man blanched. "You don't know? You must be from far away indeed."

She grabbed the bottle back from him and sipped it more slowly this time. "Yeah, from pretty far to the East of the Great River. That's how my brother and I wound up here, heard it was an easy way to filch the jewels for a quick, quiet passage back across the river. Then we got here, and all this crazy shit happened, and..." She shuddered.

"Lucky for you, you hadn't shed any blood on this town's soil. They can make it feel like they're hurting you, but they can't do real violence that leaves a mark, unless someone alive does first. Once they taste blood, they go mad for it all over again, forget they ever left the battlefield."

"How you figure all this?"

"I already told you. I was there when it started. Long ago, far to the north, high above the Wallution Territories even, near where these lands meet at the neck with the Noreaster Continent, there lived a savage, warlike tribe who'd all but wiped out one of their weaker territorial rivals, taking the children alive and raising them as slaves. Some of the descendants of those slaves escaped, and made their way southward, in a roving band that settled here, and farmed out what would be the town of Recompense. Less than a generation on, a scouting party from their former masters tracked them here, but of course the settlers weren't stupid. They'd known that day might come, and they'd made sure their strongest and sharpest were ready for battle. Strange to think that warlike folks once lived in this peaceful place...of flesh and blood, that is. For three days and nights, the warriors here held off the invaders, not only with brawn and blades, but also with... the sorcery, the necromancy, which their former oppressors had tried to stamp out of their ancestors but hadn't. Those slavers hadn't counted on how their prey would have remastered such arts by the time they caught up, enough to make a winning stand against them. Oh, don't get me wrong, there was plenty of the usual good ol' fashioned brutality on both sides. Corpses choked the streets and the forests beyond by the end of it. But the necromancy, it had other consequences.

"The souls of the fallen, on both sides, are bound to the lands that drank their spilt blood. They've watched over the town ever since, just out of reach. The survivors of that battle and their descendants have lived on in...well, I won't call it prosperity...but good lives. Once a year when the veil grows thinnest, the ghosts can almost feel the cool, damp air on their skin, so they can pretend to be living, peaceful people. For that brief time, they forget the old hatreds and meet each other as cheerful old friends... unless any of the actual living people should happen to go outside, trip on something, cut themselves, and spill so much as a drop of blood on the soil. If the ghosts taste that, they remember how they got here, and they're locked back in those old sensations, and they can't escape it 'til they've quenched it. So the townsfolk stay indoors and keep quiet. They tell each other it's out of reverence, but I know better. I remember the times when they learned that lesson the hard way.

"By the end of the battle of Recompense, only one young man of the barbarian invaders remained alive, to be taken prisoner. He was too badly wounded to put up a fight. Would have been kinder for his captors to just kill him, but they liked to think of themselves as better people than their enemies. Their leaders debated for a long time what to do with him. Once his worst wounds healed, but he didn't have his strength back, the village elders convinced everyone to let him roam at liberty, under watch, free to make whatever life he could here, long as he didn't try to escape. He never quite healed right, would never be the warrior he'd once been, so even if he did manage the journey home to his own people, they'd never have taken him back.

"Years passed while he lived docilely and obediently among his captors. Eventually they got used to him and treated him almost normal. He got older, but he noticed that he aged slower than the people around him. He watched the next generation grow up. They'd only ever known him as one more kindly, familiar face. So it was with the next generation…and the next, and the next…yet somehow, he was still here. There were even a few girls who grew to womanhood so they decided he was handsome." Kallar smiled sentimentally. "One in particular…for a while…'til old age finally caught up enough with him, so she stopped finding him handsome, so she settled down and married some young buck her own age. After that, he kept expecting to finally die of old age, but somehow hadn't yet. Must have all been part of the same necromancy that kept his old comrades and enemies around…keeping him around as another kind of ghost, 'til he…I don't know, finally atoned for something, somehow, so maybe he'd get to pass on. He just never figured out how."

"That's you, ain't it?" said Tia. "The lone survivor of the marauders."

Kallar smirked. "You're sharp as a spine-rat quill, aren't you, girl?"

"Fuck you." She took another pull on the bottle…slower and steadier this time. "Hang on, that don't make no sense. I saw what those marauders looked like. It was one of them, attacked me first, upstairs. You don't look like that…like…some kind of monster, barely even humanoid."

He smirked again. "Armor and warpaint. That was the idea, with my people, to scare the shit out of our enemies, into thinking just that. I confess, it still warms my heart, to hear the illusion holds up, even to a warrior-woman like you."

"Uh, thanks, I guess." Something else hit her. "Wait a second. You said the only reason they couldn't kill me was because no blood had been shed. But they still attacked me. Thought you said today was their one day to be all lovey-dovey."

"Yeah. Something's got 'em spooked, though, if you'll pardon the phrase." He leaned back, closed his eyes, and breathed slowly, as though searching the air for the answer. "If I were to bet, I'd say…somewhere else, throughout the grounds of this town, blood *has* been spilled."

"Oh, shit… Ketz!" Tia sprang to her feet, instantly got a wicked head-rush, and almost fell back down.

"Whoa, there, take it easy! Stay here. Wait it out 'til it's over."

"I can't. My brother's still out there, in the middle of all that shit!"

"If he is, if he's where the blood has been spilled, then he's almost certainly dead already."

"Obviously, you don't know Ketz. If he's in trouble, though, I still gotta find a way to bail his dumb ass out." She started towards the door.

"Tia," said Kallar, sharply enough that she looked back. "If they hurt you again, they'll finish destroying you…and they'll be stronger by now."

"Yeah, you're right." She stalked towards him and grabbed him by the throat. "Except I ain't goin' up there alone. C'mon, old man. You got me out of there before. You have that much influence on 'em. You can lead me safely through them, too, can't you? Think you're ready to die? I could give you that death by torture. Help me find my brother, now, or I will."

With a strange smile, he reached up and gently pried her fingers away from his neck. Even at his unnatural age, he was still alarmingly strong. "You're not being half as clever as you think…but funny enough, it just so happens you're right, or at least close enough…hopefully, for your sake. I have a sudden inkling, we might just be able to help each other today. Before we go find your brother, though…let me retrieve something."

* * * *

Tia emerged from the cellar and found the saloon empty. All the ghosts were gone…though not quite. One of the red-horned devil people stepped out next to her, except this one was still flesh and blood. His armor, now that she saw it in solid form, was ornately sculpted from some kind of flame-hardened blood-red wood. It looked a lot heavier than it had on the spirits, too. She'd have expected the creaky, ancient figure wearing it to collapse beneath its weight. Kallar only sagged a little, otherwise holding himself sturdy and proud.

Beneath the rim of his horn-crowned helmet, she saw the embers of the proud barbarian warrior of his youth still flickering in those pale gray eyes. Part of her couldn't help but stand in awe. Another part of her thought, *Damn, keepin' him around as a hostage-citizen is one thing, but lettin' him keep his fuckin' armor, not to mention that big, nasty-lookin' sword strapped to his side? Folks in these parts must be even loonier than I thought.*

She picked up her own sword as she crossed the boards, from the spot where the ghosts had been all over her, where she'd felt their weapons carving her to pieces. It was weird, not seeing her own blood, or anyone's, splattered anywhere. She shivered and hurried towards the front door. Before she stepped outside, a leathery, gauntlet-heavy hand fell on her shoulder.

She twisted free, spun and snarled, "That's a bad idea, old man, startlin' me like that."

"So is walking out there with that unsheathed." He pointed at her sword.

"That a threat?" She brandished it at him a little.

He groaned and shook his head. "Damn kids, I swear...No, just a little friendly advice, from the guy who's the reason you're not still back there on the floor." He thumbed over his shoulder, at the spot she'd just been staring at.

She peered hard at him, then shrugged. Her blade shrieked home into the scabbard.

"Smart move. Don't worry, kid, you'll get to quench your thirst before the day's done."

"Yeah, like the next time you call me *kid*."

"Don't worry, you'll know when the time's right. You'll notice my signal. I guarantee it. 'Til then, whatever happens, no matter how much your every instinct says otherwise, don't do anything crazy. Not if you wanna save your brother's life."

Outside, the clouds had gotten so dark, she thought at first that night had already fallen. Far away, light shown from the village square, shimmering pale green like some eldritch fire. The closer Tia drew, the more ghosts she saw...no longer reveling merrily in the streets, on their one day of liberty, but converging somberly towards the monolith in the square. They barely seemed to notice when Tia and her ancient companion fell in step with them.

Tia's boot stepped in something squishy. She scraped it off casually, then she glanced down and realized what it was. It was no lone stray, either. The thoroughfare leading towards the square had some fresh decorations, the juicy kind. Tia wasn't green to the sight and smell of spilt humanoid insides, but these ones weren't just spilt all over the road. They'd been draped over shop signs and other hanging fixtures, along with ragged, dripping shreds of meaty flesh and muscle that looked freshly ripped clean off the bone. Speaking of bones, a few of those crunched beneath Tia's boots too. Red slime and patches of raw meat still clung to them. Whose insides *were* they? Tia could think of two possibilities. She gulped hard and looked to her left. Kallar walked on quietly beside her.

Finally, they drew close enough to get a good look at the monolith. Tall spikes had been driven into the ground around it, in a circle, leaning outward. Thick, gleaming fleshy cords hung from the tops of each, twisting in the air. Were those more intestines? She drew closer and saw that yes, that's what they were. Damn, she sometimes forgot just how long someone's insides really were, when you scooped them out and stretched them out. Swollen, glowing pods dangled at the ends, their viney stalks braided and fused with the gut-ropes. Tia knew what those were, too, even though they didn't grow in her home region.

How do these people grow light-pears out here in this dank climate? she thought.

Whenever the ghosts passed through the glow, they grew fainter, more translucent, almost fading in and out of existence. At the center of the glow, at the foot of the monolith, a lean male figure crouched on his knees, his wrists bound in tight knots that stretched his arms wide, the other ends of the ropes tied to spikes driven deep into the ground. His shirt and coat were gone. Some kind of paint coated him from his head to his waist, ashy-white on one side, blood-red on the other...*the colors of the ghosts' skin and Kallar's armor, respectively.* When he groaned and lifted his head, Tia recognized the eyes of her brother. He met Tia's gaze across the square but didn't liven with much fresh clarity.

Tia trembled where she stood. *Holy shit, that's my brother tied up there, and he sees me just...standing here. I can see him thinking* What the hell are you waiting for, Tia? Do something! Get me out of this!

Every nerve in her body buzzed and crawled, compelling her to do just that. She took in the whole scene again, remembered what Kallar had said, and made herself stand perfectly still, for now. Sweat broke out on her forehead, despite the chilly air. Her hand crept to her coat and slowly pulled it back, away from her sword, the better to draw it fast when the time came.

Above Ketz, two fresh decorations hung on big nails that had been driven into the monolith; a stripped, bloody ribcage and above that, a severed head. On the latter, Tia recognized Gurgi's giant rotting mouth hanging open. Even in death, the prick couldn't keep the damn thing shut! Gurgi's eyelids hung open wider than ever, showing gaping-black, red-rimmed craters where the eyes used to be. The ribcage must be his too.

Amidst all the onlooking dead, only two other living folks stood present. They must have been local women, one middle-aged, the other very young. They were mother and daughter, Tia guessed. The mother strode up behind Ketz. With one hand, she jerked his head back by the hair, baring his throat. Her other hand held a thin, curved, glittery, jewel-studded knife. At the sight of the blade, Tia almost forgot everything else and sprang. Kallar's hand settled on her shoulder. She didn't round on him this time, just took a deep breath and readied herself.

"Shades of the glorious dead," the mother shouted at the spectral crowd. "My daughter and I stand before you here in penance...penance on behalf of those on this side of the veil who have dishonored the observance of your sacrifice upon this sacred day. Hereby, I anoint this bloodshed of penance to..."

"Oh, forfuckshake, Ethane," Kallar shouted. He strode towards the women and their captive. "Will you cut that lizardshit out?"

"Back off, Papa," she exclaimed. "Go back to that hole you live in. This is none of your business."

"*None of my business?* You ain't even saying those words right, or even following the right appeasement ritual." He pointed at Ketz. "You got the shade of red wrong, too, in the paint."

"Grampa, please," said the young lady. She also pointed at Ketz. "Mama won't listen to me. This man here stopped the frog-faced man from raping me. She was right there, too, but she won't —"

"I told you to be quiet, Stili," Ethane said to her daughter. "He just as likely did it because he wanted you all to himself." She glared at Kallar. "I'm speaking the words you taught me for emergencies like this...the one thing I ever got from you, from your whole awful side of the family. Now you're saying you didn't even teach me that right! You really are worthless, you know that? Should have died a long time ago."

"Won't disagree with you there," said Kallar. "Ain't my fault you didn't pay attention to your lessons, though."

"Look, Mama," Stili kept pleading, "the frog-faced man's already dead. Why look, the ghosts already made their own decorations out of him, right there..." She gestured at the hanging ribcage and head, then at the cords that held the lightpears, then further out around the square. "... And...there...and there...and...well, shouldn't that be enough?"

"You'll do as you're told, girl," snapped Ethane. "These invaders have violated the day of the glorious dead, and we must make amends with the dead by setting an example in blood."

"*The glorious dead?*" Kallar chuckled bitterly. "That's what you call them now? Seriously?"

"You and them aren't the same anymore, old man," Ethane screamed at her father. "These two were both invaders, like you once were. They looked to take advantage of this sacred day. One shed the other's blood, so here they both are. The others who yet hide within won't be safe until the glorious dead have tasted this other violator's blood, spilled by living hands in offering. You know that better than most, don't you...about that need for atonement...? If you care so much, maybe it's time you proved it." She jerked Ketz's head harder backwards and held out the jeweled knife in offering.

Kallar stared, then his face changed. He strode forward. "You know what, Ethane? I think you're right, for once. Except if I'm gonna do this, I'm gonna show you the right way to do it." He waved away the knife she offered, and instead drew his own sword, which he leveled over Ketz's neck. Across the spectral crowd, he met Tia's eyes and said, "Sorry it has to be like this, kid."

With a roar, Tia sprang forward, ripping her sword free. As she closed the distance, Kallar moved his blade away from Ketz's neck to meet hers. His expression didn't change, not 'til her sword smacked his aside and slashed at his throat. She was used to people making a quick retreat when she lunged on them, whenever she didn't open them up with her first strike. Kallar parried the slice with a crashing strike from his cruder but heavier sword. The impact rolled up her arm and rattled her teeth, so she staggered backwards. That ember of his savage youth, which she'd glimpsed in his eyes earlier, now reignited into an inferno. He came at her almost as fast as she'd come at him. Now she was the one who fell back on the defensive. As he closed with her, he lifted his blade overhead in both hands and let it drop straight at her skull. Her sword went up to block, then his strike swerved like a fish swimming around a rock. It nearly cut her in half at the waist before she checked it and danced sideways.

In the frenzied blur, she thought of her old childhood fight-trainer Jaffer: You've got youth and ferocity on your side, kid. Us old guys, we ain't as fast or strong, but we're sneaky. Seasoned cunning wins over youthful vigor every time unless you remember to watch for it.

Kallar had sure as shit gotten Tia with *seasoned cunning* from the start, saving her life just so he could bait her into this moment. She didn't have time to puzzle out his crazy old motives, because he was already redoubling for another swing. Too bad for him, she'd already gotten around him. He was cunning, but that heavy armor still slowed him down at his age…and Jaffer had trained her well for old bastards like this, at least when it came to an honest fight. Her edge lashed between the plates at his elbow, landing with a meaty crunch. Half his arm fell off and landed on the ground between them along with his sword. A moment later, he crashed to his knees. Blood spilled out of his stump like water from a ruptured pipe.

His eyes glazed as he stared up at her. A serene smile crossed his face. "I've…been waiting…so long, Tia…for someone to finally complete it for me. We all have. Must have been the necromancy that kept us here, required it…Just wasn't complete without me…Maybe I've been selfish… holding out for someone like you…someone to give me a worthy death. Call me old-fashioned like that." His face ran pale and still as the last red gush of his life pissed itself out of his pruned arm. He fell dead at her feet.

Tia stumbled left and right as the adrenaline cooled, leaving a dizzying wooziness in its place. She bumped into something that grunted and shifted. She glanced down and saw Ketz, still on his knees. Her blade lashed left and right, so the cords binding his wrists split in half.

"Thanks, sis," he muttered as she helped him to his feet. His eyes were glazed, as though from strange drugs.

"Good job, Tia," a voice whispered in her ear. "Now it's complete. Now we can all go."

She recognized Kallar's voice, looked around, saw him still lying dead at her feet. She looked around for the army of ghosts. They were all gone now.

Tia turned her attention back to Ethane and Stili. They both stared dumbfounded, then the girl broke from her mother, fell to her knees in front of Kallar's corpse. "Grandpa," she sobbed.

Ethane's eyes were empty and cold. She was either deeply in shock, or she'd just really hated her father…or hadn't given a shit about him, or her daughter, had just lived for the power-trip of this occasion, of which he and Tia had now robbed her…permanently, it seemed.

Tia stalked towards the old bitch and lifted her blade. "Now then. Where were we?"

"Tia, no." Ketz caught her by the wrist. "It's done. No one here can hurt us anymore."

Tia looked Ketz over. Other than being still muddled from whatever Ethane had drugged him with, he seemed alright. That, and the body-paint sure looked silly on him. She wondered how long it would take to wash off. "I guess you're right." She glared at Ethane. "You two are lucky my brother's sweeter than I am." She pointed her sword at Stili, who finally looked up from her grandpa's corpse. "He's missin' a coat and a sword. I reckon you know where those are?"

Stili nodded swiftly.

"So go get 'em."

"Don't listen to this foreign heathen, child," Ethane said. "Just —"

Tia pointed her blade at Ethane. "I tell you to talk, you old bitch? Stili, go get my brother's gear." The girl rose and hurried off towards her home. Tia glanced at Gurgi's hanging head and ribcage and continued, "Now, from the sound of things, you owe my brother here an apology, and a *thanks for not lettin' my daughter get raped*, while you're at it."

"Sis, c'mon," Ketz slurred, "there's no need for —"

"Shut up, Ketz." Tia's sword tip poked at Ethane's throat. "You were sayin', bitch?"

Ethane glared coldly. "You're the ones who brought the disruption here. You have no idea what you've done, what this will mean, now that the ghosts are gone, so we don't have —"

"You know what," said Tia, "I don't care. I'm already sick of this place. Hey, Ketz, soon as that girl gets back with your gear, let's go snatch that sleeshkill and wagon, cut our losses, and ride on out of here. We'll find another way home. Before we leave, though, I'm gonna head back to that saloon and grab a few of them bottles for the trail. After all this shit, I need a drink."

⨯

MOTHER SHUB-NIGGURATH

Frederick J. Mayer

"Taking Mystery to Bed"

There is no longer normal you be
everything is such a mystery
sleepy and you take everyone
darkly counting sheepish goats
never be afraid to run from the light
This dark facade ends
tarnished mirrors over heads
bed, the true reflection says go to
dead, only those who stay awake
say you've got no body tonight
She has delicate bodies
decay brings birth day cries
bestially starts worshippers to
be sucklings of Magna Mater
beloved of Goat Mother of Mysteries delight
Mystically crude of carnal creativity
All those is isn't all you see
Thrills secretive of hidden
frilly fecundity
lace of twilight
Will awaken a thousand dreams
the hybred young of goddess schemes
a copulate appetites
affectionate Shub-Niggurath
taking mystery to bed this night.

THE TOLL TAKER AND THE TROLL

Paul R. McNamee

Emily sat on her the stump at the toll gate and talked with the troll who lived under the bridge. She had been talking with it all her life. Well, she talked to the troll. It was sleeping and didn't reply. It had been asleep for generations.

No one else in the village spoke with the troll. The villagers said she was crazy. She preferred to think they were cowards who were jealous of her bravery. Her attitude didn't win her any friends but the troll was her friend, so she wasn't concerned.

"I know," she said. She bit off a piece from her bread loaf. "But I can't come play. I need to watch the road."

Her duty at the gate bored her. She wanted to climb down the ravine, splash in the creek, and be near her friend. Spending each and every day in the same spot had drained the work of its novelty. It was a far cry from visiting the troll at random moments when she wanted to get away from the village.

Not many people—other than Emily—believed the troll was anything more than a relic of the ancient times. Yet, the villagers' tenacious superstitions held on. No one in their right mind would use the bridge at night. They wouldn't say why but she knew they didn't want to risk being eaten by the troll.

Eastward on the road, sunlight glinted off metal. Emily shielded her eyes but it didn't help block the reflected light.

"See? I told you!" Emily cried out to the troll below. "Oh, I would have been in trouble if I'd listened to you and kept them waiting!"

Emily jumped to her feet and brushed crumbs from her gray skirt. She ran a hand through her curly blond hair to push it away from her face.

Strangers were appearing far more often of late. The world was growing, her father liked to say. Meaning, kingdoms were growing and spreading again.

She squinted until the moving figures took shape. A man riding a horse. Not just any horse, by goodness! A roan horse so large it could only be the mount of a nobleman. The sunlight glinted off polished armor. More than a mere noble—a knight!

A strange creature followed the mounted knight. Large and long—larger than any faithful hound might be—it rolled along, with wheels for feet on the end of its spindly legs. Bird legs. Yes. It might have been a bird. It was shaped like a duck in flight, with a round head on the end of a long neck. Yes, that was certainly what the follower must be. Emily could see stubby wings and a proud vertical tail feather.

The knight drew up at the gate. His long white bird halted behind. He had a square face—or maybe it appeared that way because of the open visor of his helmet. His eyebrows were as black and bushy as his mustache.

"What is this?"

"Toll gate, good sir."

The villagers had thought to put up a gate to bar entry to the bridge at night. Civic and monetarily minded members of the community had seen an opportunity to keep the gate closed, only opened by the key of coin.

"Toll gate? You would charge me a toll? I am a nobleman of the realm."

"We charge everyone." Emily shrugged. "Three drachs."

"Three?" The man looked around as if he might find someone to support his outrage. "Where are your elders, you flaxen urchin? This is extortion!"

Emily touched her hair. Though it was often bushy and wild, it usually received compliments, not insults.

"The money helps keep our village robust and flourishing." Emily—well, her father—received a flourishing touch of the money taken as payment for her service, too. "And keeps the troll quiet."

"Troll?"

"The troll, sir. Lives under the bridge."

The knight, encumbered by armor, leaned far to his left, rocked back, and then leaned far to his right. Emily didn't know how he didn't fall from his horse. He looked into the ravine and the creek under the bridge.

"I don't see anything."

"Oh, he's there. But he is ugly so we let the trees and the brush grow thick around him so he doesn't scare off visitors."

"I don't believe you."

"It's all there on the sign." She pointed to the wooden sign, with its dense paragraph, which justified the toll of the bridge and warned of the danger of disturbing the troll at night. "You are a learned gentleman, yes? You can read?"

"Of course I can read. Do not be impertinent, child!"

Emily decided she didn't like the knight very much. She might be a child, but she was the only one with enough courage to perch above the troll every day. Even the bravest villager knew the best course of action was to walk—or ride—swiftly over the bridge, even in daylight.

No one manned the post in the evening.

"Six drachs."

"What? What?" The man's face went red. "How dare you double your price while I speak with you!"

"Well, it is usually three drachs per traveler. Now, if you were pulling your...bird along, towing him like a wagon. It would be three. But he seems to be moving under his own power. So, he needs to pay his own passage."

"If I was exaggerating before I am not now," the knight said. "This is extortion. Do you charge a man driving cattle or accompanied by hounds in the same manner per head?"

"Five drachs, then. Three as normal and two for all the fares I've lost while you've argued with me."

The knight twisted in his saddle—no easy feat in his armor. The road behind was as empty as it had ever been.

"All the...!" The knight shouted, unable to finish the sentence in his frustration. He pointed his thumb over his shoulder. "I am of a mind, young lady. I hadn't planned on setting my dragon loose before speaking with your elders, but you have extinguished my goodwill."

"Your dragon? What dragon?"

"You have a troll. I have a dragon."

Emily leaned to her side, peering around the roan horse.

"You have a very large bird, sir."

"Do dragons fly?'

"Yes."

"Do dragons breathe fire?"

"Everyone says they do."

"I assure you they do. I assure, he does. And he flies. He is a dragon."

"He must be blind and dumb."

"Why would you say that?"

"No eyes. No mouth."

"Well, child. Why not declare his deafness, as he does not have ears?"

"Newts don't have ears. Well, they do, but they don't stick out. If dragons and newts are lizards it stands to reason your friend..."

"My dragon..."

"Yes...it stands to reason your dragon might be similar."

"Child, you are a smidgen wiser than I give you credit. Only a smidgen, mind you."

The knight reached into the sack hanging at his right leg. He retrieved an odd-looking box, studded with long and short metal twigs and knobs.

"The beast can hear me quite well."

His fingers played on the knobs atop the box.

The dragon squeaked. The dragon did have eyes, and they opened. Its eyelids must have been hidden in its strange, smooth face, The red eyes were lit with some internal fire and the dragon blinked constantly.

"Now." The knight's eyes reflected an intended malice. His grin was keen. "Allow me to show you the proper way to extort someone."

The armored man continued to play with the knobs on the box.

The dragon turned, rolling on its wheels until it pointed away from the bridge, back down the road eastward. The white beast trundled down the road, gaining speed. With a roar and a snort of fire out its backside, it leapt into the air and continued to climb upward.

The dragon turned about over the trees and then swooped down, only a few measures above the road, leaves and dust billowed in its wake.

It flew right at Emily. In her mind, the image of the duck was replaced by the image of a deadly falcon.

Emily's nerve gave way. She cried out in alarm and leapt aside. The dragon spat flame. A fireball consumed the toll gate and blasted the sitting stump into the air. The dragon swooped upward as Emily hit the ground. She felt the air knocked out of her lungs from the impact and the pressing wave of the explosion.

Coughing and wheezing, wiping hot grime from her face, she glanced up at the saddled knight.

"Now. I believe I will keep my coin." A wicked smile stitched his face. "And I will see what coin your little hamlet has to offer as protection from such menaces of the sky."

The knight kicked his horse's flanks and proceeded across the bridge.

"Troll!"

Emily crawled to the edge of the ravine and shouted again.

"Troll!"

The babbling creek absorbed her words.

She swung her body around, climbed down using the handholds and footholds she knew well. She waded into the creek, cold water up to her knees numbing her calves.

"Troll! There's a man and a dragon crossing your bridge. They mean no good. Are you just going to sit there?"

The troll did not move.

Emily felt tears of frustration welling in her eyes. Was she wrong? Was everyone else right? Was the troll nothing more than a lump of metal? Had it always only been a lump of metal from the old days? Had it ever been alive? Was the legend only a legend?

"I know you're real," she whispered. "I know you'll help us."

The troll grumbled and opened its eyes and they, too, were as red as the dragon's orbs.

Emily couldn't find the words to speak. She couldn't breathe until she realized she was holding her breath.

The troll stirred, grumbled louder, like a man deep in sleep protesting his impending awakening.

The beast lurched forward, trees bent under its low belly, cracking and snapping.

For the first time in her life, Emily was afraid of the troll. Maybe he wasn't protector of the village. Maybe he only cared about his bridge. Maybe the great beast was more of a wolf than a hound. A wolf could be tamed but you never took the wild out of one. A tame wolf might tear out his supposed master's throat as quick as tear out the throat of a man's enemy.

The troll's hard face turned and regarded her.

"Perimeter violation!"

The troll spoke! And it spoke to her! Emily jumped, folding her legs at her knees, momentarily forgetting all dangers and misgivings.

Her excitement fled as soon as she realized she didn't understand those words.

"What did you say?"

"Perimeter violation."

"I don't understand."

"Incursion." The troll seemed to think it had delivered enough information. "You are unarmed. Rank?"

"Rank?"

"Title. Designation."

Emily heard a whining sound and looked skyward. The dragon was diving toward the village. She heard the muffled blast as it unleashed its flame. People screamed.

"No title, no designation, no rank! Just Emily!"

"You are a civilian?"

"I'm a villager. Is that what you mean? I'm not any noble."

"Civilians must be protected."

"Yes. Yes we must! I'm not the one violating your persimmon..."

"Perimeter."

"...perimeter!" She pointed at the dragon in the sky. "The dragon is!"

The troll turned its neckless head. Emily had the strange impression the troll was looking up, though its face did not turn toward the sky.

Its nose lifted, pointed up. So strange to see a nose with a joint at its root. The nose rose above the troll's own eyes, and then snorted smoke with a dull thump.

Knowing trolls were uncouth, Emily wasn't surprised to see the snot come out of its nose, sailing skyward. The smoke drifting from its nostrils was a surprise, though. She far more expected that from the dragon.

More surprising was the dull roar, similar to the dragon's fire, as the troll's snot exploded when it hit the dragon's belly.

The dragon staggered in the sky, faltered but then straightened its flight. Emily could see cracks and scorch marks on its belly, but it would take more wounds to stop the beast. The dragon circled upward, dodging another snort from the troll's nose.

"Gross. Can't you swing a proper weapon?" Emily asked. Then she remembered the troll had no arms.

The troll ignored the comment. It walked from the woods on its odd flat feet and sideways toes, thrust over the terrain and reached the spot where the remains of the toll gate still burned. Emily scrambled after it.

"By the sphere of Jupiter!"

The knight had returned. His mount had halted halfway across the bridge. Behind him angry, frightened, and cowed, villagers stood at the other end of the bridge. Smoke rose where some homes had stood that morning.

"What is that beast? How dare it attack my dragon!"

"How dare you attack our village!" Emily cried in response. "This is the troll. Our troll. My troll!"

The knight scratched at his mustache and grinned.

"Ah, well. What is a mere troll against a dragon?"

He had the strange box across his lap again. His fingers played.

The dragon dove, speeding like an arrow, and loosed a barrage of fireballs. Emily dashed behind a tree. Explosions littered the ground and the top of the troll. She heard terrible sounds of metal groaning and hisses and unintelligible broken words from the troll.

The smoke cleared. The troll had lost an eye. A dent crushed into the top of its head. The troll's head turned from side to side, as though the beast was hurt and confused.

The dragon circled and its next strike would be a kill, Emily was certain.

"Troll! Oh, troll! Shake it off! Come on!"

The knight watched his dragon, and his hands moved over the box.

"Control...signal...detected...control...signal...detected," the troll muttered.

Those were words Emily did understand, though they didn't makes sense. Or did they? She knew what a signal was. It was how you told someone else something without shouting. You waved a cloth or your hand.

Control? A collar and leash or a fence or a whistle could control an animal.

The knight's box! It had to be!

Her troll was its own master, but the dragon was a slave to the knight. Emily thought it had been her own words of pleading that had awoken the troll. But perhaps the knight's signal to the dragon was some kind of language all monsters could hear.

Emily looked to the far end of the bridge. Her fellow villagers were too terrified to take action and she couldn't explain fast enough. She grabbed a short length of log. Splintered and shattered at one end, the piece of wood had been part of the toll gate. She dashed onto the bridge and ran at the knight.

He saw her coming and laughed. Behind her Emily heard the whistling descent of the dragon. She resisted the urge to look back.

She reached the side of the horse, jabbed her makeshift staff upward. The knight put his arms up to defend his face but that was not her target. She knocked the box from his lap and it flipped away onto the bridge.

"No, you little...!"

Emily darted under the horse, startling the creature. The horse bucked and stamped. She avoided the hooves and emerged on the other side. She swung the club down, smashing the box. Two blows dented and cracked the box and on the third hit, it shattered into tiny, shiny pieces.

The knight screamed in anger.

Emily whirled.

The dragon kept diving.

"Oh no!" She almost ran forward but stopped. The impact would kill her if she got any closer. "Move! Move! Move, troll!"

The troll responded but not fast enough. Its body jerked in a odd back and forth rock and it side stepped. The head of the dragon smashed into the earth beside the troll, rather than directly onto it.

The troll's escape lasted less than the moment it took for the rest of the dragon's body to crumple and crush in on itself.

The dragon exploded.

All the fire the dragon had left inside its belly ignited. Billowing round flame towered toward the sky. Emily was knocked onto her backside, her ears hearing sounds through cotton. The troll spun into the air, flipping side over side and crashing back down into the ravine where it had slept for so long.

Emily staggered to her feet. The villagers stepped cautiously onto the bridge. Their murmuring rose to gossiping noise as Emily's hearing returned.

The villagers found their courage and surrounded the knight. The ignoble noble had been knocked from his horse. He flailed on the ground like a stranded beetle. He demanded assistance, berating the people for not acknowledging their betters. His demands switched to pleas for mercy.

Emily turned from the ugly, angry mob and ran to the toll end the bridge. As quick as she dared, she climbed to the bottom of the rocky ravine.

"Oh, troll," she whispered.

Lying half in the creek, the beast was dented and scorched. One of its funny feet had torn apart. The nose was broken and bent. Its good eye, though, still glared red.

"Scan indicates Kerfen Drone is no longer present," the troll said. "Threat eliminated. Perimeter secure."

"Yes," Emily said. Her joy was mixed with fear for the troll's well-being. It appeared gravely injured. "The dragon...the drone...is gone. Destroyed."

"Cannot..." The troll's voice hissed and spat. "This unit cannot resume standby mode. Circuits damaged."

"What does that mean? Are you dying?"

"Query is not understood."

"What did you mean when you said, 'cannot resume standby mode'?"

"I cannot...rest. I cannot recharge. I will...expire."

"When?"

The troll did not answer for a long moment.

"Twenty-four thousand years. The half-life of my atomic core."

"Twenty-four thousand?" Emily laughed and smiled. "And you can't go back to sleep?"

"This unit cannot engage standby protocol until repairs can be affected."

"What is your name?"

"Tank, juggernaut class. Designation A-C-four-two-six."

"I think I'll just call you, Tank."

"This unit's designation is A-C-four-two-six."

"No, no. You're Tank. 'Tank' sounds like just the right name for a troll."

She rapped her knuckles on the troll's hard metal side.

"Hello, Tank. I've waited a long time to talk with you."

WOMEN IN WHITE
Cynthia Ward

Whenever he could, J. William Sitwell III slipped away from the house on Cumberland Hill to visit his secret lover at her efficiency apartment in Portland. Always, he brought Marie Doucette a dozen red roses, a handful of summer in the dark of winter. And always, he declared his love.

"I'd marry you tonight," William added, as they lay together in her narrow bed. "But my father's stubborn and determined to see me wed to his partner's daughter. Stella Colford is an old friend, and I don't want to hurt her with a hastily broken engagement. I don't want to be disinherited, either. We must proceed carefully or ruin our chance for a happy and comfortable life together."

"I don't care if you're rich or poor," Marie declared. "Come what may, I'll be happy!"

"I care, darling," William murmured. "I want to be a good husband and provider. So my parents mustn't know about us yet. I'll break the news to them when it's the right time."

"Of course, William," Marie whispered. "I'll keep quiet."

"I want only the best for you," William whispered, and Marie's heart thrilled at the depth of his concern. She nearly wept when he drew her close and said, "I'll love you always."

William could visit her only rarely, for he had many responsibilities to his father's enterprises and his social position. Marie followed his activities on the *Portland Press Herald* mobile site, reading it over her low-calorie bag lunch in the breakroom of Southern Maine Mercedes-Benz, where she worked as a receptionist. She'd met William at the dealership, which was owned by his father and his fiancé's father.

Three days before Christmas, Marie was eating Dannon Light and Fit blueberry yogurt with a Diet Moxie when she learned J. William Sitwell III would be marrying Stella Colford in a private ceremony on Christmas Eve.

There must be some mistake. Marie called William's cellphone. After several rings, her call went to voicemail. She kept trying to reach him, by call and text, but he didn't answer.

She drew a deep breath. Then she accessed the company's private directory. She picked up the office phone and called the number she was only to contact in an emergency.

A servant answered in a snooty English accent. She gave her name and asked for William. The servant said, "Young Master William has not mentioned you to me" and hung up. When she hit the redial button, her call went to voicemail. She dropped the receiver as if it had gone as hot as a blue flame.

Then she drove to William's parents' estate through the fury of a blizzard.

The Sitwells' private road ascended Cumberland Hill in switchbacks. For most of its length, the road passed through a dense forest of tall hemlock and black spruce. The wood ended abruptly, in storm-slashed sky. Here, a century ago, Cumberland Hill had broken in a winter storm. The section that slid into the Atlantic left a high precipice of gray granite. The Sitwells, who'd owned Cumberland Hill since the colonial era, didn't install a fence or guardrail.

Marie turned her steering wheel, trying to follow the road's sharp turn away from the cliff. The worn tires met snow-covered ice, and her car began to slide toward the edge. Despite the terror that struck like lightning, Marie took her foot off the accelerator. She didn't hit the brakes. That would almost certainly send her right off the cliff.

Her tires caught on a patch of bare asphalt.

Shivering, she continued up the steep road and found a house bulking enormously against the dark sky. She recognized the great Georgian Colonial from a newspaper story about the Sitwell family. William had made her swear many times that she would never come to his home.

A recently constructed five-car garage occupied a level area below the house, but William's silver SL550 Mercedes-Benz was parked on the circular drive, filling the porte-cochère of the imposing entrance. Marie parked her rusty '78 Dodge behind the new hardtop convertible. Struggling to slow her breathing, she stepped from her car onto the unplowed driveway and started shakily for the front door.

The fierce wind blew snow into her eyes and numbed her face. It tangled her black hair. It cut like an ice-edged knife through her short, thin coat. It tore at the exposed hem of her red silk dress, William's gift. With every hard-won step, snow fell into the tops of her fashionable low-cut boots, another of his gifts.

The servant who answered Marie's knock promised to call the police if she didn't leave at once.

Finally, Marie understood she'd lost William.

She'd lost everything.

No—she'd never had anything.

She told herself it was melted snow streaking her face as she ran back to her car.

No one saw her again for two days.

* * * *

In a small, intimate chapel decorated for a Yuletide wedding, J. William Sitwell III slipped the gold band onto Stella Colford's finger as he spoke.

"With this ring—"

"He will betray you, Stella, as he betrayed me!"

The voice was loud and oddly hollow. The guests twisted around in the pews, and the bride and groom turned away from the altar. The minister and several guests screamed. The groom's face went as pale as the woman standing at the back of the Sitwell family's private chapel.

The woman was as white as the marble altar, as white as the snow that covered Cumberland Hill, as white as Stella Colford's wedding gown. It was not only the woman's dress that was white, but her skin and hair. Water streamed from her hair and dress, as if she'd just risen from the Sitwells' indoor swimming pool.

Her limbs were mantled in ragged shrouds of seaweed. Her head was a bloated globe, with a deep pit where the nose should have been. Her teeth gleamed like polished bone where her lips had been eaten away. She faced the congregation with dark and empty sockets; yet everyone knew she saw them.

As if through a heavy mist, the back wall of the chapel was visible through the woman's body.

She raised her right arm. Several guests shrieked. She had no fingernails. She pointed the forefinger at the bridegroom.

"Beware, Stella Colford!" she cried, advancing up the aisle. "William was my lover. He said he would love me always. Yet he stands at the altar with you. How long will it be before *you* are abandoned?"

The bride turned to her fiancé. Her bouquet, a dozen red roses as bright as summer, slipped from her hand.

With shambling steps that granted an impossible speed, the white woman drew close to the couple.

William's father rose up suddenly, lunging to seize the white woman. He stumbled. His hands passed through her body as if it were a snow flurry.

"William, you were my doom," said the white woman, raising her arms. "But you swore 'always,' my love—" she stretched out her arms "—and I hold you to your vow!"

As her arms closed about him, her lover screamed. She silenced him with a ragged kiss. He struggled violently against the arm that crossed his back and the hand that cupped his head. He was a tall, broad-shouldered man, known for his mastery of golf, alpine skiing, and horsemanship. She was insubstantial. Yet he couldn't break free or take his lips from hers.

Abruptly, he went limp.

The white woman vanished. The bridegroom fell to the granite floor. He lay motionless.

The family doctor went to him as other guests called 911. Though he'd practiced medicine for decades, the doctor couldn't revive William; nor could the EMTs, when the ambulance arrived.

The medical examiner's report stated that J. William Sitwell III had died by asphyxia due to drowning.

✗

BENEATH THE CRESCENT MOON
Frank Coffman

Holding his bachall with sickle head he stood
Between the gathered folk and the sacred oak.
The bark scraped off one side: many ogham runes
Were etched into the Tree's flesh so laid bare.
He'd watched the flight of the wrens that day to scry—
From the wild and twisting patterns as they fly—
Who had been chosen as sacrificial gift.
The divining spoons had reaffirmed the choice,
And now the people answered—as with one voice,
Echoing his words, responding to his chants
The Day of Samhain, told by the rising sun,
Had come around again. Soon stark Winter's woes
Would kill the Earth. It needed to be reborn.
And, as it chanced that night, the pale crescent moon
Glowed on the blade of the sickle in his hand—
A larger arc than the symbol on his staff,
Made of pure silver, with oak leaf pattern etched.
Then a silence, as they led the young man forth,
Paler in the wan light than the rest were pale.
They knelt him before the Priest, facing the folk.
More chanting. And then—the blade was pulled across.
And though the young throat brought forth no final sound,
All heard—even the chosen one—suddenly—
The wrens crying from the branches of the oak.

I HAVE DRUNK AND SEEN THE SPIDER

Kevin J. Wetmore, Jr.

As Darren dragged him into the fourth bar of the night Mal was already over the scene. Truth be told, he had been over the scene the second week into their semester in Prague. If he wanted to bar hop he could have just stayed back in Pittsburgh. But Darren dragged him out weekend after weekend to these small bars in hopes of meeting with and hooking up with women from all over the world. A history buff (and history major), Mal would rather have been going to cultural sites. He never got tired of Prague Castle. It was eleven years since the "Velvet Revolution" and Mal loved that the nation had all this history. You could see medieval instruments of war in a museum right next to a display of Soviet-era dissidents.

"Dude, I met these two chicks from New Zealand," Darren broke into Mal's annoyance at another bar full of loud noise and smoke. "They said they were coming here tonight."

"*Dude*," Mal responded, "for the millionth time, I have a girlfriend."

"Yeah, back home, who you haven't seen in two months and won't see for like three more. If I were you, I'd be dying of semen poisoning or something. C'mon—it's not cheating if it happens on another continent."

"I'm not cheating on Janet, and I am not hooking up with some strange girl from New Zealand. In fact, I think I'm heading back to the dorm. I want to catch the train to Vienna in the morning, maybe hit up the kunstmuseum."

"Buzzkill. Hey, look at this place, though, pretty sweet, right? I figured this place would appeal to you, history boy."

Despite himself, Mal looked around. The place was dark. Like the other bars it was full of cigarette smoke, but this one was different. It was called "The Iron Door," but the only reason Mal knew that is because Darren told him. There had been no sign. In fact, from the outside, there was no indication that there was a bar here at all. They walked down a dark stairway and through a narrow alley through the eponymous metal-covered door.

The ceiling was low, and patrons sat in small groups gathered around what looked like stone tables. As he looked closer, he realized the tables were actually tombstones, or at least made to look like tombstones.

"Are those…" he began to ask Darren.

"Yeah. Kylie, the chick who told me about this place, says they are real tombstones. The owner got them when a medieval cemetery was moved in the sixties."

Mal looked around the dim room. The other bars they had been to kept the lights low for ambiance and atmosphere. This bar seemed to eat light. There were candles on the tables, and sconces lining the walls and behind the bar, but the shadows outnumbered the bright spots. The music was not the typical techno dance sound they had heard in bar after bar in Prague. In the Iron Door it sounded like speed metal being played on Romani instruments. The patrons seemed different, too. Quieter. Older. Locals. These were not backpackers, exchange students or the youth of Prague seeking momentary romance with those passing through. These were something different, something more intense. The conversations were quieter. More intense.

Darren grabbed his arm. "There they are. KYLIE!" he called across the room. Two blonde twenty somethings in the corner turned and one waved. "Let's go, man. Kylie is mine. You can have what's-her-name."

Mal sighed. Darren wasn't a bad guy. He just had a one-track mind, especially on weekends, and he wasn't interested in relationships or monogamy. He was an excellent student, though he hid it well, and was fun to travel with, which is why Mal went out with him on weekends to begin with. Darren could make friends in any situation while Mal tended to be a bit of a wallflower. Darren was one of those people who just seemed to move effortlessly through life. He never tried to be cool, he just was. People naturally flocked to him, and he was the center of every conversation, not in a self-centered kind of way. If anything, Darren specialized in getting other people to talk about themselves. Both Mal and Darren were dressed somewhat similarly tonight—jeans, t-shirt over long-sleeved shirt and a jacket, but Darren made it look effortless and hip, whereas Mal felt like he was following a style not his own, even though these were clothes he had had bought himself.

Darren was confident with the ladies, as many as possible. Mal had met and begun dating Janet freshman year and had never been with anyone else. He wasn't kidding when he told Darren he was staying faithful to her. After graduation, if all went well, he would ask her to marry him. He'd invite Darren to the wedding, but somehow doubted he'd come. They went to different schools in different states back home, and Mal had the feeling that Darren was a good buddy to the people present in his everyday life but was not much of a long-distance friend.

They crossed the semi-crowded room to the girls and made the small talk that college students in another country make, exchanging information and stories about their travels and life back home, quizzing one another about where they had been. It was clear Darren was working hard to go home with Kylie, but neither Mal nor the other girl (he forgot her name as soon as she was introduced to him) had much interest in each other. Besides, Mal kept getting distracted by the fact that they were sitting around a medieval tombstone.

They were drinking round after round of Staropramen, which a bored goth-looking waitress kept bringing them. After a while, however, Mal, bored of the conversation and of beer announced he was going to the bar to get something else.

"Anyone want anything?" he asked as he pushed back from the gravetable, A chorus of "nos" left him free to wander to the bar along the opposite wall, a veritable treasury of alcohols and spirits, some of which looked older then him. Hell, most of which looked older than his grandfather.

He wanted to try something different; he wanted an experience, not just a drink. He wanted to imbibe a genuine Czech glass of something. The bartender, an older man dressed in a Soviet-era heavy metal t-shirt, jeans and a traditional peasant's cap holding down his long, greasy hair, came over. "Co chceš?" he grunted.

"Uh…co je dobré?" Mal had only begun studying Czech when he arrived in the country and "what's good" was about what he could manage.

"American?" The bartender smiled without smiling.

"Ano, I mean yes. What do you…uh…recommend?" Mal waved his hands at the wall behind the bartender.

"Is all good. You want something different, yes? Have you had absinthe?" He began to reach for a bottle on the bar.

"I've had it." In fact, a lifelong fan of Poe, Mal had sought out absinthe his first night in Prague. Not the stuff they sell back home, but the real stuff, the strong stuff. It is an acquired taste and if he were honest he would admit he liked the experience of drinking it more than the actual drinking.

The bartender stopped reaching and turned back, folding his arms. "What, then?"

On a shelf behind the bar, high up on the left sat a single, ancient-looking bottle with a dark green liquid in it. Something else floated inside. "Is that absinthe, too?" asked Mal, pointing.

The bartender followed his finger and turned back. "Is not for you."

"Why not?"

"Very special. Very old. Not for kids."

"I'm not a kid."

"Not for tourists, then."

"I'm not a tourist. I'm a student at Charles University."

The bartender considered, reached up, and pulled down the bottle. The bottle had to be over a century old, the glass frosted. The stopper was intricately crafted in the form of an owl. Something round sat suspended near the bottom of the liquid.

"What is that?" he asked, pointing.

"You know golem? Rabbi Lowe?"

"C'mon, man. I been to the museum and the castle, I've seen the statues."

"Museum, huh? You're sure you're not a tourist?"

Mal rolled his eyes, "I told you—I'm a student at Charles University. Jsem student na Univerzitě Karlově! OK? I know about the golem."

The bartender smiled again. "Is eye of golem."

Mal looked at the bottle. "Bullshit."

The bartender grabbed the bottle and moved to put it back on the shelf.

"Hang on, hang on. I'm sorry. Je mi líto. I didn't mean it. It's just— that's supposed to be the actual eye of the golem? Really?"

The bartender looked him in the eye hard. "If you know golem, you know golem comes to life when Rabbi Lowe writes the word 'truth' on Golem's head. This is eye of golem. In absinthe. The eye and the absinthe make you see the truth."

"I thought the word was 'life.'"

The bartender breathed out, as if growing tired of the conversation. "Some tell that version. Is wrong. 'Truth' on golem's head makes it live. Golem's eye in absinthe lets you see truth."

"What do you mean, 'see truth?'"

The bartender gestured for him to move a little closer. He spoke in what seemed like a stage whisper. "You have heard 'in vino veritas', yes?"

"In wine there is truth, yeah."

The bartender smiled again. "Yes, wine makes you tell the truth. You ever drink a lot? I mean a lot. So much that you see the truth?"

Mal thought for a second. "Yeah. You know that moment where when you're drunk you think you are having a moment of clarity and everything makes sense, but then when you wake up the next day, none of that clarity is there? Yeah."

The bartender barked a laugh. "Yes, yes. Every drunk thinks he knows the truth. But this is different. The golem's eye in the absinthe allows you to see the truth of everything. When someone talks to you, you know the truth of what they are saying. When you look at someone, you know the truth of their life. You drink from this bottle and for the rest of the night, you will know the truth about everyone and everything."

Mal smiled. He knew he was being played now. "So let me get this straight, I do a shot from this bottle and no one can lie to me?"

The bartender's face darkened. "No. Is not lie detector. Instead, it allows you to see the true nature of reality. You will see the world and people as they actually are."

"Well how can I pass that up? How much is a shot?"

"No charge."

"Now I know you're playing with me," Mal said. "Free truth? Not in this day and age."

"Price is not paid in money. You will pay in other ways."

Mal was now fully playing along. "Oh, OK. So what is the price that is paid in other ways?"

"Do not mock!" The smile left the bartender's face, replaced with a scowl that somehow seemed dangerous. "You say you are friend of Czech people and you are not a tourist, but you do not take veritas absinthe seriously? Then don't worry. I give you vodka shot on the house." He went to put the bottle away.

"Wait. Wait! I'm not mocking you, you're the one playing with me. You asked if I'm American and then you offer me a magic drink?"

The bartender grew quiet and deadly serious. "Drink is not magic. Drink simply allows you to see everything as it truly is. Do you want to know the real truth about your friends over there?" He pointed at Darren and the girls in the corner, talking and laughing. "Do you want to know who they are? What they think? What they think of you? Who they are when they are alone and do not have to make a face for the public?"

He poured out a shot into a glass on the bar. He put the bottle back. He did not push the glass forward, so Mal reached for it.

"Do you really want to know who you are?"

The question stopped him. "What?"

"Do you really want to know who you are? If you drink this, you will see yourself as you truly are. Not as you see you. Not as others see you. The truth of you."

Mal paused.

"Everyone lie, yes? We learn this in Prague when communists were in charge, but you know this in America, too, I think. You know who you lie to the most?"

"Yourself," Mal responded.

"Yourself," the bartender agreed.

Mal looked at the shot glass on the bar. He stared at the liquid within it. He heard the music and felt the room vibrating all around him. All of the alcohol already in him began to rebel and he felt like the tombstone tables were watching him, to see what he would do. His inner wallflower began to assert itself again.

"You know what, I'm okay. Give me four Staropramens."

The bartender barked another laugh and downed the shot himself. "You know what, most people do what you do. No drink." He opened the four beers and handed them over. Mal held out a wad of koruna notes, but the bartender waved them off. "On me. Man not ready for truth needs a drink." He laughed again and turned away.

The rest of the night passed in a blur. Darren went home with Kylie and the other girl went with them since they were staying at the same hostel. Mal stumbled out of the bar sometime when it was still dark out to find the trams had stopped running. He had little memory of the long walk back to the dorm in the cold, but he felt like something profound had come close and then passed out of his life.

For the rest of his time in Prague he did not return to the Iron Door, nor did he think he could even find it. The city had lost some of its luster in his eyes. Something now seemed missing. He returned home at the end of term and life went on. He graduated and grew up.

Thirteen years later, he once again found himself landing at Prague Ruzyně Airport, except now it was called Vaclav Havel Airport and he was no longer here as a student. He had returned to the city for very different reasons.

He had married Janet after college, learning only half a decade into the marriage that although he had remained faithful, she had not. He learned about her serial affairs and one-night stands only after she filed for divorce to marry her current lover, who apparently had made her pregnant. Mal was in graduate school at the time, working towards a doctorate in history. His life began to fall apart and he lost his scholarship once his grades fell. He moved out of the apartment they had shared and into a studio in what his mother colloquially called "the bad part of town." He made ends meet by teaching high school history for a small private school. The economic downturn meant that last hired was the first to be let go.

He realized three things sitting in that studio with no job, no wife and no idea what came next. First, he felt like he was twenty again. Not in the good way. Not in the young and healthy and the whole future in front of you kind of way. He felt twenty in the your-life-is-not-your-own, you're-still-sleeping-on-a-used-futon, not-enough-money-for-anything-more-than-ramen-and-a-pity-beer kind of way. Second, he had no prospects in the immediate future and at the current rate would exhaust his savings in a few months. Third, the last time he was truly happy was when he first arrived in Prague at the beginning of the millennium. So he took his meager savings and purchased a plane ticket and figured if he was living like he was in his twenties while in his thirties, he may as well backpack the best parts of Europe and then come home and start his adult life over.

The first few days were about re-acquainting himself with the city. So much had changed in the near decade and a half, but not much changes in a city centuries old, either. It was like going to a high school reunion. Everything was familiar and strange and not quite how he remembered it, but the memories were comforting, even if the current reality was not—a kind of warm uncanny. He toured the castle and the old city. He visited the old dorm and the classrooms and libraries at Charles University. He spent a whole day on the Charles Bridge.

He ate cheap. More money was spent on beer and spirits than on food, but it was worth it. The spirits helped him sleep and sometimes even improved his mood, allowing him to pretend, if only for a few minutes, he was the kind of twenty that had the whole future ahead of you.

One night towards the end of his stay he missed the tram back to the hotel. He decided not to wait for the next one, but would walk back. The six beers he had with dinner were keeping him warm, a little sleepy, and a little loopy. As he walked down the cobblestone street, an alley suddenly looked very familiar and opened up a memory. He stumbled down the alley and smiled when he saw the stairs leading down to a metal covered door.

Pushing the door open, he entered the space. The differences were immediately obvious. No smoke. The music was traditional Czech music. The tombstones were gone, replaced by more traditional tables. He almost turned around, but then he saw the man behind the bar. It was the same bartender, the same peasant cap.

He crossed quickly to the bar. "Dobrý den starý přítel! Hello, my old friend!"

"Dobrý den," the bartender grumbled back, picking up a cardboard coaster and setting it down in front of Mal.

"I'm American," Mal told him.

"You don't say."

"I was here about thirteen years ago. Those tables were tombstones."

The bartender smiled slightly. "Yes, they were. What can I get you?"

Mal's eyes narrowed. "The last time I was here, you offered me veritas absinthe."

"Did I?" The bartender seemed amused. "Did you drink it?"

"No! And my life has been shit ever since! If I had just drank it I would have known that the woman I loved was a cheating liar. I would have known not to go to grad school, or I would have known all the stuff that was going to happen and avoided it. I should have drank it."

"You live, you learn. What can I get you?"

"Veritas absinthe."

"Sorry, my friend. You only get one chance at that, and you chose not to."

Mal reached across the bar and grabbed the bartender. "No! I was wrong last time. But you have to give me another chance. I will drink it this time. I want to know the truth!"

Mal felt strong hands grab him and pull him away from the bar. The bouncer had him in a tight grip.

"Is okay, is okay," the bartender said to the bouncer, who released Mal with a shove. "Fine. You want a shot, I will give you a shot. On the house. But do you really want to know who you are?" He raised an eyebrow at Mal.

Mal slumped, drunk and broken onto the bar. "Yes" he whispered.

The bartender reached up to the top shelf and brought down the ancient bottle. It was a little lower than last time, but still had a substantial amount of the liquid in it. The bartender poured out two fingers into a glass and set it on the cardboard coaster in front of Mal. He then stepped back and looked at Mal, who reached a shaky hand out and picked up the glass.

He swirled the liquid, which looked clear and cloudy at the same time. It was a rich green. He could see the reflection of his own lost and drunken face in it, beard already going grey, hairline receding, the bags under his eyes. Even before he drank he was seeing the truth of himself he realized. With a deep inhale, he downed the shot, coughs exploding out of him two seconds later.

The bartender laughed again and put the bottle away. "Good luck, *my friend*, now you will know the truth of everything. Not everyone can handle it, so be well."

Mal stared at the people in the bar. Many of them were looking at him and he could almost hear their thoughts. They were judging him. They thought they knew him. He could tell by looking at them, though, what their sins were. He started to feel sick as the drink took effect.

"Koupelna?" he almost screamed at the bartender, who pointed to a door at the other end of the room.

Mal stumbled past the people, falling into several of them before he reached the metal covered door with a silhouette of a man on it. He pushed through and fell into a row of metal sinks with a mirror above them. He looked up and saw himself in the mirror and screamed.

Ten minutes later, the bartender told the bouncer to go check on the drunk American in the bathroom. The bouncer came running out and whispered to the bartender, who ran to the bathroom and then back to the phone.

Fifteen minutes after that the three police and the medical examiner were standing over the body and the bar had been emptied out.

Inspector Fenič was interviewing the bartender, who sat on a stool next to the bar.

"So, this American comes in here and asks for a drink. What was it again?"

"A 'veritas absinthe.'"

The inspector wrote it down and then looked at the bartender. "And what is that?"

"It's just regular absinthe in a fancy bottle. I put a marble in it and tell tourists that it is the golem's eye. They buy more drinks and pay more if there is a fancy story attached to everything. Every tourist wants to think they are different and getting something ancient and magical, so I made this up and sell it to them. Or used to. I haven't done it in years, but this guy must have been here years ago, because he remembered it and asked for it. So I just gave him a regular absinthe."

The inspector rolled his eyes, but he also smiled. Cannot blame the tourist trade for sometimes taking advantage of the tourists' preconceptions and prejudices. "So he drank the shot of absinthe and ran into the bathroom?"

"Yes, and I guess when he saw the mirror he screamed and collapsed."

The inspector glared at the bartender. "And you're certain it was just regular absinthe?"

"Fero, hand me the bottle!" The bouncer reached up and handed the bartender the bottle. "Here it is—test it if you want."

"We will." Said the inspector, but still unstoppered the bottle and poured out a shot for himself, draining it in a single gulp. "Tastes like absinthe. You'll get this back once we get the lab results." He sighed. It was going to be a long night and day. He'd have to inform the American embassy. There would be a ton of paperwork.

Inspector Fenič walked into the bathroom and uncovered the corpse. None of this made any sense. Least of all that when the American looked in the mirror he collapsed of what seemed to be a heart attack. What a strange way to go. The oddest part was that the look on his face was not one of horror, but recognition. Fenič covered the face again and ordered the body removed. It was going to be a long night indeed, and that was the truth.

✗

Civil Service
Gregg Chamberlain

Sitting at the kitchen table, chin resting on a fist, Phil stared at the open letter he held in his other hand.

"Dear Sir/Madame:" it read. "We appreciate your application for a position with our company; however, we regret that..."

He dropped the letter onto the little kitchen table. It landed on the pile of other open letters that had come in the morning mail. The pile included two other job application rejections, a letter from the bank reminding him that his credit line payment was due, another letter from the bank notifying him that the mortgage payment was coming due already, plus the latest phone bill, ditto from the cell phone outfit, and the cable company about his Internet connection, as well as a polite request from the power company for payment of the last bill.

There was also a not-so-polite letter from a credit card company notifying him once again that his account was overdue and that should it remain in arrears "we shall be forced to turn the matter over to a collection service". Below that was a letter from his ex-wife's lawyer outlining the agreed-upon terms of the divorce settlement, one which, as the lawyer observed was "only proper and fair recompense for the best 10 years of her life" and if Phil could make arrangements soonest for automatic debit of his account for the alimony payments it would be appreciated. Underneath that was a letter from his own lawyer that featured an itemized bill for all the costs involved in limiting, as much as possible, any loss of blood, real, virtual or financial, while his ex's shyster skinned him to the bone during the divorce process in return for being allowed once-a-month visitation rights with Jesse.

The last letter, yet unopened, was in a long, white, and very thin envelope bearing in the upper-left-hand corner what looked like the letters I.R.S.

Just great, Phil thought. An audit. Now my day is complete.

"I'd give anything," he said aloud, as he slit open the envelope and slid the letter out, "if only once, just once, someone would do something for me."

He unfolded the single sheet of cream-coloured paper and puzzled over the glaring, and likely very expensive taxpayer-paid-for, typo in the letterhead that should have read Internal Revenue Service if not for the "f" replacing the "t" in "Internal", before starting to read the generic salutation.

Phil felt a tap on the shoulder. He spun about in the chair.

Standing in the middle of the tiny kitchen, dressed in a very conservative business suit-and-tie with horn-rimmed glasses perched on a crimson nose and holding a briefcase in one hand, was a demon.

The demon offered Phil a polite fanged smile and extended a neatly-manicured taloned hand for him to shake.

"Good day, sir," the demon said, warmly. "I'm from the government, and I'm here to help."

✗

THE SELFISH NECROMANCER
Darrell Schweitzer

Beloved,
I shall raise you up,
because our love should be eternal,
even if you're not.
Alas, there was only one draught of immortality
and I impulsively drank it.
I shall raise you up,
out of your dank grave,
and place you, radiant,
among the stars,
exactly as I remember you.
If I do it for my own satisfaction,
to alleviate my own grief,
whether or not you,
as an apparition,
can even know
that I've resurrected you,
still, give me credit.
It's a nice gesture,
the best I can do.
I shall raise you up.
Beloved.

PHISHING FOR CTHULHU

D.C. Lozar

Frank Nelson woke face down in a square room whose walls were a patchwork of uneven metal plates held together with oxidized rivets. Oval windows bulged into the room from each of the walls. A sticky yellow light pulsed through their glazed surfaces to provide the only illumination for his prison. His nostrils burned, his tongue ached, and the cloying smell of rot clung to his skin and soaked clothing. The ground he lay on was ice cold, and he could see small puffs of air when he exhaled. Muffled footsteps, indistinct voices, and manic screams echoed against the incessant sound of grinding metal. If he was being honest, Frank had the impression that some unfathomable bulk was pressing down on him, that he was trapped in a safe room moments after an Earthquake with the weight of a skyscraper above his head.

He tried to remain calm, to focus his senses, and to gather as much information as he could before letting his captors know he was awake. He assumed he had captors as he had noticed through half-open eyelids that none of the walls had doors. This made him wonder how he had gotten into such a room, how they intended to feed him, and how he was supposed to communicate. Frank struggled again to fill in the black hole in his memory, the missing page in the book of his life that could explain how a thirty-year-old, middle management, life-going-nowhere, college-dropout, could end up in a place that resembled the "Saw" movie set.

The fact that he held a serrated six-inch blade in his right hand and a reinforced steel hose in his other did little to dispel his mounting unease. Wherever he was, and however he had gotten here, Frank was in trouble.

Again and again, he swallowed a dry cough at the back of his throat until he could suppress it no longer only to have it trigger an avalanche of hacks that forced him to his hands and knees gasping for air. Distantly, he noted that the wet clothes he wore, a pair of jeans and white dress shirt, were coated in gritty, dark sand. The stuff was in his eyes, nose, and mouth, and it tasted of brine and corrosion. Forced to give up his charade of sleep, Frank struggled to his feet. His shoes were missing, and the skin on his heels was mottled and thin from prolonged exposure to water.

Frank's grip tightened on the knife as he stumbled toward the nearest wall. The hose snaked behind him until he ran out of slack and chose to drop it. The nozzle end clanged against the floor, reverberating hollowly around the room and making Frank wish he had set the thing down gently. Now, there could be no question but that he was awake and on the move.

He made his way to the nearest wall and the half-domed window that grew from it like a swollen toadstool. The bilious-yellow glow that pulsed through its cloudy surface made him hesitate, but Frank forced himself to peer through the glass into the neighboring chamber. There was a shape inside, something that resembled a human except that it was hopping jerkily on one foot. Carefully, Frank polished the window and pressed his face close to its surface. Now, he could see the man inside with his face turned away from Frank. One of the man's shirtsleeves was torn off, and his hands were filthy with fresh blood.

Frank considered yelling or pounding on the wall but instead decided to remain anonymous a while longer. He still didn't have enough information. Why was he here? Who had done this to him? Why couldn't he remember anything beyond going to work yesterday? The wall pushed against him, bulging ever so slightly inward as if conceding to some invisible pressure, and Frank backed away. Ducking under the window, moving as quietly as possible, he made his way to the next porthole.

Inside, he found a man lying on his side, seemingly unconscious. The man wore the same soaked sandy clothes as Frank and held a knife in one hand and a metal hose in the other. The hose led to one of the cell's corners. Absently, Frank wondered if this was how they planned on sending him food and fresh water. Maybe he was supposed to use it to communicate. Once he had his bearings, he'd try speaking into it and find out.

Rushing to the next window, he felt a piercing sting in his foot. Bending, he discovered that the welded steel plates on the floor had buckled inward and an uneven edge of steel had ripped open the sensitive flesh of his foot. A fountain of arterial blood pooled on the rusted metal. Hopping jerkily, Frank cut one of his sleeves off and wrapped it around the sandy wound. The improvised dressing would slow the bleeding, but he had seen bone and tendons behind the torn flesh and knew he would need stitches if not surgery.

Midway to the next window, Frank reflected on his actions. He was behaving predictably, and there was a good chance someone was watching him, even anticipating his next moves. He shouldn't make it easy for them. Defiantly, he changed course and headed to the center of the room where yet another domed window pulsed with the room's unchanging putrid light. Kneeling, he looked down through the riveted portal.

Below, he found a room indistinguishable from his own. It contained a prisoner who bent over the floor portal window of its cell in the same manner as Frank. Indeed, the man was dressed in similar clothes, had a bloody tourniquet around his foot, and held a six-inch blade in his right hand just as Frank did.

This was too surreal. It had to be an elaborate prank, a game that some warped group of friends or co-workers had devised to admonish him for some slight. Only, it had moved beyond the old-boys "gotcha" playbook he could have laughed off and now rested squarely on the page labeled "I'm going to sue your ass for giving me PTSD." Experimentally, he swept his hand over the window. After a moments delay, the man below mimicked his movement. Frank spread his fingers and watched his doppelganger did the same.

Okay. That made sense. They were watching him somehow, monitoring his movements with a video camera, and then mirroring them as part of the farce. As disturbing as that was, Frank relaxed as his mind explored the idea. Then, his heart skipped a beat as a new thought crept into his head. Just how far had they taken this joke? Had they thought of everything? If, so...

Abruptly, he twisted around to look up at the ceiling.

Above him, seen through the fish-eye optics of the portal, Frank saw the torso of a man leaning back to look up at the window in his room's ceiling, mirroring Frank perfectly. Anger welled up in his chest. There was no way a lawsuit was going to even the score. He was going to find out who had done this and destroy them. Turning back to the window below him, he imagined his twin doing the same in the ceiling above him. His fingers relaxed and tightened on the hilt of his knife and a flash from its flat surface gave him an idea. Slowly, he angled the weapon so that its blade reflected the ceiling. Adjusting it, he soon found the window above him and, within it, the face of the man peering down at him.

That face. Oh, but if he lived a thousand lives, Frank would have given every one not to have seen that face.

It had no eyes, mouth, nose, or any discernable characteristics that might identify it as anything other than an unfinished mask of clay, and yet it was profoundly familiar. It was his face, his continence, wiped clean of anything that would let him claim it, twisted into a mannequin's ghoulish stare, and yet he knew it was his.

"Oh, Hell no." Frank scrambled back from the window, knowing to gaze a moment longer meant he would forfeit his sanity, and demanded, "What kind of freak show is this?"

The walls groaned, the honeyed-light throbbed, and no one answered.

Frank did not look up.

It must have been a trick of the light, his fatigue, or some part of his brain slowly unraveling, but he knew what he had seen was impossible. Yet, he had seen it.

His foot throbbed, the walls groaned, and Frank sat down cross-legged on the floor to wait. In time, his breathing relaxed, and his heart rate slowed. He tried not to hear the muted screams that burrowed through the walls.

Eventually, he looked up at the ceiling.

The thing with his face was gone. The ceiling oval pulsed.

There was a massive groan, and the wall on the far side of the room bulged inward. Rivets shot around the room like bullets, ricocheting past Frank's head. Ducking, he scurried back. "Shit."

His hand brushed against his pocket, and he felt something he hadn't noticed at first. Glancing down, he found a moist envelope sticking out of his jeans. Desperate, he pulled it out and carefully unfolded it. He hadn't finished reading the second paragraph before he understood. His hands shook, and the letter fell to the floor.

To make some extra cash, Frank started a small extortion scam using the mail. He hadn't expected much, maybe a few hundred dollars, but the payout exceeded his wildest dreams. It wasn't a complicated con. He sent out several dozen letters addressed to the male residents of high-end communities, and then he waited. With all the sophisticated IPS programs around, this "old school" style of phishing seemed safer, even more anonymous, than the high-tech methods. Frank was careful not to leave fingerprints, and he never used the same copy machine twice. There was no way to track him down. He could have been anyone.

The letter in his pocket had been addressed to Howard at 10 Barnes Street, Providence, RI. 02906-4445 and read, "Hello Howard, I'm going to cut to the chase. My name is YellowBelly40, and I know about the secret you are keeping from your wife and everyone else. More importantly, I have evidence of what you have been hiding. I won't go into the specifics here in case your wife intercepts this, but you know what I'm talking about."

The letter went on to demand that funds, in the form of Bitcoins, be deposited to Frank's online address within ten days or the embarrassing details of Howard's incriminating actions would be sent to his wife, friends, and neighbors. Those guilty of indiscretions would be wracked with remorse and send money, a fitting punishment for their crimes. For those who had done nothing wrong, his letter served as a friendly reminder to continue to live an honest life. In Frank's mind, he was doing the world a public service.

Apparently, Howard did not see things that way. Howard was not the sort of guy you phished.

Scrawled in fine cursive indigo on the back of the letter Howard had written, "CTHULHU FHTAGN."

"Crap." Frank's grip tensed around the knife as he addressed the creaking walls. "Listen, Howard. I'm sorry about that. I don't have anything on you. I never did…I was just trying to find a way to get by. It was just business. No one got hurt. Right?"

The room pitched to the side as if a truck had hit it.

An entire wall of his prison collapsed inward, the steel pinched together by some unimaginable force. Jets of blue-green seawater spurted through the damaged partition, and Frank's eyes instinctively darted around the room, searching once more for some means of escape. His breath came in ragged bursts. "What do you want? Please. Let me out!"

He edged away from the growing pond until he found his back against one of the two remaining port windows. Swallowing hard, sweat dripping from his matted hair, knowing this window must contain even more terrors, Frank braced himself to face whatever he saw.

He looked.

The chamber on the other side of the glass was half-full of brackish water. A featureless doppelganger wearing Frank's clothes dog-paddled within a circle of horror. Gelatinous things, organisms made of bulbous eyes, fangs, and pinchers, swam around him like shadowed wraiths. The water roiled and foamed as the mannequin tried to tie a knot in a hose that closely resembled the one Frank had discarded eons ago.

One of the shapeless hideous masses dove beneath the water.

Frank yelled against the roughen glass, "look out!"

The jellylike thing yanked the mannequin beneath the water like a catfish taking a cork bobber. There was a battle, a frantic dance of splashes, appendages, and teeth, and then a dark pool of blood rose to the surface. A moment later, the ghoul pretending to be Frank surfaced holding a glob of writhing tentacles that resembled Medusa's skull only the shadowy monster wasn't dead. Its suckered mouthparts bent inward to gnaw on the doppelganger's clay-flesh while its arms tightened around his wrist like a garrote. A moment later, the mannequin's severed hand fell into the water with a bloody splash.

Turning away, Frank saw that the glacial water in his room was up to his waist. He sloshed to the center of his cell and groped around until he found the metal hose. He would beg for help. He would do whatever they wanted.

There was something inside the hose, something living, and it was crawling toward him. Remembering the indescribable lurid horrors, the globular fiends he'd seen circling his twin, he tried to crush the hose, but it was too stiff. The skittering thing inside was nearly at the opening, almost out into the water, and Frank had little choice but to meet it.

Expecting a mollusk covered in weeping eyes and uneven teeth, he blanched when an army of mite-sized tadpoles swarmed from the opening. He spat and clawed as they squirmed into his mouth, up his nose, into his ears, and slid effortlessly into the thin recesses surrounding his orbits.

Those that fell into the water expanded like ink, absorbing substance from the brine, shedding their skin only to gobble it up and sprout more eyes and teeth.

The water frothed as the first wave of oily black nats grew into the sinister monstrosities that had circled the mannequin. Frank felt another wave skittering down the hose and tried to tie it off. Then, he remembered that this was what his twin had been doing before it was —

The beast's fangs dug into his thigh as it hauled him down. He slashed at it as the briny water entered his mouth and stung his eyes. He felt it eating him, tearing off strips of flesh and denim, as it dug for the chewy tendons beneath. Forcing his eyes open, he saw the suckered appendages that grew like tubers from the thing's skull constricted around his leg, threatening to snap the bones. Frank's lungs screamed for air. His ears rang with the muted sounds of grinding metal, and he wondered absently if anyone would miss him at work. How long before they hired someone to replace him, to fill the tiny void his death would create? A day? A week?

No. Frank fought the blackness as it colored his vision. It couldn't end like this. He couldn't have mattered so little. Someone had to care that he was gone.

He reached for the formless spawn's skull, felt it squirm and twist in his grip, and struck at its neck with his blade. It let out a bubbled wail as he sawed through the elastic meat of its head stalk.

Recalling what had happened to the mannequin's hand, Frank flung the nightmare's head from him before swimming to the surface. He gasped fresh air. "I'm sorry! I'm sorry. Please. You've got to stop this!"

Another wall crunched inward as the chamber lolled harshly to the side. More rivets whizzed around the room. One slammed into Frank's shoulder, and his arm when numb. Helpless, he watched as the knife fell from his deadened fingers into the murky water. Blood poured from the open wound under his clavicle.

One after another, the nauseating yellow lights of the room's portals flashed out until only the window he had yet to examine remained. He felt the gelatinous eye-and-teeth creatures swim near him, could hear their small mouths slurping up the blood he was loosing and knew that they were waiting. They had gotten a taste of him, an aperitif, and no longer felt the need to rush the main course.

Cursing and blessing this last pulsing eldritch light, Frank swam toward the portal. Without it, he would be blind and as defenseless as a newborn rabbit in a den of snakes. With it, he risked seeing what lay beyond and in so doing lose his sanity.

"I just want it to stop," whimpered Frank. His fingers stuck to the frozen surface of the grimy glass as if it were dry ice. "This is sick. Please. If you can hear me, I'm scared. Please don't make me look."

The slowly throbbing amber light was his only answer. The half-seen vile sludge in the water nuzzled him, urging him to look, and he splashed at them. Their little mouths caught the bloody water and gurgled it down with happy chirps and puffs.

Knowing it was what was expected of him, knowing that there was no way to avoid his fate, Frank turned to peer through the aperture.

A vast expansive of pitch-black ocean met his gaze. He was thousands of fathoms below the sea, at a depth that only fish with luminescing prominences and mouths of serrated teeth dared explore. The weight of the world lay above Frank's small prison.

Below him slept a creature more immense and abysmal, more mind-shatteringly ghastly than any night terror a mortal mind could imagine or even grasp. Folded leathery wings the size of islands extended from the barnacled leviathan's shoulder blades. Tentacles the size of bridges drooped like a beard from its placid face to undulate like corded seaweed in the ocean's currents. The titan's mottled hands were spiked with vicious talons the size of school buses, and its hoary cranium shammed any rendition of what lay at the center of Dante's Inferno. This was evil, the full and unadulterated majesty of a cosmic force, the antithesis of all that pertained to good and wholeness in the universe.

What lay beyond its torso and arms was curtained by gloom, but Frank made out greenish stone blocks upon which ancient runes were carved and a gleaming monolith the size of which made his mind reel. Swimming and darting from one shadow to the next were hoards of monstrosities, unspeakable demons, unfathomable slimy atrocities which if unleashed upon the waking world would drive children to die in their mother's arms and fathers to murder those they loved to save them from a fate far worse than mortal death.

Even Frank's sudden precognition that these atrocities would one day rise to consume his race did not compare to the revulsion he felt upon seeing that the sickly yellow glow that had for so long illuminated his cell emanated from the partially open lid-slits of the Goliath's two serpentine eyes. Direct exposure to the vibration of that power unlocked Frank's soul, and he understood in an instant that his reality was but a dream to this being, his world's existence no more than a neural spasm within the slumbering beast's mind and the only thing of value he or any of his kind had to offer such a deity was their eternal suffering.

Unable to comprehend, to process the beautiful malevolence of what he now knew to be true, Frank looked away from the light.

There were five metal boxes such as his in the water, and each was encircled by one of the monster's chin tentacles. It had been these constricting serpents that had sluggishly collapsed the walls of his chamber rather than the indomitable weight of the ocean above their heads.

Inside each box, Frank saw faceless mannequins peering out into cobalt oblivion. They pounded against the portals, shook their fists at him, and screamed vainly with mouthless tongues.

"Please. No. Please. I'm sorry."

One after another, the sleeping leviathan placed each of the steel boxes between its beaked lips and cracked them open like walnuts. Its sticky pink tongue drew forth a flailing human form, a mote of infinite fear, and bit down.

Frank slammed his fists against the port window and screamed, but no noise came from his missing mouth. His head dipped beneath the rising water, and his hearing disappeared as the liquid filled his canals. In the absolute silence, he surfaced and tried to wipe the brine from his eyes only to find that they were gone.

Exploring his face, Frank found that he no longer had a mouth, nose, or eyes. His fingers met only gooey pliable flesh and came away slimy and fouled. He was one of them now, a mannequin, a clay-faced anonymous ghoul with no senses but that of touch. He tried to inhale, but it was as if a plastic bag had been pulled over his face. His lungs screamed for air, his mind panicked, and yet he did not die.

The parasitic tadpoles that had entered his body had done this to him. Their brethren, the formless spawn in the water, had never meant to consume him. No. They had been nothing but a distraction, an audience to his metamorphosis.

The shell that had been his prison split open, and the sudden crushing weight of the ocean pushed in from all sides, demanding he not exist.

Frank fought as a tongue-like protuberance found him and dragged him between the leviathan's hooked beaks. He shrieked and squealed soundlessly as the sleeping giant chewed him, macerating his bones and flesh, and still he did not die. The formless mites had changed him, preparing him for their master's pleasure, so that his rendered mortal flesh healed as swiftly as it was damaged. So it was that the star spawn chewed its human cud...

Frank woke face down in a square room whose walls were a patchwork of jagged metal plates held together with rusted rivets. Oval windows glazed to resemble cataracts bulged from each of the six walls to emit a sickly yellow glow that flickered menacingly and was the only source of illumination for the prisoner...

Knowing what was to happen, what would recur for an eternity, the thing that had been a man named Frank screamed against the clay of his lipless mouth.   ✗

RIVER OF THE BLUE CARMINA
Brandon Jimison

The river was no place for a mummy.

Kairo stood in the middle of the barge, which was little more than a large raft with a small enclosure, and second guessed his decision to float the Rio Grande in search of a peculiarly high and elusive bounty. The spirit voices whispered sweet derisions to him.

Considering the options, Kairo had little choice. He had spent three days riding all along the coast of the river with nothing to show for it but stiffness in his legs, and a bullet from an adventurous vagabond. He would hate to have to add death by water to that list of grievances.

He was dead already, of course, and somewhat alive too. It was odd business being a mummy.

His steady gaze surveyed the gentle ripples in the wake of the barge. The Nile in Egypt had never caused him anything but peace, as he had floated along its lush banks many times. The uneasiness he felt along this river was unusual for him. He didn't much care for it.

He didn't want to find out what a dip in the river would do to his dry, caked, wraps and dusty bones. His dark jacket and wide brimmed Union Cavalry hat often shielded the worst of rain, when he had been foolish enough to be out in it for longer than a few minutes. It would be of no use against the river.

It was his general dustiness and aged wrappings, which blended well into his facial features that kept his true nature concealed from the living. For the most part, folks just thought him odd. It also helped that he tended to keep in sparse company. He hoped that the small group on the barge didn't test him. They were the largest group of living people he had been around for several months.

The pole man pushed the barge out away from a fallen tree in the river. The sudden change in movement caused Kairo to shift his feet with trepidation and steady his titled hat.

"Looking a little green there stranger," The miner said.

The miner sat along the side of the barge with his feet dangled in the river. "Reminds me of the mighty Missouri. I'll be back there someday," He said.

The miner sounded as if he were trying to convince himself more than anyone else. Kairo had determined that the man was running from something fierce, or heading towards a home…could be both.

The miner kept a large, worn, and dusty bag on his shoulder or arm at all times. If anyone so much as glanced at the bag in particular, the miner's grizzled beard would bristle and he would move it to a more secure location closer to his wiry body, more hidden from view.

Kairo imagined there was gold in that bag. No matter that most seeking treasure in the West had found nothing but hardship. Gold was on his mind, and no doubt, in his eyes.

The miner feigned he didn't notice Kairo's gaze, but shifted the saddle bag from his shoulder to his front, away from view.

"There's no shame in being afraid of the water," The old lady said to Kairo, "I've seen water carry away strong men, beasts and farms. It erodes rock and brings the haughty low. Cried much of it myself."

"There is truth in your words," Kairo said.

The lady showed a gap-toothed smile. Her dress was dark as the midnight sky with fancy white trim around the cuffs and hem. She sat atop a common barrel as if she were a queen of Egypt. A black parasol shielded her from the harsh rays of the sun.

She was also a recent widow. Kairo could see the spirit of her husband hovering always near to her.

"I'm not here to be afraid," Kairo continued.

"What are you here for stranger?" The bristly miner asked from over his shoulder.

"I wouldn't mind knowing that myself," The bargeman also said, "Don't seem like you are here for a destination. You look too much at the water and shore. Looking…or waiting for something to happen."

Kairo looked to the only passenger that had not yet spoken, to add his point of view as well. The large man at the front of the barge said nothing. He had done the same since boarding. The spirit voices chattered incoherent babble regarding the man, but Kairo could see nothing to be wary about. He may be strange, but he was not the bounty.

"I'm here for a bounty," Kairo said. Couldn't hurt to tell the truth and rattle some on board. Time would come he might need to take advantage of that.

"We have a criminal on this barge?" The bargeman asked, and casually shifted his right hand to the gun tucked under his belt. He was a dark Spanish looking man with a thin mustache and a pair of scars on his face that marked him as a fighter.

Kairo let the mood on the barge simmer.

A fish leapt from the river and made a splash that cut the silence.

"I reckon the man you're after has justice coming to him," The old lady said, "My name is Bonnie Ann Carter by the way. Can't imagine any trouble I may have caused worth putting a bounty on my head. My husband died of his own accord. My son is in El Paso. I hope to see him before I see the Good Lord in Heaven."

"What about him?" The bargeman asked Kairo, with a nod at the miner.

"Tim Riley," Was all the miner offered.

The bargeman did not yet looked satisfied. He had previously introduced himself to everyone on board as Bargeman, and felt no need to reiterate. He was not wanted for anything in the States. The people he had wronged would not send a gringo to do the job.

"It's not a man I'm after," Kairo finally volunteered, "A beast."

The old lady looked towards the second barge up ahead that held the horses. The man steering that barge gave a wave.

The bargeman did not look to the horses. He had pulled his gun and leveled it at Kairo. His hand shook with fury.

"Oh no you don't. Not my prize. She's mine I tell you. Keep away from her you stinking gringo," He spat out.

Kairo's hand was already on his own pistol, holstered at his side.

"Slow down. Talk this through," He said, "What do you think I'm after?"

"The river monstrou. Blue Carmina."

Kairo made a show of slowly moving his hand away from his pistol. He hoped that the bargeman would not take a shot at him. It would cause more trouble and explanation when Kairo did not fall dead from the wound.

The bargeman's pistol remained pointed at Kairo, though his hand was more stable than minutes before.

Before either Kairo or the bargeman were able to make another move, a large hand (easily the size of a man's head), had snatched the pistol from the bargeman's hand, and tossed it across the floor of the barge. A shot fired during a particularly hard skip, which caused the horses on the other barge to become nervous. All except Kairo's horse; Pharoah, he just swished his tail with casual ambivalence.

The large, silent man had taken matters into his own hand, and then stepped back to his place at the far end of the barge. Kairo had been amazed at how fast the giant moved. He also noticed the hand of the man was unusually hairy, but could not bring any other features of the man to memory.

"What do you know about this Blue Carmina?" Kairo asked the bargeman.

A disarmed and disgruntled Bargeman answered, "She lives in the river. Sometimes things go missing. Things left too close to the water. I saw her once. Shiny and blue as a dark sea. She is my prize. I will not hurt her."

Kairo couldn't tell if the man wanted the bounty for the creature himself or loved it. Either way, it would cause complications.

The miner took that as his cue to pull his dangling feet out of the water. He hefted his bag onto his shoulder and took a few steps away from the edge of the barge.

"So, just how much is this monster worth?" The miner asked.

"Best to leave this to a professional," Kairo answered.

"How do you know the creature is female?" The old lady suddenly asked.

It was a question that Kairo had not thought of.

"Stories," The bargeman replied, "A senorita once told me I would find my most prized possession on the river. She had magic in her hand."

Kairo scanned the surface of the water for movement. He also noticed the land around them had changed in elevation. Tall canyon walls loomed over them on either side of the river, blocking the harsh rays of the sun, and any inviting purchase of land.

His right hand was once more resting on the handle of his gun. His general nervousness invited action.

"I once heard tell a story," The old lady spoke up, "Of a soldier and his wife. This soldier fought for the honor of his country and king, but never returned. His wife, now a widow, would wait by the river for his soul to be returned to her. She believed that souls of the dead traveled down the river on their way to the afterlife. She witnessed the ferryman corral and lead these souls on nights when the moon was full, and the wind howled like the coyote. One night, she saw the glint of the moon reflect off the silver locket her soldier had always worn next to his heart. She waded into the river, thinking that she would grab his hand and pull him to her, but when the water was up to her waist, she lost sight of the locket. She cursed the ferryman. She cursed the moon. She cursed the howling coyote. She cursed the war. Then she continued wading farther into the wide river until she could be seen no more."

"What happened to her?" The bargeman asked solemnly.

"She was never seen again. Folks say that she is still searching the river for the locket of her soldier, to be reunited in spirit with her love. Some say the river felt pity on her and turned her into a creature of the water to prolong her life, and her search."

"My Blue Carmina." The bargeman whispered.

Kairo thought he saw a tear trail down the man's cheek. This man would not give up Kairo's bounty easily.

A fish leapt from the calm river to make a splash somewhere in the distance.

"Sounds like hogwash to me," the miner said, "Who would drown in a river for silver? Now gold, that is worth dying for."

The spirit voices told Kairo that there may be something to the widows' story…in so many words. It was often difficult to tell what exactly the spirits voiced, but he had learned to take the general tone of their chattering seriously. It had saved him on more than one occasion.

"Never question the lengths one will go to for love," Kairo said.

He could have added that his own love, his Amunet, waited for him somewhere out there in the desert. He would find her one day and be home.

"Does anyone have anything silver?" Kairo asked.

The bargeman scowled, "I refuse to help you."

"I have only my wedding ring, Sir," The old lady said.

Kairo understood that to mean she was not going to give it up.

"I have a silver bit," The miner said, "And a bullet."

Kairo thought about going up to the large stranger, standing away from the rest of them, and asking him. However, it seemed the man wanted to be left alone, and something made Kairo eager to oblige.

"You have a silver bullet?" Kairo asked the miner.

"Won it from a man in Kansas City. He said it would protect me from werewolves," The miner pulled the bullet from deep in his bag, and held it up to examine it as if it were a fine sparkling diamond. "Never met a werewolf yet. What'll you give me for it?"

Kairo thought about what he had to barter with. His pistol, the machete at his side, the ancient scarab necklace around his neck, the cavalry hat, Pharaoh, his boots. None of these he could part with.

He finally decided to remove a pouch from inside his shirt. The pouch was tethered to his body by a leather cord. He took a piece of turquoise from the pouch. The rock was an inch thick and nearly two inches long.

"I got this off an Indian. I brought him in for scalping a sheriff, and stealing hogs to feed his family," Kairo explained.

The miner took the rock from Kairo and weighed it against the silver bullet. He eventually placed the bullet in Kairo's hand and smiled, pleased with the deal.

"Never ran into any werewolves," He said mostly to himself.

Kairo observed the light was fast fading. The river came to a bend, and the cliffs rapidly receded along the west side. He had little time to fashion his lure.

He pried the back off the bullet with a small knife, then dumped the powder over the side of the barge. He pierced a tiny hole in the casing and ran a long chord through it. He knotted the chord and tied it off like he would a hook on a line. He held the casing firm in one hand, and gave the chord a sharp tug with his other to test the strength of the knot, and the chord. Both held strong.

Under the withering gaze of the bargeman, Kairo let the chord out and swung it around in a wide circle a couple of times before tossing the makeshift lure out into the river. The casing didn't sink right away, but when it it did, he began to slowly pull the chord back to him. It returned with no event.

"Ha!" The bargeman scoffed, "The gringo will not catch my Blue Carmina with such a trick."

The sunlight continued to fade away with haste.

Kairo tossed the lure out a second time.

It returned yet again with nothing.

The cliffs on the west side of the river had started to rise, which would block what little sun light that remained. Nature and the bargeman were not favoring Kairo today.

He tossed out the lure one last time.

Immediately there was a light tug.

A coyote howled somewhere atop the cliffs, or perhaps it was the wind.

Kairo wrapped the slack chord around his arm twice and set his feet firm. He tried not to think about the increasing current of the river, or what size this creature might be, or what he would do once the creature took hold of the lure. He tried not to think on these things, but failed. The spirit voices grew silent.

A tug on the other end of the chord pulled Kairo forward a step. He thought he caught a glimpse of a shadow under the water. It was big.

The miner had turned around to watch how Kairo's fishing was going.

The bargeman kept his hands on the steering pole, but his eyes stared at the water and his feet were shifty, like he was trying to make a difficult decision, and was readying to execute it once his mind was made up.

Kairo was forced to take another step from another sharp pull on the chord. His eyes kept returning to water at the edge of the barge only a few feet away. He was having second thoughts about this plan.

He set his feet and gave the chord a sharp yank. There was no give. He took a couple of steps backward, pulling with all his strength, afraid the chord would snap any moment.

Whatever was on the other end of the chord pulled, and kept pulling, swimming away.

The chord snapped.

Kairo staggered forward and nearly tripped over his own feet. He was practically over the edge of the barge, and screaming Egyptian curses, when a strong arm grabbed him across the waist to save him. Another strong arm grabbed the chord in front of him, and whipped it out of the water.

It was the silent big guy that had stopped the gun fight earlier. He had actually lifted Kairo's feet off the barge entirely, as he was at least two feet taller than the mummy. Kairo heard a low growl in his ear, and could smell the man's earthy, musty scent.

Kairo couldn't tell if the growl was a warning or a greeting.

"Thanks," Kairo said.

The bullet casing remained on the end of the chord, seems the chord hadn't snapped, the creature had pulled away from it for some reason. The lure lay a yard away from Kairo. He reached down to pick it up as the big man strolled back to the other end of the barge. There was something about the easy wide stride of the man that bugged Kairo, but he was grateful for that stride that saved him from a watery disaster. He shuddered thinking about it.

Kairo found that the bargeman was away from the steering pole. He held a large knife at ready.

"Lucky for you," The bargeman said, "I would have cut the line anyway. I advise you not try again for my Carmina."

"Wh-What is that?" The miner yelled out.

Everyone turned their attention to the side of the river where Kairo had recently fished, and the miner pointed. The water was calm and undisturbed.

"What did you see?" Kairo asked.

"I don't know, but it was big. I just saw a fin shape poke up from the water."

The spirit voices chattered like clacking wheels along a track. Kairo rested his hand reassuringly on the grip of his side pistol, but his recent dance with a watery dive, and the thought of tangling with something born of water had caused his hand to shake. He whispered a short prayer to all the gods he could remember.

"There she is," shouted the bargeman.

Kairo waited.

He had yet to see any sign of the creature.

It was then the creature arose from the water, and propelled itself up onto the side of the barge with two long and sinewy arms. The sun had almost fully retreated under the horizon, and the tall cliffs returned along the shore, but enough light remained to highlight the features of the creature briefly.

Its scales flashed a hue of blue and green along the sides and arms with a torso of silver. There was little doubt it was feminine and humanoid in form. Thin seaweed looking plants from the river seemed woven together with long strands of black hair which hung to the creature's waist. An eel slithered out from between the hair and plopped back into the river as they watched. A bevy of hooks were lodged in the back of the creature, still attached to broken fishing line. She didn't seem to mind the hooks, or be in particular pain. Her face had little expression at all, but wide fish eyes and a slit for a mouth where small sharp teeth lay in wait. Colorful gills along her neck opened and closed in a steady rhythm.

The creature quickly turned her head this way and that as if searching for something. Perhaps it's time out of water was limited.

The bargeman was the first to speak, "My Carmina. You have finally come to me." He took a few short steps towards the creature, his arms out in a welcoming gesture.

The creature swung at him with her arm and webbed hand which ended in sharp fin-like claws, which could no doubt rend a man's flesh into strips.

She swung her arms out to the left and right in rabid frustration.

Kairo held the bullet casing up in front of him for her to see.

She locked her watery eyes on the makeshift lure, and reached towards him like a child might to a fleeing parent or a lover to her mate.

The look in her eyes at that moment caused Kairo's resolve to waiver. That look spoke to him like a kindred soul. It said *give me back my love or give me sweet death*. It was a sentiment with which Kairo had grown all too familiar.

That didn't make what he had to do next any more forgivable.

With a short motion, he jerked his gun out from holster to fire a shot between the creature's wide eyes.

The miner plucked a pick ax from his pack and took a swing at the creature with a holler. The ax punctured the creature's side and it doubled over from the force and pain.

Kairo's bullet passed over the lowered head of the creature.

The bargeman gasped in horror, and dove onto the miner in rage. The pair ended up on the barge floor grappling at each other and throwing furious punches.

Kairo took careful steps over to the fallen creature, his gun at aim.

The creature lay on her side, rivulets of blood escaped from the wound, its forced breathe in fits and spurts. Kairo surmised that if the ax were to be removed, the blood and life would flow from the creature in a matter of minutes, maybe four, maybe twenty. A webbed hand reached out towards Kairo, not in a threatening way, but imploring. The creature's wide, bloody, mouth formed silent words.

"Go ahead, Mr. Kairo, send her to her love," The old lady said, "It's what you came here for."

Kairo had no argument.

He fired two shots into the head of the creature, and she breathed her last.

She would be home now. In a way, Kairo envied her. It seemed like home was still a far off for him, though he felt a reunion with his own love, his Amunet, was closer every day. He hoped that death, true death, would be as quick for him when the time came. Death did not look kindly on being held unnaturally at bay for as long as he had been with Kairo. The reckoning would surely be swift and brutal, at least that's what the spirit voices always told him.

The particular sound of a man's head being cracked open, brought Kairo out of reflection, and back to the scene on the barge.

The bargeman sat atop the prone and still miner. A pool of blood surrounded the back of the miner's head, his eyes vacant.

"My Carmina," The bargeman mumbled over and over again.

He looked up at Kairo like a man attuned to great sorrow. When he noticed the condition of the creature, he stumbled over to her and gently folded himself around her.

"Her end was quick," Kairo said.

The bargeman's quivering fingers ran across the bullet wounds. A great sob rocked through his body from shoulder to feet.

Kairo drew his machete from the scabbard.

"I'll not take her," Kairo said, "Give her a proper burial and mourn her in peace."

"Thank you," The bargeman said through cries.

"I will need the head."

The bargeman raised bloodshot dagger eyes at Kairo, and spat at his feet, but backed away from the creature's body. He couldn't force himself to watch the deed. A strong shudder rose up his body each time he heard the blade hit its mark- THUNK, THUNK.

Kairo held the head over the water to let it bleed out, and then placed it in a sack which he had kept folded up between his back and belt. He searched through the dead miner's pack for anything useful, and found enough gold nuggets at the bottom of the pack to almost double his bounty for Blue Carmina.

The sun had fallen, and the light of the moon illuminated a clearing of the cliffs a short distance off.

"Looks like I will be cutting this trip short. You can let me and my horse off up there," Kairo told the bargeman.

"With gladness," The bargeman replied.

The bargeman returned to his steering pole. The direction of the barge shifted abruptly.

Kairo stumbled to his knee and fought the urge to lay flat. The quicker he got off this stinking raft, the better.

When the barge reached shore, Kairo gathered up the miner's pack and the creature's head.

"I hope you find what you are looking for Mr. Kairo," The old lady said, "I have a feeling that it will not bring you peace."

"Your husband says to keep a pillow for him in your bed," Kairo said.

"Tell him to keep his cold toes off me then," She said with a smile, "Ha. You do walk with death, don't you?"

"Tell him yourself, he's here."

Startled, the lady turned quiet. She turned, and whispered something slyly over her shoulder.

Kairo left the couple to themselves, eager to step on land and dirt once more. He rushed off the barge with a final leap which caused a splash. Upon reaching land, he no longer cared about a little splash. It felt like a thick blanket of fog had lifted off from him. A sigh escaped his cracked lips.

The spirit voices sang a chorus of joy, or perhaps it was Kairo himself.

Pharaoh met Kairo with a head toss and a swish of his tail. The horse was rarely exuberant, so this was a veritable bear hug and slap on the back. Kairo gave Pharaoh a couple of firm pats on the neck, then tied the newly acquired pack and sack which carried the creature's head to the saddle. He hoped he could get back to town before the head started to stink awful. Of course, it would have to stink worse than him.

Kairo noticed that the big silent man from the barge had also walked away. The large shape of the man was off in the distance already. The stride of such a man would be monstrous. He left a trail of big feet behind him. He had apparently not been wearing shoes.

"I hope my Carmina haunts you to the grave," The bargeman yelled from the barge. He stood over the body of the creature like a sentry.

"She will have plenty of company," Kairo said, mostly to himself.

He walked Pharaoh through the rocky terrain until they reached dry, flat land. The smell of the river tinted the air, but it no longer caused Kairo tremors. The spirit voices had nearly ceased their babble. The moon was round and full, spilling its gentle rays over the desert like it was a canvas in need of a masterpiece. A beautiful night for the long ride of a dead man who had rarely felt so alive.

✗

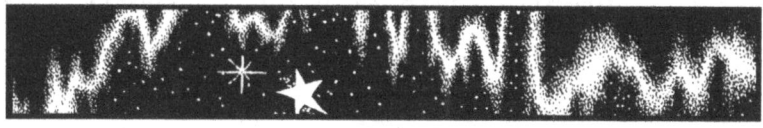

THE REPRIEVE
Darrell Schweitzer

There was an intruder in the room.

Prince Tigranes drew his throwing knife and whirled about, searching the night-time shadows. Curtains billowed from open windows, rustling gently. There was no other sound, but he *knew* he was not alone. He had an instinct for that, even as he had a talent for throwing knives. These were decadent times in Riverland, not a reign of virtue at all. While he was a man of culture and intelligence, and, he liked to think, some sensitivity, his primary talent was for staying alive. He was neither young nor old, and superbly fit. He stood tensed, like a lion ready to spring.

"Who *dares* enter my chamber?"

The reply was very soft and strangely accented, yet quite distinct. Not foreign, just odd.

"Read what is written. On your table."

Still as ready to attack as a lion surrounded by hunters, Tigranes edged over to his writing desk and picked up a papyrus. He glanced at it side-ways. In his copious spare time—for the life of a prince consists of *waiting*—he had pursued the arts somewhat himself and he could tell that the writing was tiny, ornate, and exquisitely executed, like something done by some master calligrapher hundreds of years ago. He had seen the like in the royal archives. Under other circumstances he might have paused to admire it.

"I can recite the story," said the voice. "I know it by heart. But I think that you should either hear or read —"

"Why —?"

"It has immediate relevance to your situation."

The prince whirled around again.

Now the voice was behind him. He turned again, but saw nothing in the gloom.

He picked up the papyrus and began to read, as the other recited word-for-word.

****

There was a man called Madatho, who was carried off by Death. Like all men in such circumstances, he protested that it was not his time yet, that he was afraid, that his wife and children would be left destitute, that he had things yet to accomplish in the world, and like all men he made these protestations without even the most forlorn hope.

Yet he was granted a reprieve. That is the extraordinary thing. That is why his story is worth telling.

This Madatho had heard something crawl up out of the river onto his porch, in that late hour of the night when no man of Reedland is ever abroad. For three nights the thing paced back and forth, in heavy, ungainly steps, not like a man at all, but like some heavy animal unsuited for walking on land.

For three nights, from the forbidden hour until dawn, it whispered his name in a hissing voice that did not sound at all human.

At last, when he could bear the terror of it no longer, when he was certain that his doom was upon him, Madatho flung open his shutters and found himself face-to-face with a gaping-jawed crocodile. The thing poured over his windowsill and stood up before him like a man, for it had the pale, bloated, naked body of a drowned man, though with the head, claws, and tail of a crocodile; and Madatho knew that this was Death come upon him, for it was one of the evatim, a messenger and servant of Surat-Hemad, the God of Death, whose teeth are the numberless stars, whose mouth is the night sky, who shall at the end of time devour the entire world.

He made his useless pleas, as all men do, and, to his astonishment, the creature said to him, "My master requires a service of thee. During the time spent in the performance of it, thy life shall be spared."

Madatho babbled on, "Yes, yes, anything —"

The monster told him that he must travel five hundred miles downriver to the City of the Delta, and there announce to Nakamaenon, the great and terrible king, that his life had been weighed by the Lord of Death and found wanting, and that he and all his dynasty were to become extinct.

Madatho was terribly afraid, but he could hardly refuse.

"Come then," said the monster, and it took him by the arm and hauled him out the window, across the porch, and down a ladder into a boat. Madatho wanted to protest that he needed to see his wife and children one last time, that he should pack something for the trip, that he needed money, but he knew that his first set of useless excuses were more than enough.

What followed was like a dream. There were subtle transitions, as if he'd closed his eyes and opened them again in another place, in another situation. It seemed that the Moon was high in the sky, motionless, a thin, sharp crescent, like a knife.

The monster was transformed into a kindly old man in a flowing robe. "You can call me Uncle," he said. Uncle pushed the boat along for a time with a pole, but then they were in deeper water, and the vessel was larger, propelled by twenty oarsmen—who had crocodile heads at first, then human ones—while Madatho and his uncle sat in comfort beneath a canopy.

As the river slid by, they discussed philosophy, and his uncle told him the secrets of the waters and of the skies, and taught him to read the secret language of the stars. Therein Madatho read this very tale, and knew his own destiny.

They tarried on their way to the Delta, stopping in all the towns and cities along the way, trading for goods, losing themselves in houses of pleasure for weeks or even months at a time, but always at night, as the knife-like Moon remained unmoving in the sky, and the stars, which are the teeth of Surat-Hemad, gleamed.

All his enterprises prospered, and Madatho became rich, being directed in all things by his wise uncle.

Only on a few occasions did Madatho awaken suddenly, as if from some astonishing dream, torn in conscience, filled with fear. He knew he could never return upriver, but he managed to send letters and money home to his wife and children.

Yet he had read his own tale in the stars.

Still onward he drifted, downstream, and the boat with the twenty oarsmen became a great barge of pleasure and of commerce, a floating palace, which was anchored for a full year at the City of the River's Turning, where Madatho took from his concubines another wife, and begot a son upon her. He built a golden tower for her in the river's bank, connected to his barge by a ramp, across which he would go every night to lie with her.

It was almost possible to forget his ultimate mission, but he did not forget. His uncle was always there, to whisper in his ear, and when he did, Madatho would grow silent, and sometimes weep.

His uncle taught him magic. He became a great wizard, learning to speak to the spirits of the air and to command them.

People came to him to hear him prophesy. He was their oracle.

It occurred to him to wonder whether any of this was actually happening, or if he might still be on the porch of his house far upriver, in the arms of a messenger of Death, dying slowly and horribly, and hallucinating everything else as his mind shut down.

"Does the fly, caught in amber, dream of all eternity, or does it experience but a single instant forever?" he asked his uncle.

"That is an interesting question," said the other.

Suddenly Madatho felt a great desire to run into the golden tower, to embrace his wife and look upon his infant son, to reassure himself that they actually existed.

"Alas, we are drifting," said his uncle.

Not even his magic could change the river's flow. His tale was long and leisurely, but it was not written to go on forever. In his heart of hearts he knew that.

The barge had broken loose from its moorings. He looked back just in time to see the golden tower vanish behind the curving, dark shore, beneath the knife-thin, crescent Moon.

At last he came, as had been prophesied, to the City of the Delta, and with great ceremony he stood before Nakamaenon the king, and delivered the message.

Whether he did so out of pride or hopeless resignation is uncertain, but he did deliver it. All that is reported is that he spoke softly, and his manner was dignified.

With a wave of his hand, the king caused Madatho to be hauled into a dungeon, tortured hideously and exquisitely, then crucified.

All this while he cried out for his uncle, who was nowhere to be seen.

It was only as he hung on the cross, in his last extremity, that his uncle stood below him. Now his uncle's face was that of a crocodile again, and the hands folded before him were claws.

Madatho screamed at him, every obscenity he knew.

"Ingrate," said the crocodile-thing. "You were given a substantial reprieve, in which you gained riches and knowledge, knew pleasure and happiness and even sired a son to carry on after you. Furthermore, do you see that fire in the distance? That's the palace burning. The people rose up against the tyrant, inspired by your defiance. You are their hero, their liberator. You have gained your revenge. In the future you will be worshipped as a god. What more can you ask?"

"Somehow none of that comforts me just now," Madatho said.

* * * *

Tigranes chose to be amused. He chose to laugh.

"This is a fable. My forefathers overthrew Nakamaenon more than two hundred years ago and established our dynasty —"

"I know. I was there."

The voice came from off to his left. He turned again. If the speaker was actually moving about the room and not casting his voice, he moved with absolute silence.

"Show yourself!"

"Here I am." Now the speaker was to his right. For once, he saw motion. Someone stepped silently in front of a curtain, half-visible in lamplight. For a moment the prince stepped back and stared, astonished, for he had expected a formidable-looking opponent, or even one of the crocodile-headed *evatim,* but what he saw before him was—a child, a boy, maybe fourteen or so, with an unkempt mop of hair, a round, smooth face and strange, dark eyes; raggedly dressed, in a none-too-clean tunic and loose trousers torn off at the knees. The reason he had moved about silently was simply that he was barefoot and very thin. He must have weighed almost nothing.

The prince's first thought was that this was a *joke,* that this rogue was a beggar from the street turned burglar, attempting to use a remarkably original method of talking his way out of a tight spot—but it did occur to him that the boy showed no trace of obsequiousness, and did not bow before him or address him as "Lord" or "Majesty" or even "Sir."

For such impudence, the least he would do would be to have the brat soundly beaten.

But then he noticed that the boy's bare legs were criss-crossed with faintly glowing scars, and there were more such marks on him, on his bony chest and sides, visible through his threadbare tunic, which was several sizes too large for him and open down the front. That gave the prince pause, but only for a moment.

"And what am I supposed to call you…Nephew?"

"I am Sekenre," the boy said. "I am as I seem and I am not, for I have many souls. I am a sorcerer who has lived for…considerably longer than you might think. This is not a joke. I have come to you —"

"Yes, why *are* you here?" demanded the prince, pacing nervously back and forth, twirling his knife. "To murder me on behalf of one of my numerous brothers? To carry me off into the night? Are the gods are running short of crocodiles —?"

"Because we have interests in common, you and I shall go on a journey together."

"Is that *so?*" snapped Prince Tigranes, who, quick as a striking snake, turned and hurled his knife at Sekenre.

But the boy was not there when the knife arrived. It bounced off a marble pillar and went clattering into the darkness.

* * * *

When he awoke the following morning, Prince Tigranes was still angry.

Yet there was no time for that. Precisely because his dynasty, whose grip on power was not all that certain these days, was foreign, descended from conquerors from across the sea, the court observed all the ancient rituals of Riverland with stupefying faithfulness.

At dawn, eunuchs came for him, clucking in their warbling voices that reminded him of so many pigeons. He allowed himself to be bathed and dressed, to have pins placed in his hair, jewelry on his hands, arms, and ears, great golden bands draped over his chest until he was practically armored. Someone painted his face, drawing black streaks back from his eyes, powdering his cheeks, coloring in his lips.

There were prayers and ritual prostrations, performed in shadow, and again once the curtains had been drawn, in the light of the newly risen sun.

He didn't get any breakfast. There would be a ritual feast later on, at which nobody ate anything. He barely had a chance to examine the pillar where his knife had struck the night before. There was a scratch. His strange interview had not been a dream. For that matter, the papyrus still lay half-curled upon his desk. He was not able to search for the knife he'd thrown—no matter, for he had secreted several more about his person—before he was hurried into the main palace, to appear on the balcony overlooking the great forum of the City of the Delta where the masses of the people waited in silence for the obsequies of the late king, Wenamon the Forty-Second, to begin.

Now he and his too-numerous brothers and half-brothers, all fourteen of them, raised both their hands in the prescribed manner. All of them stood in their silver robes, marking them princes of the blood, weighted down in their golden ornaments, their faces hidden behind masks of the Holy Sun—silver masks because no prince could wear a golden robe or a golden mask or the beehive-shaped crown, which were for the king alone.

In unison, they lowered their hands.

On this signal a great moan rose from the crowd. More enthusiastic common folk began to dance around the royal coffin and flagellate themselves in grief, joined by some of the eunuchs and junior priests.

It was all great fun, Tigranes thought to himself. Defunct kings were the sport of the city, the reigns being short these days and usually given to abrupt endings. All modern kings took the name of Wenamon, after a great ruler of antiquity, as if they hoped to borrow some of the other's glory; but it wasn't working. This latest Wenamon had accumulated far too many wives, concubines, and offspring, grown fat and lazy and completely oblivious to the condition of the realm, where the treasury was empty, the oracles offering only bland reassurances, and corpses of murdered citizens from sacked cities upstream kept floating by, sometimes in clumps of hundreds, to the *tsk-tsking* of soothsayers and ministers—and *then* he managed to prick himself on a poisoned needle, so the story went.

Or maybe the gods just struck him down out of boredom, to speed the game along.

The fourteen princes stood on the great, curved balcony, their robes flapping in the wind like gorgeous banners.

At least the morning breeze was cool. Later on today, it would be sweltering.

Tigranes realized he had to piss. There was nothing to be done. He would endure, as he endured so much more. Hours passed. The ritual feast came and went, and only the ghosts of ancestors, allegedly called back for the occasion from the Land of the Dead to inhabit the great sarcophagi that lined the feasting hall, were satisfied.

Then the doors to the palace were closed, and the more secret, sacred part of the rites began. (In the dark, behind a pillar, Tigranes managed to relieve himself.)

After hours more, at the very last, a solemn procession descended by torchlight down countless stairs into the vaults beneath the city, where the Black River was, that river which flowed in the *opposite* direction from the Great River of the waking world, not *out* of the Crocodile's Mouth but back *into* it—for Surat-Hemad, whose teeth are the stars, disgorges all living things into the world, only to swallow them up again. Here the dead king would begin his final journey into the afterworld upon a barge made of reeds.

Here, too, he would speak, and name his successor.

Everyone was masked. The princes all wore their solar masks. The priests and attendants wore masks of apes and fish and birds. The air was thick with smoke and incense. The procession came to the border of *Leshé*, the realm of dream, where sometimes ghosts mingled with the living, and sometimes the animal-headed figures glimpsed among the others might not be courtiers at all, but gods. *Indeed,* Tigranes thought, *if everyone is masked, how does anyone know it's really them?*

The stone floor gave way to mud. Everyone's boots and sandals made sucking sounds as they walked, except, Tigranes realized, the small, slightly-built person beside him, who *took him by the hand* with unseemly familiarity.

"Nephew?" he whispered.

The other squeezed his hand in reply.

The hand that held his was small and smooth, and such of the thin forearm as was visibly criss-crossed with glowing scars. He saw a dark robe, decorated with heron designs, and a bird-mask, and he had the impression that the other was walking barefoot across the surface of the mud without sinking, like an apparition on the surface of water.

It amused him to allow this other, this Sekenre—wasn't that a name from an ancient book?—to remain. He realized, too, that he was more than a little bit afraid, surrounded as he was by ghosts and gods and thirteen brothers who wanted to murder him, and it was some comfort to know that at least one person present was an honest impostor.

He couldn't tell his brothers apart, except for the youngest, Afkeraton, who was a hunchback and a cripple and moved like a scuttling crab.

Now came the solemn climax of the ceremony, after the late king's coffin had been placed in the reed boat that floated in the black water. The high priest bade all fourteen princes mount a little gangplank and climb into the reed boat, and there lean down over the still-open coffin of their father, where the corpse lay, wrapped in scented linens, covered with amulets, and wearing a golden mask, through which the dead man's spirit would speak one last time and name his successor.

With fourteen princes, it was a delicate matter, getting them all into the boat and properly arrayed without capsizing. Soldiers and attendants waded into the water to assist, to steady the boat, but only the princes were allowed into the boat itself.

Tigranes had lost track of Sekenre.

He looked around, and saw the impassive masks his brothers. He noted that the deformed creature Afkeraton seemed to hang back a little from the others. No matter. How could that *thing* possibly wear the beehive crown?

The air was thick with incense and smoke from lanterns and torches. Tigranes saw, drifting in it, not a few ghosts, and perhaps even an occasional god. Something with the face of a crocodile and glowing red eyes opened its enormous jaws right across from him, but then vanished, the way a shadow does when a curtain is shifted.

Drums beat. Horns blasted. There was one rattle from a bronze sistrum, and then utter silence.

The princes leaned forward, even Afkeraton. The open mouth of the golden mask seemed to widen, becoming a black abyss. There was a faint whistling, like wind. Only after a minute or two did Tigranes realize that something was wrong. Black, oily smoke rose from corpse's mouth. At first it was just a wisp, but then a great cloud, as if from the chimney of a furnace where the fire has been suddenly stoked to life—and all erupted into chaos, everyone gagging and choking, screaming and shouting as someone beat uselessly on a drum.

It felt as if burning tar had been poured into his lungs. Tigranes turned and leaned over the side of the boat, heaving. Others tumbled around him, headfirst into the water. He saw corpses floating there, soldiers, attendants, priests, princes in their silver robes.

He thought he saw Afkeraton scuttling down the gangplank, but he couldn't tell. He couldn't see clearly. He couldn't think. Then someone had him by the hand, and pulled him over the side of the boat into the water, and he was floundering in knee deep water and mud, almost blinded by the smoke, and everything else was just an impression, like a dream he'd been hurled into, all confusion, swirling shapes.

He had the sense that Sekenre was with him, dragging him away; but he stumbled, fell to his knees, and his wet robe and the mud seemed to be dragging him down. Then someone was blocking their way, someone or some thing that rose up out of the water, huge, draped in wet cloth and mud, eight, ten feet tall, like a bundle of logs or a pile of stones somehow came to life in the vague semblance of a man. This thing wore a mask, like of burnished silver, like a snarling hyena, and rimmed in pale fire.

Behind it, Afkeraton cringed, clutching the stolen golden mask from their father's corpse to himself, and pointing and *laughing* while some kind of combat took place. Sekenre had produced a knife or a short sword from somewhere and blocked blow after blow from the giant, whose weapon seemed to be a glowing crescent. Tigranes couldn't see it clearly. But the contest only lasted for a few seconds. Then the giant or whatever it was reached out with its other hand and merely *touched* the boy and sent him crashing into Tigranes, and the two of them tumbled backwards, sprawling, splashing, choking in the mud and water, in absolute darkness.

Then there was no sound at all but the dead king's ghost, wailing in protest as the black, poisonous burning consumed its body entirely.

Again, silence. For an instant, strange stars seemed to appear, but they were eyes and teeth; and all around them the *evatim,* crocodile-headed things with the bodies of drowned men rose out of the water to devour the dead.

Tigranes couldn't breathe. His lungs were burning. The air was still thick with the overwhelming stench of foul tar and he was sick from it. Then he was aware that Sekenre was trying to get him to do something, and he got the idea, and somehow he'd removed his heavy, jeweled sandals and thrown them away, and then he found that he and the boy both could walk *on* the surface of the water as if on a cold, marble floor. The two of them clung together and staggered away. He didn't know how long he went, half stumbling, half running. He felt terribly weak. His lungs burned. He had a sense of crashing face-first through reed and small branches.

It was only much, much later that his lungs and vision both started to clear, and he could almost think again, and he realized that he was in no vault beneath the city, but outdoors, in the midst of a vast reedy swamp; that he and the boy were walking on the surface of a black river; that the Moon overhead hung motionless and crescent-sharp like a curved sword; that the stars were few, far between, and dim, and the constellations they almost reluctantly formed were utterly unfamiliar.

He wasn't in the living world at all, he realized. This was the realm of the dead, or nearly so. He tried to recall what he'd read about this, what he'd learned from learned men when he'd questioned them, what sometimes even the priests let slip: that there were three supernatural realms, each progressively further beyond the world of living men: the first of them *Leshé,* or Dream, the second *Tashé,* or true Death, and the third, *Akimshé* or Holiness—this last being the domain of the gods and a very few blessed savants who reached there on spirit-journeys. But as sorcerers are decidedly *unholy,* being servants of the Shadow Titans whom the gods fear, not of the gods, it was very unlikely he would be looking upon the divine country any time soon. Whether sorcerers are entirely evil, depraved beyond redemption, or capable of at least morally neutral action depends on your philosopher, what books you read, on hearsay—and his head was much too muddled to follow this train of thought further. The best he could do was breathe deeply of the damp, cool air and wait for the dizziness to pass.

In time he realized that the boy Sekenre was clinging to him quite feebly, and that in fact he more or less dragged the boy along in his arms. He paused. Sekenre still wore a bird mask, but it was smashed, so Tigranes tore it off and tossed it aside.

Sekenre's face was pale. His eyes were rolled up so that only the whites showed. There was blood trickling out of his nose and from the side of his mouth.

Tigranes realized that the boy was soaked, not in water, but in blood. His heron-gown was dark with it.

Now the cool air made the prince's mind very clear indeed.

The thought came to him, *Why do I need this child at all and why should I trust him?* For half an instant he considered just tossing Sekenre aside and going on, but his reason got the better of him. *Going where?* He was lost here. Even if he could reach the City of the Delta again, he had few prospects there. His youngest brother, the scuttling freak, had outsmarted them all and doubtless seized the throne for himself.

Possibly, as Sekenre had seemed to imply at their first meeting, he and the boy had some interests in common.

Therefore what he did was gently take the boy in his arms. Indeed, he didn't weigh very much. Tigranes found that as long as he held Sekenre, he could continue to walk on the surface of the water, but as soon as he laid him down gently on a little island made of tufts of grass, he sank almost knee-deep into the mud. He crawled up onto the grass beside Sekenre and examined him as best he could in the dim light, tearing away his ruined gown and the ruined tunic under it, observing that scattered across the boy's bony and so frail-seeming body were a multitude of faintly glowing scars. But more by feel than sight he discovered a puncture wound in the left side of the chest that was indeed bleeding quite a bit. The whole area was slick with blood, and Tigranes's fingers came away sticky.

He tore a strip off the boy's robe and bound it around him, to staunch the bleeding, but he didn't know what to do next. Such knowledge of medicine as he had was all about spirit flows and balancing of the humors, and was entirely theoretical.

He couldn't tell if the boy was still breathing, but took the fact that the marks on him continued to glow as a sign he was still alive.

After a while he nudged his shoulder gently, and much to his surprise Sekenre coughed and opened his eyes.

"…unplugged me…" he mumbled, spitting out blood.

"What?"

"We sorcerers are a quarrelsome lot. We fight…strange wars…many wounds, which we can repair with magic fire."

"Can you…repair this one?"

"If we are not in immediate danger, it is better not to."

"I don't understand."

"It's like putting a plug into a barrel. Somebody can take it out again. Each wound is a vulnerability, if an enemy can discover it. It's best to try to heal naturally, if you can. But you never can…not all the time."

The boy closed his eyes and was drifting off again.

Tigranes nudged him one more time. *What happens if you die?*

"If I die, then my soul, and all the souls of those I have slain, which reside within me, awaken inside the mind of the one who has killed us. His name is Iod. He is very old, thousands of years, and very evil. Right now he is your brother's guardian, but I do not think…" Sekenre sighed and gasped for breath and spat out blood again. "I don't think his intentions are entirely what your brother is hoping for."

Now the boy seemed to lapse into a delirium, in which he babbled in a variety of voices and languages, and as Tigranes sat there beside him in the dark, the prince came to truly believe what he'd only regarded as rumor before, that sorcerers are composite beings, who gain their powers by killing and absorbing one another. He was willing to believe, too, that sorcerers do not age physically, and he wondered if what Sekenre had really survived as long as he seemed to imply. There was, in old books, a story about a boy-sorcerer of that name who may have been responsible for the death of Wenamon the *Fourth*—allegedly by lifting his still-beating heart out of his chest—almost a thousand years ago. The practice of naming all kings with the great name of Wenamon had only been revived in the previous dynasty, about three hundred years ago. That this "boy" might be in the habit of killing kings did not recommend him…or perhaps it did, for certainly if the now no doubt crowned "king" Afkeraton, otherwise known as Wenamon the Forty-Third, could be disposed of by such picturesque means, Tigranes would have no objections.

Indeed, he and Sekenre might yet have interests in common.

He could only sit there in the dark and wait for something to happen. He could only review his life to this point, who he was, what his ambitions were, how he had intended to live his life. He could only shake with rage when he realized that the hideous, ridiculous Afkeraton had snatched everything from him so quickly and deftly.

He drew his knees up and rested his head against them, trembling with both cold and with anger. He felt exhaustion and pangs of hunger, but he was a strong man and could endure. After a time he seemed to fall asleep, and to dream, and in this dream he was able to wonder whether he was awake or not, and he could look back at the tale of his life so far without being able to tell where the dream began, or if it ever ended. Indeed, to the end of his days, he would never know, and he knew *now* that he would never know, as if he had come adrift in time, and past and future were all part of the same stream. Adrift…as the current carried him, as it carries all created things, back to the ultimate source of both life and death, which is the belly of the Devouring God, Surat-Hemad, whose mouth is the night sky, whose teeth are the numberless stars.

Here, under the fewer, dimmer stars of the deathlands, he dreamed, and awoke within his dream, or dreamed that he had awakened.

There were ghosts with him, there on the little island. He saw pale faces among the grass, and drifting shapes like mist. He saw some of them gathered over the sleeping Sekenre, and they spoke to the boy in a language Tigranes did not know, but recognized, as the universal language of the dead, which is spoken and understood only by corpses and ghosts, by sorcerers, and by the most profound of sages.

Once or twice Sekenre made some brief reply, in that same tongue.

Then, as the dream or the awakening progressed, the sky lightened just a little bit, not into a sunrise, but more as if a second, full moon were about to appear. But it didn't. The knife-crescent remained where it was. Perhaps it brightened a little and the stars dimmed, or else his waking (or dreaming) eyes adjusted.

Time passed. He did not know how much, but perhaps a great deal, if there was such a thing as time in this place.

Someone touched him on the shoulder. He looked up and beheld a maiden there, clad in a gown the color of moonlight, her hair long and pale, her face exquisitely beautiful and, perhaps, slightly glowing. (Or else that was a trick of the eye.)

She bade him get up, and he got up.

He demanded her name and she said that it was Tsais, and that she dwelt on a barge with her father, Yazdigerd.

"Is he a sorcerer, then?"

"No, a philosopher."

"How did you find me?"

"Your friend called me."

"My friend…?"

Tigranes looked down at Sekenre, then back at Tsais, who had turned away, as if to leave. He bent down, picked up the boy in his arms, and carried him, ready to walk again on the surface of the black water, but then he saw that Tsais had a boat. She bade him sit in it, and he sat, with Sekenre limp in his lap, while Tsais stood at the back of the boat and drove it through the water by slowly moving a single oar from side to side.

They slid through the black marshes, amid the mist and softly whispering ghosts. More than once he saw what he first took to be crocodiles, but knew to be *evatim,* lying in the water, watching the boat as it passed.

Then he saw what he first thought was a rising moon ahead, but it was not. It was a barge, hung with lanterns.

Silent servants in masks tossed them a rope and helped them aboard. While Tigranes was already too benumbed with wonders to question anything anymore, he did notice with some disquiet that the servants were all hollow behind. Their bodies were open at the back. They were like sails, filled with wind; made of air, and there was no wind.

After Tsais had directed him to leave Sekenre upon a bed in a cabin, where the servants would care for him, he was introduced to the philosopher Yazdigerd, who proved to be a short, stout, bald man who looked more like a clerk or a wine-merchant than a philosopher.

Yazdigerd laughed about this. "Well, what is a philosopher supposed to look like? Long hair and beard, long gown, a grave manner?"

"Yes, I suppose so," said Prince Tigranes.

The other shrugged and motioned for the prince and for Tsais to sit at a table on the deck.

"Sorry. What you see is what you get."

"Is it?" said the prince. "Is it ever?"

"An interesting philosophical question, as we philosophers like to put it." Then he leaned forward, and his manner changed, as if to say *but all joking aside,* and added, "But more importantly, remember that *what you have is what you've got."*

The servants brought them food and drink, a fine banquet, of genuine food from the earth of living men. As Tigranes tasted the meat and sipped the wine, "How can we know that any of this is real?"

"Are you less hungry after you eat?"

"How can I tell?"

"How can we tell anything? Perhaps were are all being slowly digested in the belly of an enormous crocodile who has devoured the world, and our entire lives from birth to death and beyond are all an illusion."

Tigranes took a piece of bread and bit into it.

"What we have is what we've got."

"Precisely." Yazdigerd turned to his daughter. "Don't you agree?"

Tsais said something Tigranes could not quite make out.

"Don't talk with your mouth full, dear."

* * * *

So it was that Tigranes, who had been prince of the Delta and had aspired to be king of all Riverland, came to dwell in *Leshé,* the country of dreams, which is on the borderlands of Death. Benumbed as he was to all wonders by now, he nevertheless learned much, and came to understand how one can inhabit the country of Dreams, how philosophers and sages reach there through stern discipline and exercise, and how sometimes the most unfortunate wretches find their way there too, as an escape from their miseries.

"I could well be," said Yazdigerd, "not a philosopher at all, but some petty official cast into a dungeon for an offense, and left there to rot, all the while dreaming that I am here, on this barge, on this river. Or it could be that I am on the barge, dreaming I am in the dungeon. Sometimes I have that dream. It disturbs me. I endeavor to awaken from it as quickly as possible."

Yazdigerd was not a Riverlander at all, but came from a country far to the east, where the king's rule was strict and harsh, and any number of petty officials wound up in dungeons.

For an indeterminate time, they drifted on the black river, beneath the crescent Moon and pale stars, into realms Tigranes had never imagined existed. Yazdigerd traded for rich goods in cities of pale white stone, where not all the folk were human, but many had the heads of birds and beasts. The two of them became fast friends, and adventured together in the black mountains, in the night regions beyond the river's edge, and hunted fabulous beasts there, including one monster, whose bones were only known on earth, but here quite alive, so large that once, in remote antiquity, a king had caused one of the creature's *teeth* to be hollowed out and serve as a royal warship.

When that king died, Yazdigerd explained, he sailed into death in that vessel, which is why no such thing has ever been seen in the world since.

Sekenre's wound slowly healed, and he eventually joined them in their philosophical discussions. Someone had either repaired the boy's robe or provided him with another one. Now he was always clad in ankle-length, dark gown, embroidered with herons. He went barefoot, moved absolutely silently, and could walk on water. Sometimes Tigranes spied him stepping over the side of the barge, and vanishing into the darkness and distance. Sometimes he saw him, far away, conversing with ghosts, or with the *eva-tim,* and looked on him with certain dread when he did this, but again he reminded himself of the philosopher's advice, *What you have is what you've got,* and he realized that Sekenre had never harmed him, and that he and the boy might indeed still be allies.

But this was a cause of unease, that he did not know what Sekenre was truly thinking; that he could not hope to *comprehend* what the boy was thinking, or planning; nor could he ever learn all that Sekenre could learn.

He watched with fascination as Sekenre produced a book from somewhere and wrote in it, in that same intricate, beautiful script which he had seen on the papyrus the first night. But he couldn't read it. The boy let him turn the pages, which seemed to go on forever. It was some kind of illusion, or magic. The book was not very thick, but its pages seemed infinite.

Sekenre smiled at him, in that odd, solemn way of his, which was very much like the manner of a child who could not quite explain something. "I can't read it all either, but I think that someone within me can."

For the most part Tigranes allowed himself to be lulled into the state of things as they were, remembering the philosopher's advice, and he watched the dark shore pass by, and he wondered at the sights he saw. Once, he, Yazdigerd, and Sekenre together walked into the air and came to the Moon, which appeared before them as an enormous crescent, like a vast sword. They approached from behind, out of the shadow, and stepped into the sunlit country of the Moon and there saw golden hills and golden rivers, golden towns, golden people and golden gods. They gazed down at the Earth from there, and saw how tiny it looked, how slightly absurd, like a blue marble a child might roll in a game.

But it was in *Leshé,* in the darkness of the river of dreams, that the real miracle occurred. Tigranes found himself spending more time in the company of Tsais, his host's daughter, and he made excuses to converse with her; and before long he felt stirring within himself such emotions as he had never before known.

In time—though there is no way to determine time beneath the motionless crescent Moon and pale stars, in the country without sunrise—they knew that they loved one another, and he took her to wife. Then for a further time, which might have been a fleeting instant, or years, he dwelt with her in a golden tower by the shore of the river, while her father's barge was moored there; and he had a son by her, who was named after a sage of her father's country, Vahran; and still they lingered in perfect happiness while Vahran grew until he was almost as tall as Sekenre.

Then Tigranes asked his wife one night, as they lay in bed together, "Is any of this real? I've dreamed that I was a prince in another place, whose brothers tried to kill him, who was wronged and cheated out of kingship, and whose whole life had been a matter of subtle waiting to kill or be killed. But, am I the prince dreaming I am as I am now, or am I as I am now dreaming I am the prince?"

"I have no idea," his wife says. "Father likes to chew on that sort of thing. Don't let it bother you. Go to sleep."

* * * *

Tigranes's undoing came from a specific cause, which is why it is worth telling.

He could not put the thought from his mind. Then his son asked him one day, "Father, who are you really?"

Tigranes joked and said, "An interesting question. I am myself."

But another time his son said to him, "Father, who are you?"

And he said, "I'm…not sure. Don't let it bother you."

Then, realizing he wasn't getting anywhere, his son said to him, "Father tell me a story of who you once were," and then it all came pouring out of him, and he spoke of Riverland, and of his depraved, incompetent father, Wenamon—whatever his number was; the prince couldn't remember at the moment—and his thirteen brothers, including the scuttling freak, Afkeraton who had seized the throne through blasphemous murder. As he spoke, he trembled with rage, and unconsciously felt about himself to see if he still had any throwing knives concealed on his person.

When he had told a considerable amount of this story, Tigranes wept, and Vahran, frightened at what he had done said, "It's just a story Father. I don't need to hear any more of it."

But it was too late. Weeping still, Tigranes left the room and the tower. His wife Tsais encountered him, and he turned from her, weeping. He encountered his father-in-law, the philosopher Yazdigerd, said to him, "Consider what you *have*. Think only on that."

"I can't," Tigranes said. "I'm sorry, but I can't."

He left the tower. He walked along the golden gangplank onto the moored barge.

There Sekenre sat at a table, playing the game of *ma*, which involves moving black and white stones across a board. It usually takes two players, but the boy seemed to be playing it by himself.

"I have to go back," Tigranes said, weeping, trembling with rage. "I have to settle things."

"Ah," said Sekenre, moving one black piece. "I fear we have broken adrift."

The prince looked back once to see the golden tower vanishing around the dark curve of the river.

He saw that they weren't in the barge at all, but in a reed boat, and a charred one at that, which stank of poisonous tar. But it floated. It would do. They drifted in silence while Tigranes thought harsh thoughts, considering all he had learned, making his plans, like a player of *ma* thinking out his campaign many moves in advance, all the while revealing nothing by his face or his actions.

Then there was no boat at all. Perhaps it sank or they stepped out of it. He and Sekenre walked barefoot on water, then on mud, then they came to a muddy shore in a chamber far underground. From there they followed a corridor, ascended many flights of stairs, and, miracle of miracles, emerged into a courtyard beneath a *full* moon and multitudinous stars.

He had not seen a sky like that in...years. He paused at the wonder of it, but only for a moment.

There were gibbets set up in the courtyard and empty corpses dangled from them, devoid of their ghosts. The façade of the palace looked to have been burnt and only partially rebuilt.

The great bronze doors opened at Sekenre's touch. No guards came to stop them. Perhaps they were invisible, or time was somehow, still suspended. Sekenre made fire with his hands, and held out a flame on his outstretched palm, and lighted their way with it.

They ascended more stairs. They traversed corridors and galleries. They saw statues everywhere of beast-headed and bird-headed creatures, and encountered such creatures in the flesh; and humans too, most of whom moved about fearfully. But no one seemed to notice the two intruders.

They came to what Tigranes knew to have been the royal bedchamber of the kings of the Delta since time immemorial.

Within the canopied bed lay his brother Afkeraton, now and for many years also known as King Wenamon the Forty-Third, who sat up astonished when the doors to his chamber slammed open and Prince Tigranes entered.

The king was very old, white-haired, feeble, trembling.

"Your life has been weighed and found wanting and now must end," said Tigranes.

"You...you!" The King pointed a trembling finger. "My brother Tigranes has been dead for seventy years! It cannot be!"

"Sometimes things are not as they seem, My Lord," came an icy, utterly chilling, utterly inhuman, third voice from the shadows beyond the bed.

Tigranes, who was never without his throwing knives, even after so long, had gotten one out and was ready to slit his brother's throat with it, drew back as an immense figure arose from out of the darkness, a thing with the face of a snarling hyena—it was not a mask this time, nor entirely, living flesh, but more like molten metal that was alive—and massive, ungainly limbs beneath its flowing robes like a body that was strangely designed, yet immensely powerful. This was *Iod,* a sorcerer far more ancient and powerful than Sekenre, and as a consequence in a considerably worse state of repair, with almost no trace of his original humanity left, every piece and aspect of him broken, repaired, replaced, made stronger, if less like a man.

Sekenre drew his short sword and faced off against Iod, who wielded a glowing, curved blade that looked like a slice cut off the Moon.

Unnoticed, Tigranes eased his way around behind Iod. This was all part of the prince's plan. He'd thought this through.

But as it worked out, Afkeraton had a plan of his own, not to mention surprising strength still left in his aged, twisted body, for it was he who slid a gleaming blade of his own out from under his pillow and leapt from the bed, not at his brother Tigranes, but onto the back of the monster Iod. Afkeraton wrapped both legs and one arm around Iod, and with a stroke of the other neatly sliced off Iod's head.

With a roar like an explosion, the gigantic thing that had been Iod the sorcerer collapsed into dust and fire, into swirling, tattered remains of cloth; and in that instant, because he had slain a sorcerer, King Afkeraton *became* a sorcerer, as the countless murdered souls and countless magics within Iod poured into him. His body writhed where he had fallen. His jaws snapped. His mouth foamed, spitting fire. His feet rattled against the floor in a series of wild kicks.

Tigranes, seeing what had happened, adjusted his stratagem instantly, and, before his brother could recover any control of his own body, drove one, two, three of his throwing knives into his brother's heart, then slit his throat for good measure.

Blood splattered everywhere. Now Tigranes, having slain the sorcerer his brother had become, *was himself* a sorcerer, and a thousand outraged voices roared into *his* mind and a thousand years of magic and vile deeds and hideous memories poured into his mind like a vast avalanche, and he too writhed and coughed fire and was so distracted that it took him quite a while to realize that Sekenre had picked up the gleaming Moon-sliver sword and chopped *his* head off, but sealed the open neck with the fire of his hands, so that he—Iod/Afkeraton/Tigranes—*wasn't dead,* just helpless, without a body. He had time to understand that Iod had been the terrifying tyrant who had made King Afkeraton his slave and that Afkeraton had long been looking for the chance to do precisely what he had done, but it took him quite a bit longer to figure out that because he wasn't actually dead, the contents of what had been Iod were going to stay where they were, and not pour into Sekenre.

* * * *

Indeed, Sekenre explained that to him later.

"It is more than I could handle," the boy told him. "I—that part of me which is still Sekenre—would have been lost like a leaf borne away in a vast tide, and I would have become wholly a monster. I believe it is my great accomplishment that I have not."

The head, Tigranes's head, spat fire. "And whom did *you* murder, to become a sorcerer yourself?"

"To begin with, my own father. His soul is within me now, and it is his wish, too, that I not become, wholly, a monster. I try to honor him."

Then Sekenre stalked out of the palace, and if anyone saw him, a barefoot boy in a dark robe, splattered with blood, carrying the still living but slowly burning head of a prince who had been missing for seventy years, well, enough bizarre and terrifying things had taken place in the City of the Delta of late that no one was about to question this one.

Out in the desert, Sekenre summoned the birds of the air, and they bore him up by the thousands, like a dark, swirling cloud with a single throbbing sphere of light within it, which was the burning head, and they carried him far out into unknown lands, where stood a haunted, immemorial city almost entirely swallowed up by the sand. There he climbed to the top of what had once been a bell tower, and using the pommel of his own short sword as a hammer and one of the throwing knives as a nail, he affixed the head of Prince Tigranes to a rafter by the hair.

The head screamed at him.

"You could have perished when your brother intended," Sekenre said, "but you were granted a considerable reprieve. What do you have to complain about?"

For an instant, that which had been Tigranes predominated, and wept, and said, "All that is of small comfort to me now. Was any of it real? Did I really love Tsais? Do I really have a son?"

"Yes, and Tsais will mourn for you. Yes, too, you have a son, and when it is time I will bring him forth into the world, for his destiny is very great."

The head spat fire. The voice was still that of Tigranes, but angry now.

"Was all this part of *your plan?* Did you plot this from the beginning?"

Sekenre got out his book, which he carried in a satchel around his neck, worn under his robe. He turned the beautifully illuminated pages.

"It's all here, but I didn't understand its meaning, until you showed me the way to the ending."

The head screamed at him some more, in a stream of garbled obscenities and curses, in a hundred languages all at once. It was Iod. It was some monstrosity from within Iod. It had many other voices.

"When it is time," Sekenre said, "perhaps in a thousand years, when I am ready to do it without becoming a monster, we shall resolve this. For now, you must wait here."

He closed the book and put it away. He descended from the tower and walked into the desert. The warming sand felt good on his bare feet. It was a sensation he hadn't felt in a while.

He sat down on a dune and watched the sun rise.

✗

THE DARKENING MERE
Scott J. Couturier

Here lurk apparitions passing queer —
the water chills at all times of year.
Black & sussurant, leaf-bestrewn,
its surface arrests the racing moon.

Brittle branches stretch down to dip
into the darkness their desiccate tips:
Gnarled here grows tree & weed,
fey things rustling in the black-shot reeds.

Down the stream drifts a tiny boat:
Cupped leaves of umber bear it afloat.
Aboard are sprites clad in black pall
conducting a forlorn faery funeral.

Pucks gather on the root-clad shore
as gull & heron screech their sorrowed store.
The black water receives a faeling corpse:
faint cries keen with inhuman remorse.

Deep within the darkening mere
all manner of prophecy may appear —
the flicker of antique times long-passed
or visions from the far-flung future cast.

Staring down into the frigid depths
one may see the manner of one's own death,
or hear again a lover's forgotten sigh:
yet some see a mere inverse of the sky.

The sun, in setting, breathes out his light.
The mere plunges into the delight of night.
Wisps rise, summoning travelers to bathe —
black water molded by the moonlight's lathe.

Step in & wince at the bone-deep chill
which burns colder than a Stygian rill.
Dip down & under, as the werelights fain:
You will grin, but not come up again.

JUNGLE ORCHID
Kyle Opperman

She was a jungle orchid, sweet and rare,
With tropic blossoms in her long, black hair—
The purple phalaenopsis, fang and flair
Suggesting deadly beauty.

With panther-stealthy steps, she walked the ways
Where waterfalls veil all in rainbowed haze—
Where unknown orchids ghostly faces raise,
With perfume strange and fruity.

At night she knelt at secret tiki shrines,
To offer flowers, seashells, fruit, and wines,
While torches flickered on their carved designs,
And made them seem to quiver.

Sometimes at sunset, she was seen to dance
Upon volcanic cliffs, as in a trance,
And all who met her mystic, magic glance
A rosy sigh would give her.